# THE BEACH HOLIDAY

Nina Manning is the author of ten psychological thrillers, including worldwide bestsellers *The Daughter in Law* and *The Bridesmaid*. Her most recent is *The Beach Holiday*. Nina is also the author of *The 3am Shattered Mums' Club* and the sequel, *The 6pm Frazzled Mums' Club*.

Nina studied Psychology and Criminology and is a trained chef; she has worked in private households and catered an intimate afternoon tea for HRH, King Charles III.

After moving from Dorset to Inverness, Scotland, Nina is inspired by the dramatic backdrops of The Highlands. When she is not writing, she can be found romping in the woods with her dog and family, plotting more books.

## Also by Nina Manning

*The Daughter in Law*

*The Guilty Wife*

*The House Mate*

*The Bridesmaid*

*Queen Bee*

*The Waitress*

*The 3am Shattered Mums' Club*

*The Beach House*

*The 6pm Frazzled Mums' Club*

*Her Last Summer*

*The Dinner Party*

# THE BEACH HOLIDAY

## NINA MANNING

HODDER &
STOUGHTON

First published in Great Britain in 2025 by Hodder & Stoughton Limited
An Hachette UK company

The authorised representative in the EEA is Hachette Ireland, 8 Castlecourt Centre,
Dublin 15, D15 XTP3, Ireland (email: info@hbgi.ie)



A CIP catalogue record for this title is available from the British Library

Paperback ISBN 978 1 399 74558 1
ebook ISBN 978 1 399 74560 4

Typeset in Sabon MT by Manipal Technologies Limited

Hodder & Stoughton Limited
Carmelite House
50 Victoria Embankment
London EC4Y 0DZ

www.hodder.co.uk

*For the beautiful people of Mana Island, Fiji*

# PROLOGUE

What was prevalent was the dark streaks of blood all through the sand, and the smell. The smell of blood. She was lying on the beach, amongst the chaos and the wreckage. She looked so serene and I wondered how I could walk away and just leave her there. I bent down by her side. I observed the blood across her dress, and down her legs. I sat back on my heels and held my hands in a prayer fashion. Then I held them out in front of me and saw the blood all over them. I could see it even in the half-light of the moon. I only had a few more minutes; I needed to get away soon. I looked behind me, to the shore where the small motor boat was moored, all ready for me. I looked once more at her lying on the sand. The dark stains marred her clothes; I was barely able to see what the pattern once was.

What would become of her? I wasn't sure. But I couldn't think about it anymore. I had to take myself from this island and forget about her and everything that had happened here. What I had been responsible for. I stood and pulled my rucksack onto my back so I had two free arms for balance to wade out to the boat and get on board. I knew every second counted now; they would be coming for me. I looked down at her almost lifeless body once more, then I stepped around her.

I moved towards the shore, then I slowly waded out into the shallows until I reached the boat. I threw my rucksack inside and climbed on board. I sat down on the plank of wood nearest the engine and before I started it, I took one last look at the island. This was the last time I would see it close, or ever again I was sure. Now it was time to go.

I looked at the body on the sand and something told me that she had gone – she was no longer of this earth – and as I started the engine and the boat began to chug away, I kept looking at her and didn't take my eyes off her until she was just a tiny spec on the small stretch of sand in the faraway distance.

# 1

## THEN

*Fiji*

The sky was drenched a russet orange. Streaks of pink sliced their way through, fighting for space amongst the tangerine canvas. I could only see the sun, only the array of colours sitting behind as it made its way to the other side of the world. It was such a beautiful display that I didn't want to turn away; I didn't want to miss one second. There were guitars and a ukulele being played in the bar by three local men. They sang out harmoniously. I heard the music and I watched the colours in the sky; this felt like the closest to God I would ever get.

I could hear my name being called over and over until I turned. It was Dana, my friend. She was Polish and I had met her three weeks ago when I arrived and now it felt that we had known one another all our lives. She worked on the market too here, in Nadi in Fiji. She sold flowers; I sold chocolate.

The pay was dismal, but it was all I needed. I had given up everything to be here. I didn't need anything. Possessions controlled you and I had been close to being in that position, becoming that person, staying where it was safe. Before, it ate me up like the disease, affluenza, the way it had so many of the people I knew back in England. Bruno, the man I had thought I was in love with, was very like them and, little by little, like someone chipping away at a piece of wood to carve it into something, I felt myself becoming someone I did not like or even recognise.

I would be sitting at a dining room table or in a restaurant, and someone would start a conversation about their kitchen, telling me all about how they'd just had theirs fitted or were getting it refurbished. They would talk about the cost of a radiator, the only one that could do for that particular kitchen . . . That kitchen that would fulfil their every desire once it was complete was the impression I got. It was going to be *the fucking kitchen*. But how long would it keep them happy? I'd been given tours of people's kitchens after they'd had them fitted, after months of hellish endurance of finding the right person, sourcing the correct handles and knobs that would make every bit of difference to their incomplete life. That knobs' sole purpose was to complete them. Then there was the anecdotes of the incompetent joiner and other tradespeople who had been involved in the saga. The agonising wait for the material, only for the wrong ones to show up. But it was here now, in all its shining glory. The hub of the home was complete. The kitchen of dreams had landed.

'We're getting a disco ball for the ceiling. For our kitchen discos!'

Subtext, because we are so cool but we really try not to be, at least not so that anyone would guess.

'So what's next?' I would ask partly out of curiosity about what mundane and banal way they would be spending the next three months of their lives and partly to be polite, to keep the conversation going somehow, whilst I finished my wine.

'We're going to transform the basement into a games room. And a gym.'

I want to see the world, I thought but did not say. I had mentioned it to Bruno a few times. Each time he pretended he hadn't heard me or changed the subject.

Bruno would smile and squeeze my hand, his way of reinforcing what they were saying so that I might get on board and feel all the feels over a pot of Farrow and Ball. I would always smile at him, put him at ease and hope that I never had to have a conversation about moving in together so we became one of them and told the same decorating anecdotes on a loop at various social gatherings. I guess I always knew then that he wasn't the one for me, even before he did what he did.

So there they were, the people I once knew, putting up floor-to-ceiling mirrors inside a twelve-foot-square windowless box room whilst I listened to what could only be described as heavenly music, whilst feeling as though I was on the brink of touching actual heaven.

The bar I hung out in most evenings was three hundred metres from my tiny flat, which I rented for $37 Fijian dollars a week. It was a basic room with a bed, a portable electric hob – which I occasionally think aligns next to 'the kitchen of dreams' – a table in the corner, and an adjoining toilet and shower where I washed my dishes, clothes and myself, though not all at the same time. It's small but it's where I have come to call home. Fiji is now my home.

Why am I here? Why have I not bought a home, and stuffed it to the gills, so it resembles that interior design Instagram post I saw? Because it never felt right. I always felt like I was acting in a play, as though all the lines were set out for me to say; I just had to add some spirit to them to make them sound believable. We were still kids, playing at being adults, it felt. Pretending that this was what we all wanted. What we needed to fulfil ourselves. I questioned it daily and often at these soirees I had attended with Bruno. I would regularly veer too off-piste for anyone to get on board, which would warrant hushed tones referring to me as a 'conspiracy theorist' and then as time went on, and we attended more dinner parties, I would start to feel him watching me, and then he developed a look, one just for me it seemed. It was telling to stop being me, to fit in and say what they all wanted to hear.

He had tried to mould me, to make me like them. But I would not yield.

It wasn't that I hadn't tried. I watched *Love Island* and *Married at First Sight*. I walked around IKEA and did Tough Mudder and Park Run at the weekend. I ate out at the sushi restaurants and went to kids' birthday parties even though we had no kids. I did it all; I made sacrifices so I could please Bruno. Because I thought I had to do those things to be considered a proper grown-up, accepted and liked. Ultimately, I was doing it for him, to save us, even when I could see the end. But where was the room he made for me? My wishes, my dreams and hopes? Well, there was no room for them in his cluttered life of rugby trophies and chrome and mirrors. The mirrored wardrobe where he could watch us as we made love, next to the crack in the wall where his fist had landed inches from my face that first time. That last time.

'*We* should get a glitter ball, babe.' He had suggested after that dinner party. I had laughed so loud, but the shock of his skin hitting plaster had knocked all the laughter out of me.

He started telling me he had tried so hard with me, but I wasn't going to budge. And then I made the fatal mistake of turning my back on him. The second blow, at me this time, was unexpected and harder to accept than any narcissistic trait he had suffocated our relationship with.

I found Dana among a crowd around a small table where the three men merrily played their instruments, and they smiled and smiled as though they couldn't stop if they tried. I recognised the song because I had been here in Fiji long enough. Dana was high. She took something – I don't know what. She pulled me closer to where I had stopped and perched at the edge of the wooden cabin.

'Come and dance. Come and dance.' We weaved our way back to the table. I still felt awkward knowing that people were looking at us. That Westernised conscious effect was somehow still ingrained in me, as much as I had tried to resist. But I would rid myself of it, one day at a time, until I could be my most authentic self without a care. Dana was different; she danced like she didn't notice anyone around her. How did she do that? How did she always manage to be so unaffected by life? I knew I had spent far too long in the company of Bruno's friends who were so desperate to be someone else that they had forgotten they needed to live first. Well, no more of that for me. I was here and I *was* going to live, and I wasn't going to care anymore.

I took Dana in my arms and swung her around. She threw her head back and laughed, and the people at the table looked up and smiled. There was a woman in the corner of the bar, her mahogany hair tied up in a bun with a large headband covering her forehead. She was grinning, smiling at us – at me. I held her gaze for a few seconds longer and then looked at Dana again as we spun. When I looked back up, the woman was gone.

That night, when I went to bed, I dreamt heavily. A faceless woman and I in a clinch. I presumed it was Dana, but it could have been someone from my past. She pulled herself away from me and began to walk away. Quickly at first, then slowly. She turned just before she stepped onto the sand and looked down at her feet. They were bleeding. Then she started running towards the sea and was out of sight quickly. I ran after her but she was gone. But I could still hear her. Her voice whispering my name.

*Sadie, Sadie,* over and over until I woke up.

# 2

## THEN

I woke up sweating. This was normal now as I lived so close to the equator. I thought about the dream immediately. It would sit with me until midday as most of these dreams did. I dreamt heavily because of the heat. The air was so dense I sometimes wondered if I was even getting enough oxygen, but here I was, thriving it seemed.

I was just about to head into my fourth week here in Nadi, marking almost a month since my arrival, since I left England. I received emails from my older sister each week, filling me in on what was happening back home. Mum and Dad were both too busy to email, but they called, and I called them. There had never been a plan in place; I had considered possibly visiting Australia and New Zealand for a few weeks, asking if the chocolate company would hold my job at the market until I returned. I liked it here. But I feared I would stay and never see any of the surrounding countries.

I took a cold shower, dressed, and headed to the café on the corner where I took my coffee and pastry each morning. The café assistant greeted me with the usual '*Bula*' and I sat by the window watching the street come to life: vendors setting up stalls, cars and taxis beeping and narrowly missing one another. A fan whirred on the counter; guitar music played softly through a speaker.

'Hey.'

That voice. I had become accustomed to it. My body froze because he had already asserted power over me, just by having that tone in his voice that I found threatening. He was here intermittently throughout the week. I hadn't seen him for four or five days and I'd presumed he had left the country. He came next to my table. He stood too close to me.

'Tony.' I barely turned to speak to him and regretted even using his name; it probably gave him a sense of entitlement. Something he didn't need. Something I tried not to give, but I was only human, and sometimes I slipped up, too.

'Hey.' Somehow he had moved even closer to me. He had never been this close to me before. I could smell the spirits on his breath and seeping through his skin, and not just from one day of drinking either; this was a constant stench that oozed from within him. Tony was a bum. A drunk. How he ended up here, in this part of Nadi, was a mystery. I had never seen anyone like him here yet; no one else had that fragmented look about them, as though they might split open any moment.

'You not working today then?' He sat in the seat opposite me and my head jerked slightly to acknowledge his presence.

He had once gotten riled at me when I tried to ignore him, so I figured this was the better way. He was about five foot seven, not much taller than me. I wasn't sure about his accent. Was he Aussie, or Kiwi? There was a British twang there too.

'No. I work in the mornings,' I said carefully, trying not to reveal any more information than was necessary. Something I had learned from a friend who had been attacked by a man out of nowhere. She'd had counselling for months and was still heavily affected by PTSD but one of the things she took away from the experience was that nugget: never keep the conversation going longer than you want it to continue.

'Ah, so you're free in the afternoons?' Tony leaned in closer, his dirty hands pressed on the table between us. I could feel his breath on my face. 'You know you should come with me, on my boat. I can get a boat. Me and you should go island hopping.'

I stiffened at the prospect of being alone in the Pacific Ocean on a boat with Tony; this was the most forward he had ever been and I hadn't ever given him the idea that I would like to spend time with him. I wasn't about to tell him that today was my day off either. I paused to consider the right words. The ones that could offend him or encourage him had to be eliminated. And I was back there again with Bruno, in the weeks leading up to the day I left, choosing the right way to say what I needed to say, wondering which words would provoke a reaction. Walking on eggshells to prevent him from getting riled up. How was it that because I was female, I had to keep making these amendments? Why did I have to think carefully before I spoke for fear of upsetting a man?

'Thanks, Tony, but I have a boyfriend, and I don't think it would be honourable to go out on a boat with you.' I felt ashamed of myself that I couldn't just say: 'No, Tony. I do not want to go out on a boat with you.' To hope instead that he would read between the lines. But men like him either couldn't or chose to ignore them.

'I didn't ask if you had a boyfriend, did I?' I felt Tony's spit land on my arm. Despite the searing heat, my skin prickled with cold.

'Hey.' Another voice, a female, this time.

I turned to my left to get a proper look at who had called out, and at first glance, I recognised her. Had she been the woman from the bar last night with her mad mahogany hair? She had an air of supreme confidence. Her hair, which had been tied up last night, was now loose and wild.

'What's good to drink around here?' She was talking to me. She was engaging me in conversation. She was trying to block out Tony and make him feel invisible. It was working. He stood up and went to the bar, looked out of the window, pretending that he was unfazed by this interception.

'Rum and Coke is always a safe bet,' I said.

'And who said I'm looking for a safe bet?' She stood close to my table.

'Well, it's probably too early for that. Or kava. You can usually get it here.' I rambled, looking at Tony. He was getting up. He stumbled over to the bar, pulled out a stool, and fell into it.

'I usually have a coffee. The coffee is good,' I said just as the café assistant set down a cup in front of me.

The woman smiled and for the first time I noticed a tiny gap between her two front teeth. I thought about a friend she looked like back home. But it was a friend I knew when I was with Bruno and then his face was suddenly there in front of me. Even though I had fought not to bring him with me to Fiji. I faltered for a moment as I shook the image away.

'And you? Can I get you anything?'

I pointed to my coffee. 'I'm good.'

'Enjoy.' She winked at me, then walked to the bar.

It was almost midday and she had been in the bar for over an hour, sitting by herself, scrolling through her phone. Occasionally her face would screw up as though she were reading something with real intention. I had brought a book and read a little, but I was struggling to concentrate on the words. A shadow cast over the pages. I looked up to see her standing over me. She leaned in and lifted the book to reveal the title page.

'*The Great Alone*? A book set in Alaska seems a highly appropriate novel to read in thirty-degree heat.' Her voice was softly tinted with an American accent, worn down by years of travel noting by the way she was dressed in faded harems and by the way her hair was beginning to form into dreadlocks at the sides, which I could now see as she was closer.

Her confidence and her ability to start a conversation impressed me. She also talked about books, which were my weakness. I was rarely without one these days in Fiji.

'I'm rereading it. It's not so much the setting, but the atmosphere, the constant threat that the family faces. I have never been one for a beach read. I like something I can get my teeth into.'

The woman nodded enthusiastically. 'I like this in a woman.'

I wasn't sure if she was hitting on me. I wasn't particularly au fait with same-sex flirting, although I had attracted both sexes in my life.

I held my hand on the book, not sure if the time was right to close it. Was this conversation going anywhere or was she simply passing by and was an avid reader herself? She had just acknowledged my favourite Kristin Hannah book.

'The world has a shortage of strong women. Leni is a prime example of the sort of woman we are missing. We need more like her.' She pulled out a chair and sat down this time. I took this as my cue to shut the book, marking the page with a small fold.

'Have you visited any of the neighbouring islands? I know your man there was an enticing travel buddy.' She laughed. We glanced at Tony who was slumped in his chair, looking as though he might pass out at the bar.

'Not yet. I was waiting for some time off. I've only been here for a few weeks. I have a job.'

The woman raised her eyes. 'A job. How very responsible.'

I didn't have a response. I was not feeling particularly quick-witted; the heat of the day had taken its toll on me. I should have gone home an hour ago, but for some reason, I kept on reading, glancing intermittently over at the woman who was now next to me. Perhaps I had been half expecting her to approach me.

'Well, that's interesting that you haven't been to any islands yet. I mean, I don't think you can say you've actually been to Fiji unless you've left Nadi.'

I nodded. 'I agree. I have put making money ahead of sight-seeing. I was thinking of heading off to Australia and New Zealand for a couple of—'

'Why?' The woman cut me off and leaned forward. 'You've just said you haven't seen any of the islands and you want to go to another country? The islands are the very essence of Fiji. You think this is nice? You haven't yet arrived in paradise.'

Again I wasn't sure what I was supposed to say.

'I'm travelling to one of the islands tomorrow. You could be my guest.'

'Oh, I don't know, I can't just leave my job and let my boss down.'

The woman turned her whole body towards me. 'I saw you when I arrived, and you did not strike me as someone who was a conformist.'

'Oh,' I said.

'No, you look to me like someone who is trying to escape the past and maybe looking for a little adventure.'

Didn't everyone come here to escape the past or was she just really good at reading people? I pulled my mouth into a semi-smirk. The woman smiled. Her green eyes sparkled. Strands of her long red hair blew in the gentle breeze that was coming through the gap in the window that I had opened when the morning hit midday.

'Are you? Looking for an adventure?'

I briefly thought back to why I was here. I had run from Bruno who had tried to make me into someone I was not supposed to be. If I had put up with the comments, if I had just accepted that was all I was to amount to, then I would still be there now, going to dinner parties, saying what everyone wanted to hear. Being the woman that Bruno needed me to be.

Yet here I was, putting invisible boundaries in front of me, telling myself I had to stay when I really didn't need to. I had escaped Bruno and his boundaries; I had nothing to stay for. I could get another job or flat just as easily. I thought back to a conversation I'd had with Bruno in the early stages of our relationship. I had listed the countries I wanted to visit. He had laughed it off and in a mock-southern American accent told me: 'No woman of mine will be galivanting off around the world.'

I had told him we could go together. He had told me he had a job and responsibilities. 'God, Sadie, it's time to grow up.'

Bruno's voice was replaced by the woman's in front of me.

'This island, it's called Totini. It's a boat ride away. It leaves at 1 p.m.' She grinned, then turned and walked out of the bar. Just before she reached the threshold, she called over her shoulder. 'I'm Avril by the way.'

I talked about it with Dana that night. We sat in our usual haunt as it filled up with punters, all eager to get merry, drink and dance.

'This is our calling; this is where we need to be.' I pointed out into the distance as the sun was setting.

I looked at Dana and a smile had crept over her lips. Was she, like me, trying to contain her excitement, like a small child who had been promised a treat for good behaviour. Perhaps, like me, she didn't want to believe it was true, that we had arrived in Fiji but we had yet to truly experience paradise.

'It could be just what we need,' Dana agreed.

'I want to see so much and try everything,' I said.

I suddenly felt the burning desire that Avril had infected me with this afternoon and I wanted, no I needed to go, because for the year and a half I had spent with Bruno's berating and complete lack of optimism for my future, he wasn't here anymore. I needed the space between us, so I could really forget about him. So his voice would stop in my head every time I had doubts or worries. I needed to keep moving until I found that place where I could truly be myself.

The boat was leaving at 1 p.m. I already knew I was going to be there at a quarter to, ready to experience the next part of the adventure.

**3**
**NOW**

The light stings my eyes. Why is it always so bright in the mornings? After opening them for a millisecond, I close them again. I think if I shut my eyes I am also blocking out the external noises. I can hear the world around me getting up and getting on with their day. There are only two things I want to get up for, two things that there seems purpose for. One of those is my weekly session with Dr Bhaduri. I even make an effort and put on a dress and do my hair. Even though I feel self-conscious; is the dress too bright? I feel eyes on me everywhere.

But today is not another session with Dr Bhaduri. I will have to wait another three days for that. The weeks feel long but I spend time thinking how to block out the external world, and the noise of everyday life. I know he has expectations, and I am not fulfilling those expectations. But I go each week because I like him. And it fills the long days. He makes me feel warm inside when he speaks. I have missed the warming tones of the voice of a man. His voice is like caramel. Even when he speaks the name I am assured belongs to me, but I barely recognise it these days. I hear echoes of it from my past. Sadie Adamson. But it won't resonate properly with me. It is just a bunch of syllables that I no longer associate with who I am.

Who am I?

Who have I become?

I am nothing.

*You're nothing.*

I often think of all the things I *should* say to Dr Bhaduri and maybe this is one of the many things he would want to hear from me. That there is a voice that still haunts me. I went somewhere to escape it but sometimes, it is still there. Probably because of what I have done.

I usually let the words evaporate and disappear from my mind as quickly as they arrive. Other times, I feel an uncontrollable rage. The emotions are so close to the surface sometimes it's like I can touch and taste them.

Am I a violent person? The constant whirring thoughts, they drag me from my bed each morning and hold me hostage all day before they become my nightmares. I sleep but the images come with me to my bed.

I am so tired even the dreaming exhausts me, then it stays with me, day and night: a strange tiredness that is neither here nor there. I occasionally try to lie down during the day to sleep, but as soon as I lay my head on the pillow, the desire to slumber is gone.

Eventually, I find the energy to get out of bed and pick my way across a mass of discarded paper. I try to look away from what is scrawled all over them. I had been writing again last night. Some might call it journaling, or free writing. Maybe I would have done the same under other circumstances. I scribble so fast that no sooner have I finished on one piece than I have cast it aside and begun another. I will need to tidy that all away. Someone could see that and then what would they think of me? Messy? Inconsiderate? No, something much worse than that.

These days I am exceptionally conscious of keeping the tiny spaces I inhabit neat. I don't need to spread my belongings around. Besides, I don't own anything. It helps me think better so I pick up the papers and push them into the corner of the wardrobe, ignoring the piles that have already accumulated in there. I find my way to the bathroom and to the sink where I wash my face. I look at myself in the mirror. I am not yet thirty years old, and it appears to me that I am looking at a reflection of a woman twice my age. I must remind myself daily of my name, age, and where I live. Or I am sure I will go completely mad.

The noises around me become louder and I feel a crushing sensation in my skull. I touch it to make sure something isn't constricting it because surely there must be. I turn on the tap and even the sound of running water is too much. I need fresh air. As I reach the door that leads outside, there is a far-off scent of bacon frying. I feel my mouth fill with saliva. I am going to retch.

Today I know I will meet Jane. She had just appeared there one day on a bench a few metres from the front of the house, overlooking a mass of fields. I feel like she is an angel. I'm not religious or particularly spiritual but I am looking forward to seeing Jane again. Because now she sits there and waits for me, every Tuesday. It has become our thing. I have a thing and it feels good. I feel almost alive. I used to have so many things, every day used to be a vibe of some sort. Now it's just me, and a head of swimming thoughts.

Jane is older than me by about five years. She likes to talk, she says. I let her do all the talking for the first few weeks and then I began to talk back. She seems to like that, and it feels good to talk to someone and have them listen when they aren't getting paid to do it. I appreciate my sessions with Dr Bhaduri, but it is his job to sit with me for an hour each week. Jane is just a person like me, who saw a bench and was able to form a connection with me, and I feel lucky. Lucky Tuesdays I call them. I feel as though I need something to cling to although I'm not sure why. It doesn't matter, does it? Nothing matters.

I move tentatively towards the bench. I am worried if I hurry Jane will turn, see me coming and leave. It's hard to know why Jane likes me, and I fear if she knew the real me, the person I had been a few weeks ago, she wouldn't want to sit with me on Tuesdays. If I approach cautiously then I can be on the bench before she realises what is going on. But I don't know why I am always so worried. Jane is a very accommodating person. She makes me feel very relaxed. And I think she wants to be there; I think she is genuinely interested in me. But then I once thought that about many other people, and it keeps turning out that they don't actually see anything in me at all. She does seem interested in my story though. If only I could be the one to tell it to her. To everyone else who wants so desperately to hear it.

I sidle up to the bench and sit down as she looks over at me.

'Sadie! Hi.' She always seems happy to see me.

'Hello, Jane.' I look down at my feet and realise I am wearing odd socks with my trainers. Jane follows my line of vision. She blows out a laugh through her nostrils. I smirk shyly. Will she think I'm mad?

'How are you today?' She has a flask of coffee and begins to pour out two cups. I skipped breakfast again. It is becoming a habit. The stench of bacon hadn't helped. A couple of coffees will bridge the gap until lunchtime.

'Thank you,' I say, taking the coffee. That is the routine we were in already, me and Jane, a couple of girls, just hanging out on a bench, listening, talking. I feel a twinge at lost friendship. I have many lost friendships, but one in particular has brought me to where I am today: living each day without any purpose. But Jane and I have been able to strike up an easy rapport and I know I can't be completely incompetent, can I?

Jane has told me so much about her life in a short time. She likes to tell me things and I like to listen. It is like a comfortable storyline that feels so achingly familiar, the normality of it all. And I don't have to do anything except sit and take it all in.

I take a sip of my coffee. I flinch. It is hot, and I feel the tingle of heat on my lips where it scalded them. Jane doesn't notice. She is looking across the field full of cows. Longhorns – Jane had told me their name. I could have guessed from the length of the spikes on either side of their head. They are magnificent beasts.

Jane has told me a lot about herself. She has been married. Twice. She has one ten-year-old daughter who lives with her dad, but Jane sees her twice a week and for more extended periods during the holidays. She spent a summer in France, alone last year, learning how to make wine, and she reads a book a week. She has been a teacher, a yoga instructor, a party planner and ghost-wrote an autobiography for an English actor; she did a degree in creative writing and met him through an old school friend.

I know so much about her. She has yet to ask me any direct questions.

'I love all animals.' Jane sips her coffee and looks at the cows. 'I mean, look how happy they are. Just living life so unconsciously. Not knowing what the next hour or minute will entail, just chewing and breathing.'

I look at the cows and try to see them as Jane does, but suddenly one cow's neck is sliced open. Blood is streaming from the wound, like someone is standing behind pouring red liquid from a jug. My heart pounds hard in my chest; my hand goes to my neck. I glance at Jane, and she is looking on unperturbed. She can't see what I see.

'Don't you think?' Jane's voice is loud.

'Yes, yes, I guess.' I look back at the cow. It is happily munching the grass, not bleeding to death.

My heart rate slows. It's not the first time that has happened, I remind myself.

Jane's smile is so comforting. It has been hard to know what to believe recently. My mind plays tricks on me, and the dreams are so vivid sometimes I question whether I am conscious or asleep.

'How are you feeling today, Sadie?' she asks after a period of silence.

I take a deep breath and a moment to think about her question. It feels as if I've had a lot of time to think these days, yet sometimes there is nothing there. I seem to have everything I need around me: a roof over my head and food to eat. All in all, I am not sure how I am feeling, so I try to focus on the present moment, not daring to mention the things I see from time to time, like the cow just now.

'I feel content enough,' I say, because being with Jane feels better than being alone. Jane smiles back at me as though she is sharing a secret with herself.

We sit in companionable silence. I have been meeting here with Jane for three weeks and seeing Dr Bhaduri for three weeks. There is no reason to think about anything else than what is going on right now.

I look at Jane and smile to give her the impression that things are just fine.

I know what Jane and Dr Bhaduri want to hear.

I just have to decide when I am going to tell them everything.

# 4
## THEN

I arrived fifteen minutes earlier than the time Avril had said to meet last night. I left Dana at the market at lunchtime, our parting words to one another to meet at the dock by 12.45.

'Will you be there?' I asked, and she said something back in broken Polish; words she had only ever saved to use with friends from her own country perforated her usually impeccable English. But she had been smiling, and so I had been reassured. Of course, she was going to be here. Why wouldn't she? It was such a great opportunity. But the minutes inched forward, and before long, I found myself staring at a path that Dana wasn't walking down. I thought back to her parting words to me that morning. Words that I now knew were doubts. That smile had been her way of appeasing me. She was never going to come.

I turned and faced the small dock again. This time, I spotted Avril standing at the edge of the water, her face bright as she chatted to the skipper and pointed to a boat big enough to seat ten. I looked back at the path hoping to see Dana so I wouldn't have to do this alone. I could still leave; I didn't need to go. But when I turned back, Avril was looking my way, waving me over; she looked happy I was there. I took a deep breath, and blew it out. I pushed my rucksack onto my shoulder, kicked off my sandals, picked them up, and padded across the sand.

'I knew you'd come!' she said cheerfully, holding her arms out.

'Oh.' I moved towards her, and she fully embraced me, letting out a long breath. Her scent was a mixture of coconut and spices, with an undertone of body odour – a scent I had become accustomed to smelling wherever I went. No one could escape it in this heat.

'I just knew you'd come,' she said again.

'How did you know?' I asked as she helped me into the boat.

'I just did. I have a sixth sense for this kind of thing. You struck me as someone who needed to be here today.'

I suddenly wanted to open up and tell Avril everything about Bruno and how he had been in the end. About how I was here because he wasn't and because I wanted to get as far away as possible from him and the people who reminded me of him, and I had chosen Fiji for that reason. Everything else I was making up as I went along, including getting on a boat and heading across the South Pacific Ocean to get to an island with a woman I had just met. But something about it felt right because it wasn't all set in stone and planned out how Bruno had tried to control our lives, or by telling me that travelling was immature. And that was what I needed. Chances and opportunities.

There were others already on the boat and I smiled nervously at the man to my left as I sat down next to him. Avril sat on the other side of me, her chin pressed into her hand as she stared to her right, towards the horizon.

'Relax,' Avril whispered without looking at me.

I attempted to smile at her and trick my body into feeling relaxed, but it was an amalgamation of fizzing energy and gut-churning nerves. I had no idea what to expect, and as Dana was a no-show, I felt the vulnerability seeping in. Why didn't Dana come? Why did I decide to come alone? I didn't know Avril and I had no idea where this island was.

My mind was awash with images of my new home. Would there be other people there? What would they look like? The boat engine started up and it was loud. Suddenly, I had a hundred things in my head I wanted to say to Avril – questions about the trip, the island we were heading to – but I knew trying for a conversation over the rickety sound of the old boat engine would be futile. I had been trying to be spontaneous. But maybe I was pushing my luck too far this time. Just getting away to Fiji was a huge step and now this. Was I trying to be someone else? And was I that person she so clearly saw in me? Someone who was ready to take control of her life?

The boat began to move, slowly at first, picking its way through the maze of moored boats, some of which had seen better days and looked as though they would surely only survive one more storm. Young Fijian children swam in the murky shallows, waving and whooping at us. Then as we began to pick up speed I let out a long breath, which I felt I had been holding since I boarded the boat. Avril didn't move again for another fifteen or so minutes. She just stared intently at the horizon. I wondered what she was thinking.

What was I thinking? I had just upped and left my nice little apartment and job and it was unlikely I'd have either to return to. I wondered what Dana was doing now. Was she thinking about me? Regretting not coming? I felt a pang of regret that I was leaving behind what little I had – who knew what I would have on the island.

Avril turned and looked at me. 'You okay?' she called over the noise. I wondered if we would even make it at this rate; I was sure the engine would give out any minute. Water sprayed up the edges of the boat, the odd droplet landing on my face, and there was a cool breeze now we were far enough away from land. I had been trying not to think how I was feeling until now but as we got further away from the mainland, I realised I was scared and unsure whether I had done the right thing, but I refrained from telling Avril. Avril, who seemed so cool and relaxed.

'I'm good,' I said, then I gulped hard, which must have given away how I was truly feeling as Avril cast her eyes over me.

'We'll be there in about forty minutes.'

I nodded. I could handle that. I glanced at the man next to me and the three Fijian women opposite me. I wondered what they would all be doing when we reached the island. Perhaps they'd be visiting relatives.

'Thanks . . .' My voice broke from the dryness of my throat. Avril handed me a fresh bottle of water from her backpack. As she did so, I homed in on a small woven blue material bracelet on her wrist. It was the sort I made when I was a young girl and exchanged them as friendship bracelets, only this one had embellishments: tiny little silver charms. My eyes focused on a small cake with a cherry on top.

I gulped back the water.

'Thanks.' I had become aware of the Fijian women opposite me, who stared at me quite openly and without a care. Did Avril know them? I wondered what business they might have on the island we were going to.

The rest of the questions fizzed away on my tongue, and I let them evaporate. There was too much to say and I would have to wait, be patient and see what was in store for me at the other end.

I took out my phone, saw there was some reception and bashed out a text to my mum's phone then copied and pasted it to my dad's phone.

> *Hey! I'm leaving the mainland for a while,*
> *heading to an island. Not sure what to expect,*
> *but met a cool girl. I'll be in touch soon. Love you x*

Eventually, the motion of the journey sent me to sleep. Working so early at the market meant I usually napped mid-afternoon, anyway, let alone if I was being lulled to sleep in the middle of the ocean.

Like all the dreams I'd had since I arrived here, they were vivid and enigmatic. I ended up back at that night, where I had sworn I would stop taking myself. When I arrived home from work, I listened to the message from Bruno I had been saving, thinking it would be an invitation for dinner or him telling me he was coming over with a bottle of wine. There was an edge to his words that I had never heard from him before. And when he finally came over it was not to give me a meal or take me out for a drink. It was no wonder I felt as though I needed to heal because the end of the relationship broke me, so I was not sure how I was supposed to recover. I knew I had made him angry. But I also knew that I hadn't. I also knew I would be walking away that night for the final time. The only resolution I could accept was that you never really knew someone the way you think you did.

*You're such a disappointment.*

The thrust of the boat penetrated my body, jolting me awake. My arms shuddered as I gripped the handrest. Avril looked over at me then she stood up and edged her way into a small gap so the man next to me was forced to move. Then she placed her hand over mine. She didn't say anything and neither did I. I just felt the powerful grasp of her hand on mine – and everything in that grip said, it's okay, I've got this. I'm in control.

The boat shuddered to a halt. The Fijian women got up and hitched up their skirts, ready to step off the boat. Avril was pulling her backpack on and then looking at me eagerly. I couldn't believe we had barely spoken since we left the mainland. I grabbed my massive backpack, which was almost the size of me, and Avril began laughing.

'Good job you're wearing shorts, hey?' Avril said as she pulled up her trousers and stepped out of the boat into the shallows. I followed suit, my backpack grazing my backside.

'Wow!' I looked around. This was truly paradise. So very different from the mainland. The water was turquoise and clear, the sand whiter than white. The sounds were different here, nothing like the noise on the mainland. Here it felt so very calm. Once we were on the shore, I dropped the bag on the sand and sat down. There were a few huts set back from the beach. Children swam in the shallows. The women greeted other women and talked loudly in Fijian or Hindi. There was a gentle buzz about the island that I liked. It felt like it could be somewhere I could settle for a while, somewhere I could feel safe and protected.

'Don't get too comfy,' Avril said. 'The next boat leaves in a few minutes.'

I looked up at her, where she was standing over me. 'What?'

She laughed. 'We're getting another boat. This isn't Totini.'

I looked around again. 'It isn't?'

'No. This is the first island. We need to get another boat. On the other side of the island. It's a short walk.'

'Oh.' I quickly stood and then hurried to keep up with Avril. It seemed like a pretty innocent comment, but my mind reverted back to yesterday when she had said it was a boat ride away. I was sure Avril hadn't purposely tried to trick me, but either way, she had lied and already I began to wonder whether there were any other lies to come.

# 5

## THEN

The second small, simple boat hurtled across the waves towards a tiny spec of an island in the distance. We had been aboard for thirty minutes and there was another thirty to go from what I could gather from the snippets of English I had heard the driver and his skipper speaking. We were the only four aboard, and I had my mobile phone pressed tightly in my bra against my chest, as I had felt the unease with which these strangers helped us onto the boat. With the language barrier came stalled social skills, and so grew the intensity of their stares. I prayed this was their attempt to interact and not the prelude to a long and grizzly murder.

I tried to catch Avril's eye a few times, but she was leaning on the edge of the boat staring at the horizon again. Mesmerised. She seemed far more relaxed than I felt but maybe I should step up to the post and be the confident travelling buddy she probably needed me to be. Especially once we hit the ground again.

I focused on the spec of land up ahead and I began to feel a flutter of relief that we would indeed have our feet on solid ground again very soon. To distract me from how fast the boat was travelling, I thought again about Avril and how I knew very little about her, yet I did sense that she was seeking a deeper connection with something or someone. That was her mission, which was the journey she was on. And now I was on that journey with her.

I wanted to do something different, to prove to myself that I was worth something more. More than a handful of poorly constructed insults spat at me in anger.

The island was becoming bigger and bigger as we descended upon it, and I grappled with swaying emotions of dread and excitement as I looked at the lush greenery, rustic beach, and sparkling white sand.

Eventually, the boat powered down almost to the shore, and the driver and skipper began saying something to us in Fijian whilst pointing their hands at us and then at the shore.

Avril was up and alert, looking at me.

'Paddling to the shore again from here; they will carry our luggage.' She began to throw one leg over the edge of the boat and then the other until she was submerged up to her thighs.

'You got all that information from a few hand signals?' I said, surprised yet impressed.

I followed suit and felt the warmth of the South Pacific Ocean lap at my legs. I ran my hands through the water and looked up at the perfect blue sky. If I thought the last island was perfect, I truly now had arrived in paradise. I took a moment to absorb the intensity of what was happening and how far I was from the mainland. From real civilisation. There were no huts on this island. No children swimming in the shallows and only a couple of men mooring a fishing boat. Once we were ashore, I stood and looked around and then at Avril, who was standing with her hands on her hips, surveying the island.

I turned back to the boat and watched as the men waved at us, then turned the boat around and sped away.

I looked at Avril, who had begun pacing the island. She looked nervous now. If there was one thing that would disperse my nerves, it was seeing someone else on edge and knowing that I could calm them by appearing relaxed – even though right then, I felt anything but relaxed. I approached her and touched her arm. She stopped pacing and smiled at me.

'Hey,' she said merrily although I could see the tension in her eyes.

'Are you okay?'

'Sure. Tired though. How about you?'

'Same.' I looked around again at our surroundings, the island where we would be staying for the foreseeable, and wondered what we were to do next. I had presumed someone would be here to greet us and for a few panicked seconds, fear overcame me. What if no one came? What if we were stranded here?

But before that thought had time to embed itself, I heard a whistle and two women appeared and were walking along the beach towards us. Avril and I stood patiently and waited for them to reach us.

One had dreads that reached her lower back and she wore a long strappy white dress and had bare feet. The other was wearing a dirty grey-looking vest and khaki shorts, a tanned muscly upper body and short brown hair. Both had naturally brown skin.

'Hey, Mamasita!' they both said in what sounded like Spanish accents, slightly out of sync with one another. Avril walked to them and the three of them fell towards one another, their arms tightly bound in a circle, their heads pressed against one another, as though they had just become one. I could hear low mutterings; I presumed the women were exchanging their greetings. It was an unusual sight, not the way I had seen women embrace back home, arms flung around one another haphazardly, sometimes dragging one another off their feet, squeals of joy. This was something else. Refined. Restrained, yet somehow so intimate. I watched, not wanting to intrude as the moment drew out.

'Hey,' I said, stepping forward, 'I'm Sadie.' The circle unfurled.

The short-haired woman beamed. 'I'm Mary; this is Kali.' She pointed to the dreaded-haired woman.

I threw out my hand in expectation of a handshake. Mary looked at it, and a strange expression clouded her smile. She looked at Avril for a split second, then she approached me, took my head in her hands, and pressed it against hers. Her forehead was damp with sweat. She let go, then Kali moved forward and repeated what Mary had done. I wasn't sure what I was supposed to say so I stayed still and tried to smile but it felt like an inane grin.

She turned to Avril. 'And how are you? How was your journey? You must be exhausted, both of you?'

I let out a long sigh. 'We are, completely, aren't we?' I looked at Avril, but she had locked her eyes on Kali and didn't seem to have heard me. The two women seemed to be exchanging words with only their eyes. They sensed I was watching them and Avril looked at me.

'You must be hungry? I have a fresh platter of papaya and mangoes waiting for us,' Kali said.

'Sounds delicious. I've been fantasising about a cold glass of beer and a fan.' Kali and Avril exchanged another glance and I felt silly for saying that.

'Okay, well the heli is waiting around the corner. Shall we get going?'

I choked out a laugh. 'The what?'

I looked at Avril for confirmation that I hadn't just misheard what Mary had said. Heli. She said the heli was waiting.

'As in the helicopter?' I asked.

Avril looked at me and shrugged her shoulders as though this were an everyday occurrence.

Mary turned and began walking followed by Kali, and then finally Avril turned with a wink. I trotted to catch up with them.

'So this isn't Totini?' I said to Avril.

'No this is Kenco Island. I'm sorry for any confusion.' Avril turned and smiled at me but she was marching with such ferocity I was struggling to keep up. I noted suddenly how strong her calves looked in her rolled-up harems as the muscles flexed with every step. I grabbed her arm.

'Hey,' I said. She stopped and swung around and stared at me. 'What's going on, Avril? You told me it was one boat ride. We've done two and now we're going on a helicopter? Do I have to pay?' I thought about the few measly Fijian dollars in my backpack and the small figure in my bank account.

She said nothing but looked at my hand on her arm. I let it fall away.

'Just one more ride. This is the last. I promise.'

'So one more ride?' I asked, now feeling despondent.

'Yes, one more.'

I then thought back to what Avril had said that afternoon in the bar in Nadi. She had said it was a boat ride away. I was sure of it. I couldn't help but wonder why she would have not fully explained how far away the island was.

'And once we're there, you can relax, have something to drink, get settled in your accommodation.'

I liked the sound of the accommodation. But I was unsure of getting inside a helicopter with three women I barely knew and moving out into the middle of the Pacific Ocean. I had no idea what to expect but surely there would be little in the way of communication and certainly no Wi-Fi.

All I knew was that I was going to be grateful when I did arrive and that I would make sure that I was showing gratitude. Avril was, so far, a bit of an enigma. But I had taken the chance. I had put my trust in her. I just needed to have faith. Because I was getting further and further away from anywhere I could call home or civilisation as I knew it.

# 6
## NOW

I know it's lunchtime, and that I should be hungry but I'm not. I look at the plate of vegetables in front of me. They are earthy and red and as they hit my stomach I feel my mouth fill with saliva. I think I might be sick. I take a long drink of water, leave the plate where it is and find my way back to my bed. The bedroom is cool. There is a fan on. Did I put that on before I left the room? I can't remember. I lie down on the bed and the sound of the fan is so familiar. I've done this before: lain in a hot room with a fan whirring loudly until it lulled me into a melodic state, drunk on heat, unable to move from the humidity. The images swirl around in my mind, and I push them away. Not today.

I find a stray piece of cotton on the bedsheet and play with it until it begins to burn at my fingers. I look at the sheets; they seem so unfamiliar.

A bell trills loudly around me. A doorbell? I should get up to answer it. It rings again. I feel so tired. I stay still and hope that whoever is there will go away and leave me alone. I only want to speak to two people: Jane and Dr Bhaduri.

I doze off and when I open my eyes a man stands at the side of my bed.

'Sadie,' he says and his voice is close by and far away at the same time. I try to reach out and touch the tattoo on his arm and he fades to nothing. I sit up, grasping around at the space where he had been. I was not supposed to see that man's face ever again. Yet here he is, creeping into my subconscious, coming to me when I am at my most vulnerable when I am sleeping.

I want to see Jane again, but it was only yesterday I saw her. I must wait one whole week until she and I can meet at our usual spot. How on earth shall I fill my time until then? Eating. Sleeping. Thinking.

I pick up the paper pad that I keep next to the bed. I let my pen wander across the page, pressing lightly at first, and then slowly, I gain traction until I find I am scribbling, and the pen is pressing hard into the paper as it speeds across the page. Before I know it, I've ripped the page from the book and thrown it on the floor. I start again with another page and another until a dozen pages later, the pen flies across the room and lands amongst the discarded pages. I look at them and what they hold. I jump up, disgusted with myself. I quickly gather them up in my arms, open the wardrobe, and put them inside, on top of a pile that will soon reach my stomach. I slam the wardrobe, out of sight, out of mind. But Dr Bhaduri wants to know what I know.

Terror clutches at my throat, and I try to breathe deeply, but to no avail. I have done something so dreadful, that not even I have the words for it.

# 7

## THEN

I stepped inside the helicopter, knowing this was my first time but not wanting to draw attention to that fact. I eyed the other three carefully and managed to smile and look comfortable on cue. But there was a part of me that wondered if this was real. Or had I just suddenly found myself in a reality TV drama? Perhaps this was a game, a challenge I had to endure.

I was surprised to see it was a woman who was about to fly us to Totini; then why wouldn't it be? Avril greeted her at the front, and the two of them talked for a few moments in hushed tones. The woman was dressed semi-smartly in a white shirt and khaki trousers. She donned a large head set and was relaying some important information, and Avril was listening intently and replying with short answers. Avril then squeezed her shoulder and sat down opposite Kali and me.

Kali looked at me. I thought her expression might break into a smile, but it didn't. She looked away after a second, and I realised she was assessing me.

The heli took off as my stomach dropped and then flew back up. Avril caught my eye and I smiled through gritted teeth.

We flew over a vast expanse of water, and I tried to spot land, but there seemed to be none in sight.

I ignored the tightening in my chest – a pang of claustrophobia with a sprinkling of agoraphobia as I looked at the vast ocean surrounding us and the four unfamiliar women I was now travelling with. I was now so far away from home and had no real quick or easy way to get back. I began to wonder back to the days before I left England for Fiji and I reminded myself why I had left. No matter how much I tried to assure myself this was all good, that I was okay, that this bizarre situation I had suddenly leapt into and was now right in the middle of, was okay, I realised I was only here because of one person and that was Bruno. His behaviour and his actions had been the catalyst to my booking the flight without a moment's thought. Of course, Fiji and Australia and exotic places had been on my radar, and I had imagined that one day I would travel to see them, but not under those circumstances.

And then I began to wonder if this was all part of the plan; the big cosmos, the universe, had already mapped out my exit from this world. It happened all the time. I read once of someone who had survived a near-fatal acid attack and recovered, only to get cancer. I had run away from an abusive relationship only to die in a helicopter somewhere over the South Pacific Ocean.

I must have been far away with my thoughts as I hadn't noticed land coming into sight until Avril patted my knee and jerked her finger out of the window at a tiny yellow and green spec in the distance. I felt a flutter in my stomach, something halfway between fear and gratitude. Maybe not today. Maybe I wouldn't die today.

The first thing I noticed about Totini when I stepped out of the helicopter and onto the tiny landing pad, and after a minute or two had passed so that the helicopter engine had cooled enough, was the silence. It burned my ears it was so loud. I had never been anywhere as silent . . . And it was as if Avril, Mary and Kali knew this too. They barely moved as though they were giving me a few minutes to adjust and to soak in the stillness. Eventually, I dared to speak.

'Wow.'

They all looked at me at the same time and smiled.

'It should be called that, right?' Mary laughed. I looked at Kali and noticed she was staring again.

'The silence,' I said. 'It's hurting my ears,' I gushed.

'It can do that. But only this side of the island. Through there—' Kali pointed '—is camp. Things can get a little noisier there.'

'Camp?' I asked, realising I had never exactly been sure what I was to expect when I arrived.

'Yeah, there's more of us,' Mary sang merrily.

I breathed out loudly and it seemed to echo between us. I wasn't sure if it was a sigh of relief or I had been holding my breath.

'I have to ask,' I said and eyes were on me again. 'How? I mean, do you own this island?' I asked specifically to Avril this time. 'Because we are a little out of the way here, right?'

'I have an arrangement,' Avril said softly. 'But, yes, essentially, it is ours. No one can bother us.'

'Unless we want them to,' Mary said, taking my arm softly and encouraging me into a spin.

There were smiles all around. Even Kali's expression cracked into something other than a frown. Then Mary picked up my massive backpack and walked ahead, carrying mine and Avril's bags like a caveman. I took a second to steal a glance at my phone.

Damn it. No reception. And no reply from either my mum or dad. But my message had reached them, thank goodness. Maybe there was a spot on the island where I would get something.

'You'll get nothing here. We're way off the grid,' Kali said disdainfully.

I felt a shiver of fear that I was uncontactable and unable to contact anyone else.

'Okay,' I said.

'You'll get used to it. It's nice, Sadie. Freeing. Remember, that's what we want?' Avril chipped in and put her arm around me, and I thought it strange she was talking about us as though we were one entity. As though our opinions were already in sync.

Avril left me and went back to the pilot. She began speaking with her again. She pointed to a row of small huts where the beach curved round. I stood and looked at the huts, marvelling at their simplicity.

Kali began to walk towards Mary.

'What are they?' I called after her so she stopped and looked around at me. I pointed at the huts and looking back at Mary, shielded my eyes with my other arm. Kali looked as though she were considering them for a moment, as though she had also just spotted them for the first time.

'Stores,' Kali said promptly. Mary and Kali exchanged a glance and again I felt like the silly tourist.

I looked expectantly at Mary, hoping for more information.

'It's essentially a drop-off and pick-up point. Saves time going into camp.' The women began walking again.

Mary had satisfied my curiosity, and now I was intrigued to see camp as it had already been mentioned twice. I imagined a wholesome place, with plenty going on, a fire pit always burning, and the hub of the home. I smiled to myself as I thought of all those dinner parties and soirees and how I was about to enter one of the most rudimentary kitchens on the planet. 'So how many live here?' I asked as I caught up with Mary. Avril was still talking with the pilot as we walked away.

'Thirty-one.' The number slipped off her tongue. 'And that includes you.'

'I'm included already?'

'Of course. Why wouldn't you be? You came all this way.' Mary grinned. 'Besides, when you see the camp, you won't want to leave.'

We walked through a clearing of trees; coconuts hung from many of them, and I felt my heart burst with happiness at such a beautiful, iconic sight. I had seen little if anything that looked the way Totini did back on the mainland. I smelt the campfire before I saw it. And when it finally did come into view as we rounded a corner, it was nestled amongst a circle of rocks, emitting a plume of smoke that carried the hazy late afternoon light. There was a buzz around the camp, a faraway sound of music, a steady beat. Yet in the foreground, something softer. And then I saw a woman sitting cross-legged by the fire, cradling a cherry red acoustic guitar. She plucked away gently, looking down at her fingers as they moved across the strings. I watched her intently as she provided the score to this moment that was branding itself into a core memory. She lifted her head lightly, and her expression was already braced for a hint of a smile, as though she had felt me watching her.

'I can show you your digs, or you can chill?' Mary was still holding my rucksack and Avril's bag. I realised Avril was not with us. I wondered if she was still on the beach talking with the pilot.

'I wouldn't mind a quick freshen-up,' I said, looking around and noticing that Kali had walked away. She was already on the other side of the camp, in conversation with a long-haired brunette. They both looked my way, and I sensed some animosity there. I presumed finding my feet and establishing myself here would take time. Perhaps Kali felt I was a freeloader and I wouldn't pull my weight. I was going to have to prove myself to her, I thought.

Beyond the campfire, rows of huts lined a walkway. The foliage and woodland grew wild beyond that.

'That's the other side of the island that way, used mainly for cattle grazing. We don't go over there unless we have to,'

Mary said as we wandered along. I wondered which hut would be mine.

'We have you in with Clara. She's fun. You'll like her. Sporty. She's at the other end of the beach right now, probably kayaking or windsurfing or something.'

'Windsurfing?' I said.

'Oh yeah, we have it all here. A proper activity centre. You'll never get bored. Even if there weren't activities, there is a lot of work to do. We're in the middle of a new building project, plus the cleaning, the cooking, the hunting.'

'Hunting?' I questioned again, realising I probably sounded like a parrot. 'You mean fishing?'

Mary smiled; I noticed that her teeth were crooked. 'Sure.' She grinned. 'You like fishing?'

'I only sold chocolate on the mainland. I guess I should have tried to pick up a better skill.'

'You have all the skills you need here right now,' Mary told me sternly. 'And we can teach you anything else you need to know,' she said softly. 'Here we are.'

We stopped walking. We were outside a hut with stairs leading to the door. 'Go on in and make yourself at home. Yours is the bed furthest away, but you'll see. Clara is pretty neat to be fair.' Mary looked back at where we had come from. 'Dinner should be ready in an hour or so if you need to rest.'

Mary handed me my backpack. I almost buckled under the weight; I was so weary. I didn't expect to sleep, but I wanted to.

'Okay?' she asked.

'Sure.' I heaved it onto my back just for the few steps into the hut.

Inside was dark and cool, with enough shelter from the trees to keep the sun off the huts for most of the day but to allow light in during the evening. This was the time of day the sleeping quarters needed to be cool. There were two beds, not very high off the ground on either side of the wall, and two side tables in between, but there was still sufficient space. There were two wicker baskets against the wall to my right; one was stuffed full of rolled-up clothes, and the other was empty. These were our wardrobes. There was one fan against the furthest wall, but it wasn't on.

I heard noise from outside my hut, raised voices. I pulled the curtain aside and saw Avril a few feet away. A woman was up in her face, shouting and pointing her finger. She was tall, slim and blonde, and was wearing blue Nike shorts and a hot pink Nike vest. Avril stood firmly, not budging an inch, even though I was sure she could have swatted her away. She was listening to her but wasn't fazed by her behaviour. I couldn't figure out what was being said, but eventually the woman stopped shouting and started crying. Avril opened her arms, and the woman fell into them. But it seemed like an obligation to Avril, that she needed to do this. That this was part of her job here on Totini.

As the woman collapsed into her, Avril's head turned towards me. I dropped the curtain and stepped back. It was obvious that there would be heightened emotions, even somewhere as perfect as Totini. With now over thirty people living here, it didn't matter how harmonious the surroundings were, we were humans with complex minds. Perhaps she had received some bad news from back home. I then thought about my family and took my phone from my pocket. Still no signal. Kali had already told me not to expect any, yet I still hoped for a bar or two to somehow appear. Kali was right. We were as far off the grid as we could possibly be right now. I looked instead at the final message I'd had from my mum.

*I do wish you were with Bruno; I would feel so much better about all of this.*

I hadn't replied to that one. Mum existed in a world where I had callously thrown away my relationship with a man who was kind, giving and financially stable. The latter was true. And it seemed it was perhaps the only reason she wanted to see me settle with Bruno. I hadn't been able to bring myself to tell her the truth. I think it would have hurt her a lot more to know what Bruno really was, than the idea that a marriage was off the cards. I'd slipped away quickly to avoid the confrontation with my family. I thought my sister might understand, but it had all happened so fast, Bruno's final act that brought me to Fiji. I didn't have time to even try and explain it to her. It seemed like a lifetime ago. As I stood in the hut, I realised it would be easy to forget those closest to you when you were thousands of miles away. But somehow, Bruno's words remained.

*Disappointment*.

I decided to leave my things as they were; as tired as I was, I wouldn't rest. I was eager to meet people and not feel like the new campmate for too long.

I left the hut and headed back towards the smell of the fire. I absorbed some more of my surroundings from the outskirts, hopefully sinking into the trees where I didn't stand out too much. The weather was different here on the island. The mainland was stifling and often unbearable, carrying the scent of car fumes and food trucks. Here, there was some relief with the sea breeze all around us, yet the heat still wrapped itself around me and held me in a clinch, hopefully until sunset when there would finally be some relief.

One hut was standing by itself, which I hadn't noticed before. It was set even further back from the camp. It looked more prominent than the others. I wondered what it was used for. If it was another store. Hens walked freely around me, and a large rooster paraded around the campfire, confidence oozing from him as though he knew he wasn't about to become someone's dinner anytime soon and that he had the pick of all the hens. There were signs of activities, things that had been going on before I arrived: washing hanging from a line between two trees, a pile of coconuts waiting to be husked. I saw a large pot sitting next to the fire, and my stomach grumbled. I wondered what was in it. Then, just a few metres away, was a large machete leaning against the trunk of a tree.

'That's a big bastard,' I whispered to myself.

I heard voices between the trees behind me, and a small group of women walked through and into the campfire. Two small children, about four and six years old trotted next to one of the women. More people emerged as a gong was rung for dinner. I imagined that after some time living in such a place, your body automatically knows when it is time to eat. Before long, the camp was buzzing, with a pre-dinner vibe; it looked like a small soiree, a gathering before some sort of event. Except the event was simply dinner. But already I liked that about this place, that eating was significant enough that everyone came together to do it at once en masse.

I looked at the arrivals and began to count. I saw Avril amongst the group now, and I counted thirty-one, including me. I looked hard at every person gathering around the fireplace, and scrutinising each of their faces one by one until I was completely sure. But even then, I was confused and found it hard to comprehend that every single one was a woman.

Where were all the men?

# 8

## THEN

'We like to think of ourselves as a very elite group,' Mary said to me as the group of women gathered around the fire. The smell of the dinner was a few feet away from me, and I was ravenous after many hours of travel.

'Was it a conscious choice or did it just happen?' I asked Mary.

Mary sucked in a long, slow breath. 'That's a very good question. One I believe that Avril has a better answer for. But it has been a long day for you already, and we are hungry. We must eat. Please sit.' Mary pointed to a seat fashioned out of a selection of colourful cushions at the very pointy edge of what I now realised was a triangle-shaped seating arrangement, the flat base at the bottom of the camp, the tip pointing towards the huts and the trees and forests beyond. The seat at the top was where I was expected to sit.

'It looks like a place for someone important,' I said.

'A new campmate is the most important guest of all.' Mary signalled to the seat again. It remained empty as the other spaces filled up with eager diners. Already her demeanour towards me was more welcoming than Kali's.

A woman in a purple hair turban placed a steaming stew into wooden bowls. She looked a lot older than the other women, I could tell from the way her skin had lined from age, but she still had an air of youth about her. She smiled at me from afar and motioned for me to sit in the most delicate way anyone had ever done so before; it was mesmerising. I felt a sensation that I was at home, that this was my mother and that I was going to be looked after.

A few glances came my way as I sunk into the cushion, which was surprisingly yielding and encasing around my rear end. I was handed my bowl of food, and I felt humble, suddenly smaller somehow, that this community had existed all this time without me. Now I had wandered into it, and I was welcomed without any questions.

'Everyone,' Avril spoke loudly and the group fell silent. 'I want you all to welcome our new campmate. This is Sadie and she is going to be staying with us. I hope you will all give her a warm Totini welcome and help her get settled.' Avril began clapping her hands and suddenly the whole group was clapping. I felt a rush of joy. I don't think I had ever heard an applause like that, which was just for me, before. The applause fell into a beat and then I realised they were chanting. I couldn't make it out, a three-syllable word that sounded like coowee nee. Finally it faded and spoons were picked up and the women began eating.

There was a hushed conversation around the campfire as everyone ate, politely. Avril was sitting opposite me and now and then our eyes would meet, and she seemed to be checking in with me. She looked about the circle often as she ate, rarely letting her eyes drop down to her lap where her food was. And I realised after some time that she was surveying the whole group. She was watching over them, these twenty-nine other women, as though she were the teacher and they were her students. I had often wondered how such a commune would operate and now I knew the answer. I was suddenly part of one, thrust into a new way of life overnight. It was obvious that Avril was the leader. I was in awe of what I was a part of here. So many women, all living seemingly in harmony. Was that possible?

I was handed a cup of kava, the drink of Fiji, which if drunk in excess could cause you to become quite drunk, or even lead to hallucinations. I wasn't ready for that on my first night on the island. I had drunk kava before but never went overboard. I took a few sips and passed the cup on.

'So you're new,' a girl to my right began. She had dark skin and an Australian accent.

I smiled wearily. The kava had given my travel tiredness a little kick.

'I am. How long have you been here?'

'Six months.' She squinted as she thought. 'Seven months, yes seven months.'

Seven months was a long time. I hadn't considered how long I was going to stay or even how long I was welcome.

'So what brought you here? I mean, I'm trying to get my head around this being an all-women commune.'

'It is pretty mad, right?'

I laughed. 'Yeah, like we have to come all the way here to get away from them.' I laughed a little harder and then I noticed that the woman wasn't laughing, only smiling at me.

'I'm Sofia,' she offered and I wondered if she would do the same thing that had happened to me with Kali and Mary and press her head against mine, but she didn't even offer her hand.

I glanced over at Avril then, as though I could sense that she might be watching my interaction. And she was. I looked away and back at Sofia.

'It is nice to meet you. I'm Sadie.'

'Oh, this is nice; our names, they're similar.'

I smiled. 'Yes, they both begin with S,' I agreed.

Sofia was sweet. She seemed quite naive, and I wondered if this was why she had been brought under the wing of Avril here on the island of Totini. It would be nice to get some sort of clarity about the roots of this island, and I was sure tomorrow would bring just that. For now, I was just going to sit back, take it all in and go to bed tired, full of stew and kava.

I listened to Sofia chat with me about her life here on the island and her interaction with some turtles yesterday, and I was soothed into a lulling state. When dinner was over, more kava arrived, and this time, I didn't hesitate. A few women came and said hello to me, they must have mentioned their names but I was far too drunk to remember. The day had well and truly taken its toll. Finally, a woman bent down in front of me. She had blonde hair tied into a ponytail, and she wore a Nike sports vest and shorts. Even through my drunken and tired haze, I recognised her as the woman who had been shouting and then crying with Avril outside my cabin earlier.

'Hi, I'm Clara.' She looked at me curiously. 'Let's get you to the cabin.'

'Clara!' I grinned. Now I could hear I was drunk, I had already sensed it in my body.

This was Clara, with whom I would be sharing a cabin. She was young and very pretty and, wow, so very strong. She pulled me up from my sitting position, where I had feared I would end up staying the whole night, and then cradled my arm through hers as we began walking back to the cabin.

'The first day is exhausting. I remember getting here, and it took it out of me; I slept solidly for, like, two days.' Clara had a strong American accent; from the way she looked, all sporty and tanned, and her accent, which I recognised from spending time in LA, I presumed she was from somewhere in California.

We reached the cabin and Clara helped me up the steps.

'This is so kind of you,' I said and I realised I was slurring my words now. I had drunk more than I realised when the kava was passed round a second and third time.

'That's why we have cabin buddies,' she said.

'That's nice,' I said as I fell towards my bed, Clara holding me a little to help break the fall.

She looked over me. 'Okay, you'll be good.'

She left the hut. I must have fallen into some sort of slumber, because a little while later I heard the cabin door creak open and Clara came in. I saw her strip down to her underwear. She took three long gulps from a bottle of Fijian water and then climbed under her thin sheet.

I was falling back to sleep when I thought about what Clara had said and how everyone had a room buddy. Who was Clara's room buddy before me, and where was she now?

# 9
# NOW

'Are you sleeping?' Dr Bhaduri asks.

I shrug. 'I do and I don't. Depends if I'm tired.'

He nods and writes something on his notepad. I have an urge to lean forward and look. I wonder if this is normal. I wonder if I am normal. I wouldn't be here now, sitting in a room with too much mahogany furniture and the stench of lily of the valley overstimulating my senses if there wasn't a word for what I was now. I scan the room for one of those triangle plastic containers with the slits in them and the sickly yellow gel in the middle. My eyes fall upon the offensive object, expelling the scent on a shelf in the corner of the room. I was sure it wasn't there last week. Smells are our biggest memory evoker; that I know for sure. I was sure this smell of lily of the valley was bringing with it images of an auntie. Maybe a grandma. I couldn't quite catch the memory; it came close and then seemed to disappear into nothing.

'So sleeping is not too much of a problem,' Dr Bhaduri asks again, and I suddenly wonder if I'd answered wrong, if I should have said I wasn't sleeping at all. Was that the response he was looking for? Would that tick some boxes on their little forms? Of course, there was the dream, the recurring nightmare. But it wasn't as often as it had been, and I would always wake at a reasonable hour in the morning.

He shifts in his seat. I wonder if he is bored of all this. How many times have I been here now? Three, maybe four times. Our conversations keep to the same lines of questioning and the same few problem-building skills to give me the tools I will need to deal with what has happened to me. But that would only work when I knew what had happened surely? And they are trying to enter my subconscious and find out what happened leading up to the day I was found floating in the South Pacific Ocean. It's all in my notes. I am retold the same story at the beginning of every session. I knew there was more I needed to say, more I should be doing to help myself. Then I wouldn't need to be here, wasting all this money; wasting all this time. Dr Bhaduri's time. He looks as though he has a lovely wife at home who cooks him a delicious meal every night and irons those pristine white shirts he wears every day. My body does an involuntary jolt, a side effect of not sleeping properly, never knowing if I am in a dream or fully awake.

'Are you okay?' he asks.

I nod. 'Fine.'

But I can't look at him; I need to look away for a few moments. I find a mark that looks like a scuff or a burn on the carpet and focus on that.

What will happen if I just come here each week and nothing changes? Was I then to be certified completely mad?

'And any flashbacks, sudden memories, or images?'

I think of the pile of paper stuffed in my wardrobe with the scribbles on them. The images flash in front of my eyes like a film reel. I must have been quiet for too long because Dr Bhaduri speaks.

'Sadie? Any flashbacks?'

How could I tell him what was on the paper, what I had drawn, what had come from my memory?

I think about what might happen if I talk about those things I drew, that I still draw like a woman possessed who can't get them out of her head.

I imagine explaining that I have been drawing pictures of the things that haunt my dreams. That will open Dr Bhaduri's eyes to something new. He will probably stop looking bored and uncross his legs, maybe lean forward, and say something like *tell me more*.

It intrigues me how such a thing can change everything in an instant. But I cannot find the words to explain it. So I shake my head.

'No. Nothing.'

Dr Bhaduri knows we have barely scratched the surface. He knows there is so much more to explore and that it will come out eventually.

I wonder how much time I have left.

# 10
## THEN

The sound of roosters crowing gradually roused me from sleep and I wasn't surprised to see on my phone that it was only just after 5 a.m. My phone was down to its last bit of battery, and I knew after that I would have to rely on my body clock and the position of the sun to know the time, unless there was someone with a watch on the island. A half-hazy light filled the cabin as I realised I had left the curtains open. I felt surprised that I had fallen into such a long and deep sleep. I was used to the heat already, having lived in Nadi for over a month, but it was a new bed, albeit comfortable enough, and new surroundings always challenged me at first; it would often take a night or two to adapt. Clara's bed was empty and her bed neatly made. It was if she hadn't been there at all. The half drunk bottle of water remained next to her bed. I stepped outside of my cabin, needing to be near the water's edge. I also knew I would catch the sunrise, something I had not experienced enough since I had been here. Living just that far away from the beach meant I had become lackadaisical in my attempts to immerse myself amongst the natural beauty of the landscape.

I pulled on a T-shirt and light sweatshirt, which both smelt of the fire from last night's dinner. I thought of the kava; I had drunk way more than I had intended, yet still, I was sure I had been sensible with my portions, not wanting to be tripping out on my first night on a new island. When I reached the water's edge, the stillness of dawn thrilled me. The sky glowed pink and orange, and my spine tingled as a warm breeze grazed my bare legs. Waves gently lapped at the shore and I looked out across the expanse of sea in front of me, unable to believe there was so much of it between me and anyone I knew back home. Yet the sight and feel of it all, knowing that I was here and I had only to share it with a handful of others, excited me and I fell to the ground and let the waves lull me back into a melodic state. I was still wrapped in the warm fuzzy blanket of sleep that I found it easy to bring myself back to an even breathing rhythm.

And even though those thirty other women were just a few hundred yards away from me, I could have been entirely alone. I imagined for a moment that I was alone and solitary, like a castaway. I wondered what I would do and how I would survive. Even with my campmates around me, I was still in a situation where I needed to consider my survival. I was no longer on the mainland; I no longer had a job or income. I would need to do whatever everyone else here did to survive, and I hoped I could adapt. I had come to Fiji to escape Bruno, yet he had still penetrated my thoughts for the last month. And sometimes, much to my annoyance, images of the better times plagued me at moments when I was feeling weak from lack of sleep or just too much alcohol. Or now, when I had thrust myself into another new situation just a few weeks after fleeing the country. But for the first time, since I had crossed the International Date Line, I felt a simmering of contentment, enough to recognise what I had done, what I had achieved. I had come far enough away and not just in miles. We no longer shared the same day, which felt like I was further away. I felt like one of those people creating mantras for their life and sticking to them.

*You're nothing.*

He was still in my head, but already his words were a little quieter. I could finally hear my own words and thoughts taking shape. I knew that the power of this island could make space for me to heal and I had only been here a matter of hours. I had seen it on the faces of the women who were here already and I knew that could be me too.

'Wow.' I breathed the word out loud. I thought I heard the words echo back at me, and I looked around to see if I had missed someone approaching. Sometimes the quiet played tricks with my ears, I was so unused to silence at that level.

The beach was empty, a prospect that might have terrified me a year ago because I had been used to sitting in the houses of others, listening to their DIY anecdotes, feeling as though I needed to be surrounded by so many other people, even though I had nothing in common with them, just so I could feel less alone because that was how I thought I needed to be. Society had taught me that I needed constant distractions and affirmation for the smallest of achievements. I thought about the other women sleeping in their huts. I thought about the kinship, the sisterhood I was about to be a part of. I hoped I would finally be surrounded by like-minded people who only needed the basics to get by and who had lifetimes of stories to tell.

First, I wanted to speak with Avril, to ask why she didn't tell me before that it was a female-only commune, or that we needed three modes of transport to get here. Did she think that may have deterred me? Now I was here, though, and the initial surprise had worn off, I was content to share the next however long of my journey here in Fiji with only women.

I looked to the left and to the right and tried to envisage how big the island was. I guessed at about two hundred acres in size. Fairly small compared to some of the other islands I had heard of and also Kenco from where we had just come. I imagined I could walk around it in two hours. I looked up to see a small hiking trail that led up to the highest point, which was probably about eighty metres, and led to a small cliff that overlooked the front beach, but it also looked dangerous. There were lots of rocks on the way down and if you fell I imagined it could be fatal. Yet, I was excited by the prospect of getting up there and exploring and I knew I would want to check that out as soon as possible, whilst being extra vigilant. I couldn't get any further off the beaten track, yet somehow I wanted more. The sky had begun to change colour again. Golden streaks of light were breaking through a thin layer of cloud, a golden ball was peeking up from the horizon and I could see the sky had lightened to a dark blue.

'It's beautiful isn't it?'

I saw a pair of legs. I looked up and a woman in denim shorts and white vest standing next to me, her hands on her hips, her shoulders thrust backward, looking out towards the sea and beyond. There had been a lot of us at dinner and I couldn't place her face. Despite my tired and drunken state last night, I noted how all the women who were there seemed to curve into their surroundings, as though the island and they had become one. They all had a worn-in look.

'Hi.' She held her hand out to shake mine and I jumped to my feet to greet her standing.

'I'm Precious.'

I smiled at the name.

'I know,' Precious said. 'It's pretentious as hell. But I'm own-ing it. It's my birth name; I'm not a hooker or a stripper.' She laughed and her eyes twinkled.

I clung to her hand, not feeling I needed to let go immedi-ately. She was slim all over, with thin arms and slender fingers. Her long brown hair was neatly tied back into a ponytail. It was nice to hear an English accent.

'I like it. Sorry if you've had to say that to everyone you've ever met. I'm Sadie.'

'I've said it once or twice.' She laughed again and we dropped hands. 'It's nice to meet you, Sadie. I retired pretty early last night, so we didn't have the pleasure. But there are a few of us here so I'm sure you were spoilt for conversation.'

'The conversation,' I said. 'What was that again? After sev-eral kavas I could barely remember my own name. My room buddy put me to bed.' I chuckled.

'Ahh, the kava. I rarely participate myself. Only on special occasions. Not that last night wasn't a special occasion, I just really wanted to be up early with a fresh head today.'

'I imagine there must be loads of special occasions what with thirty women on the island.'

'Oh, more than you would think.' Precious raised her eyebrows, suggesting a sense of wickedness, and I imagined the women celebrating birthdays in true style. I felt a shiver of excitement at the prospect of the soirees and conversations ahead of me.

We both looked back at the horizon in companionable silence. Then Precious lifted her skinny arms over her head, her shoulder bones clicking from the stretch.

'Has anyone shown you the island yet?'

'I was here just before dinner yesterday so, no.'

'Well, that is good. I was a castle tour guide in my teens and I consider myself the best woman for the job here, don't let anyone tell you differently. I imagine Avril wanted to do it.' I detected a bend in her tone when she mentioned Avril's name. 'But I beat her to it, so come on.'

Precious began walking the opposite way from the camp to the open stretch of beach. She sounded as excited as a young girl, and her enthusiasm was infectious. Despite my heavy head from a day's travelling, I found myself trotting excitedly after her.

How fast a sunrise is, I thought, having never seen that many before in my life. I had always imagined them as a long process. But before I knew it the sun was up and ready to serve the day as if it hadn't been hiding all night.

'I've come here often,' Precious said. 'To see the sun rise. It doesn't get boring.'

'That's good to know. I was amazed. I'm glad that the wow factor isn't going anywhere.'

'The wow factor,' Precious repeated. I could hear a smile in her voice. I wasn't sure if she was mocking me.

We found ourselves at the curve of the island and sands even whiter than the ones I'd seen on any beach so far. Baby blacktip reef sharks were swimming in the shallows, and I stepped towards the waters and paddled as we walked, watching how they dared to swim close to me before swerving away. As we walked I saw perched on some rocks, almost entirely hidden by foliage and small bushes, streaks of wood. It looked like some sort of outbuilding or another hut. I moved from the water and pointed it out to Precious.

'What's that up there?'

'It's what was left over when a small tribe was living here some thirty or forty years ago. I think it was used for storing medicines. And now, Ula lives there.'

'Someone lives there?' I asked.

Precious was looking away towards the sea as I strained to see the hut as it was almost entirely encased by foliage.

'Ula. She prefers to live alone. It's her choice. We just let her get on with it.' There was little warmth to Precious's tone.

'And do you visit her? Does anyone check on her?' I could hear the concern in my voice, the desperation that I needed to know this faceless stranger was okay. Yet also, I felt a sense of unease, that someone lived segregated from the others. How could that ever be the case? Didn't the women look after each other?

'She prefers to be alone. She knows where we are if she needs us,' Precious said with a matter-of-fact tone.

I looked at her, waiting for an expression of concern or empathy, but there was nothing. I felt sadness for Ula, who was in that solitary hut. The island was remote enough without segregating yourself even more. I already knew I would want to visit Ula, but I could sense that the desire was tinted with danger. I hadn't been told that visiting her was off-limits, but it was obvious that she wasn't a real part of their community, and I wanted to know why.

Then another question that seemed so glaringly obvious needed to be asked. I hadn't got the reply I needed last night.

'Why is it an only-female camp?' I asked.

'Circumstance. That's how it began, and men just didn't fit. Avril has wanted it this way ever since. She will talk to you more about that, I'm sure.'

Precious was somewhere else again, her mind wandering. Her answer made sense, especially as I had escaped a man who had been physically and verbally abusive. I could understand that other women might not want or need to be around men. And already it felt right, as though it were all meant to be.

The hut came fully into view as I continued to look up, yet it was still hidden by some foliage. Despite the searing heat, I felt a cold shiver down my spine. I didn't like the idea that someone living on Totini was not part of the group. My mind was full of questions. Why had she decided to segregate herself? Had they tried to get her back? Had she been forcibly removed? I had so many things to ask, but none of them felt appropriate at the time. They wouldn't form into sentences that I felt comfortable asking right now. I had a sense that Precious did not wish to talk about Ula. But that would not deter me.

Precious and I had walked halfway around to the other side of the island, but Precious stopped abruptly. A sound rang out, a screeching like a bird.

A woman was standing at the edge of the forest on the small patch of sand, about four hundred yards away, one hand on her chest, one on her hip. She didn't move. She didn't wave. Precious stared at her. The woman looked back at us.

'It's far too hot to go any further. We tend to stick to this side of the island. There isn't much else going on that end, except the cattle grazing.' Precious turned and looked back the way we had come. I was tired so I didn't protest but I knew I would have liked to have gone all the way, to see what the back end of the island held. Where the forest had grown together into a cone shape that stretched right to the edge of the sand.

'What does she want?' I looked at the woman. She had relaxed her stance and was standing with her hands by her sides. Another screech.

'Sadie,' Precious said with intent, and like an obedient child I caught up with her.

The walk back was quieter, and I felt questions about the woman were not welcome. The sun had fully come up, the flutter of cloud had disappeared, and the sky was a bright sheet of blue. Sweat was pooling in the small of my back. I wanted to get back to my room and fetch my costume and take a dip.

'There's a shortcut here.' Precious pointed to a small path that fed away from both the beach and the mountain, which led up to the hut where I had just been told Ula lived.

'Okay.' I followed Precious, grateful for a little shade as we quickly found ourselves amongst a thin, wooded area. I dutifully followed.

I didn't know Precious, yet I sensed an edge to her voice before we had turned around. The incident with the woman, the way she had been standing there alone, seemed odd. Precious hadn't greeted her and the woman hadn't greeted her back, yet they'd had some telepathic moment, and for whatever reason Precious had not been keen to continue the walk because of it. For now, she seemed to be rushing to get us through the clearing and back to camp. She could just be hungry, I thought. I had not eaten anything; I was ready for breakfast. Considering we were so far away from modern society, there should not be any restraints or hierarchy amongst us, yet I felt there was a sense of control. Which I supposed was different.

Precious was quite far in front of me. The leaves were brushing against me and I wasn't used to it. Combined with the sweat on my skin, I could feel it becoming irritated.

I heard a twig breaking. I spun around to the edge of the clearing where the trees were thicker and dense. I saw a flash of something, someone? Camouflaged into the forest but not quite. My eyes quickly tried to focus, and my senses were heightened. My heart began racing. This was fight or flight in the rawest of conditions. But as soon as I had seen it, it was gone along with a quick rustle of leaves. I looked up ahead at Precious, ready to call out to her, to say I had just seen something, but it was probably just a bird and I would have made a fool out of myself trying to draw attention to it.

Precious navigated us back through the middle of the woods and back to camp, and by this point, I was tired. Precious abandoned me at camp, next to the fire and eating area. Someone was already stirring a big pot of something steamy. The young girl and boy from yesterday were playing in the ashes by the fire. The little girl looked at me and smiled. I waved.

I watched Precious as she walked hurriedly to the larger hut, which hung back to the right of the camp and just away under the trees slightly. She walked up the steps and onto the veranda.

She tapped lightly on the door. The door opened after a few seconds. A sleepy-looking young woman stood there in vest and pants. She could only have been eighteen or nineteen. Her hair was long and hanging over her shoulders. Avril appeared behind her. She was wearing a long T-shirt, her hair scooped up on top of her head. Avril rested her hand on the girl's shoulder and stroked it, a tender touch . . . The girl turned and went back into the cabin, leaving Avril on the threshold listening as Precious spoke to her. I had acknowledged the calmness that Avril emitted. Whenever she was approached or whenever she was speaking with someone, she never seemed to lose her cool, look alarmed or seem out of control. She was centred. I knew then that I wanted to hone that trait for myself.

Precious, on the other hand, had run her fingers through her hair a few times in a manner that suggested she was stressed, and immediately, I thought of the woman at the far end of the beach. The way we had stopped walking and turned back. The strange stance with her hand on her chest. I thought, if you wanted to alert someone to something without making it obvious, could that be a way? I felt my gut twist as I began to sense that something could be happening and I wasn't to know if it was serious or not. I had no idea what the protocol was for any kind of emergency. I was miles from civilisation and my phone was about to die, taking all possible communication with the outside world with it.

# 11

## THEN

Avril came out of her hut dressed a few minutes later. A few women were mooching around camp, and I had stayed close by because I wanted to know exactly what was going on.

'Avril.' I reached her before she headed for the back of the camp where the stores were, a kitchen prep area under a canopy. There was also a large gong that had been rung for dinner last night.

'Is everything okay?' I asked tentatively, not wanting to show any sign of unease myself.

'Nothing for you to worry about,' she said calmly and continued on her way. I caught up with her.

'I just hoped we could have a chat today, you know.'

She stopped and looked at me. Then her face broke into a sympathetic smile. 'Of course, Sadie, I'm sorry, I have neglected you. Of course, we will talk today. Ask me anything you need to know. I just have to deal with one thing.'

She moved towards the gong, lifted the hammer and played out several beats, emitting a sound that carried across the camp. It wasn't the same simple double gong that had been sounded for dinner last night, it was a more complex sound, but short nonetheless. She laid down the hammer and turned to me and smiled.

'After breakfast okay?' she asked and I nodded.

'Sure, of course.'

I waited in camp and as I did I saw women arriving in droves. The gong sound must have woken them from their beds and they were being drawn to the camp. It was still early, not yet even 7 a.m., and from the tired looks on the faces of those who were making their way to the campfire, they did not look as if they were ready to get up. Was this usual practice, to be woken at a certain time?

Avril was now over at the prep area speaking with three other women dressed in similar beige and green combat shorts and vests and baseball caps. This was interesting, I thought. I approached a woman with the headscarf at the fire. She was putting water on to boil.

'Morning,' I said.

'Oh, hi, Sadie, isn't it?' She grinned. I noticed she had two missing teeth. I tried not to flinch at the sight of them. As a result, she spoke with a slight lisp.

'Yes, it is.'

'I'm Ray.'

'Hello, Ray.' She was one of the older ladies in the camp but she had an easy look and way about her.

She arranged the kettle in place over the fire and wiped her hands on her skirt. 'How are you settling in?'

'Okay,' I said, distracted by the three women and Avril talking. Avril seemed to be giving them instructions now. Her hands were making short sharp slices in the air in front of her then to her right. She pointed to the left and then made the sign with two hands, one sliced over the other, as though indicating something final, or something was over. 'I was just wondering what was going on this morning, why we're all up so early.'

'Protocol. Avril does this once a month or so. Training. We all need to be in one place to be accounted for.'

'Training?'

Ray waved her hand around. 'It happens rarely. We're on our own out here, so you know, we have to be prepared for any eventuality.'

It made sense and I was already imagining pirates. I supposed it was possible that anyone could just rock up. How did thirty-one females protect themselves in the middle of the South Pacific?

'Don't worry, you'll get to see everything that goes on in time. Avril would like you to relax for the next few days, just acclimatise.'

I wondered if it was going to take me a little longer to acclimatise when there was so much going on around me and so many things I didn't quite understand. Like why was Ula living solitary, what was the woman trying to signal to Precious this morning, why did Avril wake everyone so early and what sort of training was going on? I wanted to understand more about the island; I knew I was being impatient, and all this would come with time, and soon I would know why Avril had chosen to create an all-female commune. I had been promised time with Avril this morning, but I was almost certain that whatever the woman was signalling to Precious earlier was why Avril had raised everyone early and was now prepping some of the women.

'Would you like some porridge? Tea?' Ray asked.

'Yes, please.' I didn't want to turn down food, but I had lost my appetite. I watched as the three women and Avril disappeared through the other side of camp. The way they were headed could have been where Precious and I had arrived had the woman not stopped us in our tracks.

Ray began spooning porridge into a bowl.

'I'm just . . . would you excuse me for a second?'

Ray smiled. 'We've been asked to stay within camp,' she said quietly yet quite firmly, and with a grin still on her face. So that was what that gong had spelled out to all the campmates, except me, who was unfamiliar with any commands. I was unfamiliar with most things it seemed.

'Oh, sure, I went to the beach early. I just need to freshen up before breakfast.'

I hurried across the camp until I passed the prep kitchen stores and all our cabins. I could see where the forest set in again, but also a small clearing, a pathway that would lead into the trees. Not a large one from what I had seen and worked out from seeing both sides of the island but big enough that you could get lost in, if you weren't familiar with it, as I was not. I was taking a bit of a risk here, but then I took a risk arriving alone in Fiji, coming here to Totini, and putting my faith in Avril.

I could sense that I was going in the right direction, although there were no sounds ahead of me, and all I could hear was the gentle swish of the foliage on either side of me as it brushed against my skin and clothes, and my breath, heavy and hard. What was I expecting to discover that was making my heart race at such a pace?

I slowed down, never really knowing what I might come across or discover. It was getting hotter by the second; once the sun was up in Fiji that was it, you were cooking. I felt sweat around my neck and temple. I would probably get lost; that was the obvious outcome here. And there would be a search party out for me. Would there be a special gong for that? I thought of many things as I walked, and the image of Avril with the girl on the veranda of her hut this morning made me think about the relationships between other women here and in a place removed of all men, what their agendas were. I wondered if many had taken up celibacy, that they were glad to be away from the constraints of a relationship where sex was always an expectation and not the antidote to a happy marriage. I thought about Clara and how she was sweet with me last night, how I wanted to see her and thank her and how I was also looking forward to getting to know her more. It had felt like such a long time since I had really felt a proper connection.

I stopped suddenly. The path had opened up into a clearing. I didn't know which way to go; I couldn't see any more path. But Avril and the other three women had to have gone somewhere. I bent down and found a large stick and a heavy flat stone on the ground to my left. I moved them in front of the way I had just come from, and I began to walk around the clearing, looking for a way to continue. I heard a crack. The classic foot-on-stick sound and I swung around expecting to see Avril or one of the three women. But it wasn't any of them.

Instead I found myself standing face to face with a man. He was topless, wearing a pair of ripped shorts. He was hunched over; his face was slick with grease, sweat and dirt. Immediately I thought of pirates. The short gong sound. Terror gripped every inch of my body and I couldn't move or speak. The side of his face was bleeding, but on the other side was a large cut, an older one that hadn't healed properly. He was probably tall, but he was carrying himself in a way that made him look as though he were injured and in pain. His eyes were wide as he stared at me, and something in that stare told me he didn't want to hurt me. He looked as though he wanted to say something to me, but he just raised his finger to his lips.

'Stay where you are, Sadie.' Avril's voice. I swung around to see her behind me pointing a rifle at the man. I whipped back around and two of the three women were behind the man. He turned to dash but two more rifles appeared in his face.

'Turn around,' one of the women spat and now I could see it was Precious, her long sleek hair tied up and wearing a baseball cap. This was a different side to the woman than the one I had experienced on the beach earlier. Then the man turned back to face me. I could see now for the first time that there was fear in his eyes, and something else, a look of hopelessness.

'Take three steps back, Sadie,' came Avril's command and I did as she asked, so that we passed each other. She was now in front pointing that massive thing at the man, and I was behind her.

'Get on the ground,' Avril commanded and the man sunk to his knees. 'Hands behind your back.'

The man obeyed. Someone moved forward and I saw it was Kali. She produced some rope and quickly tied his wrists. The man was dragged to his feet. Precious kept a rifle aimed at him. Avril gave a nod and they kicked him forward, the two women stayed behind him, and disappeared into the forest.

Avril kept her rifle aimed at the spot for a few more seconds, lowered it, and turned to look at me.

'An unwanted guest,' she said coolly.

'Does that happen a lot?' I asked. My voice came out a little shaky. I had been here less than twenty-four hours and already there was so much to take in. Should I be feeling more worried?

'Not really. Rarely actually. But we must always remain vigilant.'

'So I have a lot of questions,' I said.

'Sure,' Avril said. 'This evening, we will talk.'

We watched the sunset from the clearing in the camp and ate a supper of vegetable chilli with garlic rice and green beans. I was feeling sleepy but I wanted to stay awake, to have the conversation I was promised with Avril. I had been thinking about the man all day; about that look on his face and how quickly he surrendered. How had he got here? I hadn't seen the other side of the island yet. Was that where he had moored his boat? Avril, Kali and Precious had been so efficient at dealing with the situation. But I wondered where he was now and what had become of him. What happened to those who came to the island uninvited?

'How long do you intend to stay with us, Sadie?' Ray, the older lady with her signature headband, was speaking to me. I was quiet for a moment, mulling over her question.

'Well, I was invited here, so I guess until I've outstayed my welcome.'

'There's no such thing as that here.' Ray laughed and flashed me those gaps in her teeth again.

'You will reach a point where you have everything you need. And you will realise over time that amounts to just a handful of things. Food, shelter, relationships with people who care about you and who you care about.'

'And that's it?' I laughed. 'That sounds pretty simple.' But I knew that was the only reason I had come here in the first place.

Ray shifted. 'Here comes the kava; take it easy tonight, Sadie.'

I watched it being carefully carried in a large wooden jug. Half coconut shells were being handed around.

Ray was handed a coconut and it was filled halfway. She gulped down the entire contents.

I smelt the overpowering earthy scent with a bitter spiced undertone taste as I drained my coconut cup and placed it on the ground.

The next thing I knew, there was music from a speaker. I turned and saw an old boombox cassette player, probably running on batteries. Women had sprung to their feet. I recognised the song as Abba's 'Dancing Queen'. Ray jumped to her feet and held her hands out to me.

'Come on,' she squealed.

And I was up. Dancing felt easier after the shot of kava, and I found that being in Fiji made my bones and muscles feel constantly supple, as though the warmth had made them so.

Within minutes, I felt my body relax even more than it had due to the heat and humidity on the island, so when a full coconut arrived again, I didn't hesitate to swallow it down.

I had seen Avril moving around the circle, and when I turned around, she was in front of me. She put her hands on my face and stroked my hair back.

'Sadie, look at you. You're glowing. Totini is doing you good.'

'I love it here,' I said as I looked around at the big all-female disco that was happening around me. 'Everyone is so chilled, so happy.' All thoughts of the man were behind me and no one else seemed to be making a big deal out of it. Precious and Kali had dealt with it without a fuss, and I didn't need to question it.

'Why do you think that is?' She slipped one arm on my waist, her finger grazed the skin between my vest and skirt. I felt my skin came alive under her touch, my drunken mind suddenly alert. Behind her, the young girl from her cabin was grasping at her shoulder. Avril turned and lifted her up into her arms, the girl's legs thrust around her waist, and Avril grabbed her buttocks and nuzzled into her neck before swinging back around to face me.

'This is my Lola,' Avril said. 'Have you met my Lola?'

Lola was looking into Avril's eyes as though she were the only person here on the island.

'No, we haven't met.' There was no interaction from Lola. She seemed young and was clearly obsessed with Avril.

'I promise, I'm all yours tomorrow,' Avril said. 'It's been a bit of a weird day.'

I nodded. 'Of course.'

'Good,' she replied. 'You're not going anywhere?'

'No.'

'Good.' Avril winked and walked away. Lola slipped down her body and into her arms. The two kissed passionately before disappearing into their cabin.

That night in my own hut, Clara and I sat up in our beds, legs crossed like we were at a pyjama party.

'So, you came from England?'

'Yes, I worked on the mainland first, selling chocolate, and I met Avril in a café and she asked me to come with her.'

'And so you did? Just like that?'

'I did,' I said. 'And you? How did you find this place? How did all these women find this place?'

'I was in Australia. I met Avril there. She was looking for more women to join the commune and so we came.'

'We?'

Clara looked down at her hands and squeezed them. 'I came with someone, but she left.'

'Oh, I'm sorry, you seem sad about that.'

'She was my best friend.' Clara looked up, her eyes sparkling with tears. She waved her hand. 'Anyway, that was last year. I have you now.' She smiled.

I listened to the soft sounds of Clara sleeping, thankful I hadn't been lumbered with a real snorer. I was on the ledge of consciousness, about to fall into the valley of sleep, when the image of the man from the clearing came at me. I gasped and opened my eyes. Clara stirred but didn't wake. I couldn't unsee that look. It hadn't been hopelessness; it was pure defeat. It was the look of someone who knew there was no escape. I fell asleep unable to shake the image of the sadness that his expression had carried.

# 12
## NOW

I wake up sweating. It is not a pleasant experience and so I shower straight away. Once I am dressed in a simple summer dress, I step outside. In a few strides, I arrive at the bench.

My bench. Jane is already waiting for me, and I begin to feel my heart lift and swell a little. I have felt despondent the last few days since my last meeting with Dr Bhaduri. There are things I was sure I was supposed to tell him, but I just didn't know where to start. The words are so muddled in my mind that the images swim and dart around like skittish tadpoles. Maybe I should try and speak to Jane about them instead? She has told me so much about herself already in such a short time, which is nice. I really appreciate her warmth and kindness. It is exactly what I need. I feel safe with Dr Bhaduri yet that moment I had at our last meeting has shaken me a little. But our meets are a necessity from his perspective and so I must continue to go.

I slide onto the bench next to her and she gives me a full smile.

'Good morning, Sadie. How are you today?'

'I'm well. A little hot,' I say as I shift about trying to arrange the dress so my legs don't stick to the bench.

Jane pours the coffee as she always does.

The coffee is tasty and exactly how I would make it for myself, although I can't remember the last time I made one. So it's nice that someone has thought about me and made one for me.

We don't see many people from this bench when we sit here. We have a view of a large plain of grass and beyond that a river that disappears between some trees. The cow field is to the right, but they aren't in it today. I wonder where they might be. My surroundings make me melancholic, like I am yearning for something, but I am not sure what. Maybe I will mention it to Jane and see if she ever gets those feelings. But I like how we can just sit. In silence for much of the time. I'm not bothered by the silence. I don't feel the need to fill the gaps with small talk.

Jane tops my coffee up again and offers me a biscuit, but I decline.

'I have a bit of dilemma I'm battling with today,' Jane begins. It's not unusual for her to talk this way; she usually has a lot going on in her life. Unlike mine, which appears relatively calm to everyone else; except in my own head things are a little busier.

'Oh?' I say. I'm never really sure what to say to people these days. I would be happy staying silent if the truth be told but people tend to look at me funny when I do that. So I try and say the right thing. I'm not sure if I get it right all the time though.

'Yeah. I need to tell someone something important today. But I'm not sure they are ready to hear it.'

'Sounds complicated,' I say, trying to take it all in because it did sound complicated. It sounded like one of those soap operas I had been watching on the TV at night.

'Ah yes, this one is very complex.'

'I guess if something needs to be said, it should be said,' I reply but thinking about my own muddled brain, filled with information I need to be rid of. I knew I was not the best person to be giving advice.

Jane looks at me and smiles. 'You're right. I just want it all to be okay. I like to try and fix things.'

'Sounds like it's one of those things that will sort itself soon enough,' I say, not even thinking about what I am saying. The words just seemed to come out of me.

Suddenly I feel Jane's hand on mine, and she is squeezing it. I look up at her. I think I see her eyes glistening with tears.

Then she laughs and takes her hand away. 'You're so perceptive; you know that?'

I laugh too. I'm not sure what she means. I'm not sure about much.

We sit quietly for a while.

'The weather certainly has turned out nice.' Jane is speaking again and my train of thought drifts away. 'Too hot for some maybe. For me actually. I don't manage too long in the heat.' She pauses before she carries on. 'But some people can. Some can spend hours in the sun. I envy those people, the ones who live in a really hot country or have lived in a hot country.'

My body jolts at her words.

The heat.

The humidity.

A flash of a face is in front of me then gone as quickly as it arrives. Blood on sand. A scream from far away. I can't reach them. I need to reach them.

I drain my coffee cup and stand up. I know I don't want to talk about heat or humidity.

'Thank you for the coffee, Jane; it was delicious as usual. Same time next week?'

I don't turn to see Jane's face as I leave, for fear it could be the same look of disappointment I see on most people's faces each day. I may have left Jane in the cold with my brash exit, but her words about heat are still penetrating through me. I can almost feel the sun burning my skin. I rush back to the bedroom, where it's cool, where I can push my face into the pillow and block out the memories that keep coming and coming. And soon I know I will not be able to hold them back.

## 13

## THEN

The roosters woke me again. I felt as though I had been in a coma. My head was throbbing with what? Heat? Tiredness? I couldn't figure it out. My body was also aching and as I stretched out one arm I could see a long red scratch from my wrist to my elbow from the forest yesterday. I searched the room for water and found a bottle with a few dregs left beside the bed. I gulped the remaining liquid down.

I wished more than anything that Avril would fulfil her promise to me today.

Clara's bed was empty again. She must be up and running at dawn. I leaned down to my phone in my backpack. It was officially dead. I hadn't seen any of the women with phones although Avril had one when we were travelling here. Was there somewhere to charge a phone here? I had seen generators for refrigerating food but there was no Wi-Fi. Maybe I could hitch a ride back to the neighbouring island and pick up some up there if I really wanted to call or text anyone, but I had messaged my parents and let them know I was travelling again. These were all the things I told myself, but the niggle in the pit of my stomach was trying to intervene, telling me I needed to be connected to the world. But I knew it was my Western roots poisoning my organic experience. I needed to learn to live freely. That was what I wanted, wasn't it? That was one of the main reasons I had run from England, to escape the constraints of life with Bruno.

I eventually gave up on sleep, crept from the cabin and picked my way down the path to the camp and then back out onto the front beach.

This beach wasn't quite as beautiful as the one further up by Ula's hut. It had a more rustic feel; it was used more often for campfires and there were some cricket posts made from driftwood stuck in the sand waiting for a game to resume at any point. I felt unsettled as I fell onto the sand and tried to concentrate on the sky turning from a bright orange to a light turquoise as the sun rose. It was cooler out here than in the cabin and I was sure I'd be able to fall asleep here for an hour. I wondered what my third day here would entail. I began to ponder how the camp was divided into tasks and duties, how they filled each hour and made the time count yet lived without expectations or rules.

But the mere thought of work made me realise I was still tired. I laid my head on the sand, curled into a foetal position, and felt the weight of sleep.

I woke suddenly to the sound of a child's laughter. I sat up, disorientated, unable to remember why I was on the beach and not in my cabin, and then I remembered the beautiful sunrise. The sun was higher in the sky. The temperature must have been getting on for the late twenties already.

A few feet away from me were the two children on the island, the young girl and boy. They both had dark hair so maybe they were siblings. They were playing on the sand; there were no adults in sight. Just then, I noticed, out of the corner of my eye a small object a few inches away from me. I reached out and picked it up. It was a rudimentary doll carved from wood and about six inches high. It had a basic round head and straight arms and legs, with a face scratched into the front of the head, which a child itself could have done. But it was the hair that was the most prominent on the doll. Several thick strands of the blondest locks had been attached to the scalp area. I inspected the head and I could see it had been done with strong glue. I touched the hair, reached to my own long light brown hair, and touched it. The texture was identical. This was real hair. Not unusual, I presumed, to create a toy out of whatever materials were to hand and one of the women must have given up a few extra locks to help make the doll. But I thought back to the women I had seen and met in camp. There were only two women I had seen tending to the children, I was sure one or both of them was the mother and they both had dark hair.

'Hey!' I called croakily to the little girl. She turned from where she was knelt next to the boy. 'Come here.' I waved her over. She came without hesitation and stood in front of me. I sat up and handed her the doll.

'Is this yours?' I asked.

'Yes,' she said with a slight lisp.

'Does she have a name?'

'Deny.'

'Deny? That's a lovely name.'

She took the doll from me and ran off, laughing as she did, until she rejoined the boy and settled back into the sand.

I heard a voice from the clearing in the woods and looked up. It was one of the mothers I tried to cast my memory back to a few nights ago when I was introduced to everyone, but it was hard to remember names on so little sleep whilst acclimatising to new surroundings.

The woman looked at me and smiled as the little girl and boy went running over to her.

'Breakfast is ready,' she called to me this time and I waved my hand in thanks.

As I walked back through the woods, I could hear a cacophony of sound coming from the camp. The clanking of pans, people calling to one another, the cockerels still making shrill calls, and then the welcoming smell of the tomatoes sizzling over an open fire. As I reached the woods, I saw the iron kettle hanging above the fire, and a large pot of something simmering on the other side. I stepped carefully over to the pot and peered inside. There were about two dozen eggs inside. I looked to my right. On a large board was a huge loaf of bread. Then I noticed an oven fashioned from bricks and clay and realised that was where it had been baked. I felt a small swell of joy rise through me and for a moment a sense of complete contentment: as though this was it, life was happening as I wanted and needed it to and I had finally arrived.

After breakfast, Avril still hadn't emerged. I ate my eggs and tomatoes as though it were my first proper meal in a year. Clara appeared as I finished.

'And how is our newest member of the camp?' she asked, showing me where the dishes were washed and left to dry, ready for dinner. I could smell body odour – was this how I would soon smell? Was this the signature cologne of the camp? I didn't mind it and I realised I had always liked it, both on myself and on others. But it hadn't felt acceptable to be aroused by it back home where men I knew covered themselves in every type of spray and aftershave. Bruno was a serial showerer, sometimes twice a day. Now I thought about it I wondered why we continued to mask our true scent. But then living in the UK, we masked a lot more than the way we smelt.

'I'm well, thank you. A little tired. My body is used to the heat, but it feels different here.'

'Everything is different here.' Clara laughed and I laughed with her, a light relief of comedy amongst the swell of questions still thick in my mind.

'I don't suppose we can charge phones here, can we?'

Clara looked serious and then laughed again. I was still for a moment and then I laughed with her again. Of course not, I thought. What a ridiculous notion. Why would the community want their beautiful island exposed to the world?

'You get used to it,' she said earnestly. 'It's not as bad as you think.'

I shook my head. 'Oh I know, I was never obsessed with my phone, and I always wanted to be somewhere I could just switch off.'

'Well, you've found it.'

I found it hard to imagine someone like Clara fitting in and literally switching off. She didn't have the same worn-in look as the rest of the women here. They all looked as though they had a part of the island living within them, as though the sea and sand had made their way into their skin. Clara looked as though she were visiting with her smart sportswear and her pristine tied-back blonde hair.

'You look tired though,' she said conveniently just as I was thinking how well-turned-out she looked. 'Your body will soon catch up with the different pace of life here and you'll be sleeping like a baby in no time. Have you had enough breakfast?'

'I have, thank you.'

'Did you try our eggs? The hens lay so many. That used to be my job, to look after the hens, feed them, put them away each night – so they lay in the morning in the same spot.'

'So what's your job now?' I asked keen to know. I was thinking about what my role might be in camp.

Clara looked away and mumbled something about helping Avril out with things now. She didn't want to discuss it, or it was menial maybe? But what could be more menial than looking after hens?

'I think you'll be very happy here, Sadie. We need a strong woman like you here.'

I laughed. 'Strong,' I repeated.

*You're nothing.*

'Often we don't see what others see in ourselves. You are more than what you think you are. I hope your time here will show you that. One of the things Totini urges in us all is to let go of all those doubts and constraints you have put on yourself. Labels. You know the thing Western society does to you without you knowing. Here you can feel and be whomever you want. You can experience whatever you want. You can try new things and not feel shame. Do you know what I mean?'

I looked at her and nodded, feeling her words, wanting them to embed into me. I wanted to lose all inhibitions and to live each moment without any feeling of fear or worry.

'Right, I'm tired. I need to have a nap.' Clara stretched and I was keen to know what job she had that got her up so early, meaning she was tired by breakfast. I watched her walk away back to our hut.

'Okay, I'm going to head back to the beach for a while.'

We parted and I took a slow walk back to the beach. I felt I needed to keep looking out at the horizon, to get my bearings. This was where I was right now, on Totini, and I wanted to live in the moment as much as I could. I reminded myself to do this daily on the mainland, but it felt more important to do it here because of the beauty and serenity of the place.

After some meditation, I went back to the hut. I opened the door and found Clara hunched over with her back to me. She straightened as I entered the room, and I saw her slip something into her rucksack and then she turned to look at me. Her eyes looked bloodshot. Had she been crying?

'Hey.' I sat on my bed and crossed my legs.

She turned all the way around to face me. 'How was the beach?'

'Still there.' I smiled. 'I feel I need to keep looking at it like I can't quite believe I'm here.'

'I know.'

'You were up early this morning.'

'I like to run,' she said quickly, 'and walk, before it gets too hot. It's the only way.'

I nodded. I hadn't thought about exercise, but I knew I would need to keep my body moving; early mornings seemed the best time.

'Maybe I'll join you one morning.'

'Maybe,' Clara said, not sounding convinced. 'I run fast. I like to do it alone.' She looked at me. 'But we can go together some mornings?' She flashed me a grin and I didn't feel as though she was trying to avoid being with me.

'I've always been an early riser,' I said. 'But it was hard to get up this morning after the travelling, and I'm still not really adapted to the temperature even though I've lived in Fiji for a month.'

'It's easy to rise early in paradise,' Clara said and we both realised how cheesy the line sounded. Clara laughed and I was pleased; we both had the same sense of humour.

'Well, what shall we do today then? Sit, walk, sit some more?' I laughed.

'I know, it'll take some getting used to, this slower way of life.'

'I presume I'm expected to do chores?' I had already imagined myself cooking on the open fire.

'This week they will just let you bed in. Don't worry, you'll be busy enough soon.'

'Yes,' I said yawning at the mere mention of it. 'I might take my book onto the back beach. Fancy joining me?' I asked Clara as I slipped on a bikini.

'I think I'll try and grab that forty winks. You were right – I was up particularly early this morning.'

I picked up my book from next to my bed and walked to the door. Clara was looking at her rucksack. Whatever was causing her sadness today was in there.

I headed through the woods the way Precious had taken me back yesterday. It was about a good twenty minutes to get to the other side of the island through this stretch of wood and when I arrived, I was not disappointed. It was still as spectacular as it was when I saw it yesterday. The island then stretched out and formed into a larger sphere on either side of this spot where denser forest lay in between both sides. I was happy with this spot for now. There was plenty of time to explore the deeper sides of the island. I put my towel and book down and decided to get in the sea for a quick swim. Nature's bath. It was luke-warm and I lay down on my back and let the water take my weight as I floated.

The ease of lying in water whilst it supported my whole body was exhilarating. The sky was cloudless. I turned over and swam out further, seeing shoals of fish beneath me. Then I took off following the shoreline and swam until I felt a pleasant ache in my arms and legs. It felt good to move my body. I stopped to tread water and looked left to where I could make out the speck that was my towel on the sand. Then I looked to my right and realised I had swum far enough to see the panes of wood through the foliage up on the hill. That was the hut that I had enquired about with Precious yesterday. That was where the woman Ula was.

I swam to the shore and stepped out, dripping onto the sand. The heat would dry me in minutes. I walked to the foot of the hill and tried to make out if there was some sort of path that led up to the hut, but I couldn't see one. The hut was barely visible even up close, as so many bushes encased it.

The words of Precious rang in my ears – Ula was looked after; it was her choice to live alone and so on – but curiosity had the better of me. I wasn't sure if I wanted to see her or just her dwellings. Either way, I had an urge to catch a glimpse of something. I got the impression I was supposed to leave her to her own devices but I was finding it difficult to accept that someone would and could live solitary here.

I pushed my way past a few shrubs and found that it opened onto a tiny pathway. A spot where it was apparent people had walked up and down a few times and so some of the brambles and shrubbery had cleared a space.

I felt a branch slice across my leg and winced at the pain. I would need to get back in the water to get some salt to it.

I found my way into the slight clearing. It was tight. It couldn't be used very often. I wondered again why Ula was living here alone. Had she really made that choice herself?

I began up the incline, my heart pounding with the exertion; it was steep, and with every step my muscles throbbed and my mouth became drier, the sun burned my neck.

I reached a point where the hut revealed itself a little more. I could see how worn down it was, much more so than the huts back in the main camp.

I dared myself to go a little closer, to walk to the other side where there would probably be a window alongside the front door. But as I approached the hut, I could see things on the outside of it: a pattern of sorts. As I got closer I could see they were handprints. Red handprints all over the back side of the house. Some were faded to barely anything, whilst some were bright and bold as though they had been put there fresh today. The newer ones overlapped the faded ones at specific points. The more I looked at them, the more confident I was that they had been made with blood. I felt my gut twist with unease, and I shivered despite the heat.

I tried to make myself walk around the other side of the house, but my body had frozen itself to the spot knowing I wanted to see more, but knowing I should retreat, head back down the incline, back to the beach that now seemed like a sanctuary. But the more I stared, the more I wanted to know. The same feeling I'd had when I had seen the other side of the island that they rarely used and when the man appeared in front of me. I wanted to know. I needed to know. I took three tentative steps, so I was halfway along the side of the house; there were more handprints along the side of the hut.

What if this woman was injured or in pain? What if those handprints were blood from an injury? But they looked too uniform and neat, as though they had been placed there purposely as decoration or as a statement of some kind.

I had barely taken one more step before I heard an animalistic noise coming from inside the hut. My heart lurched and I pushed my hand against the wood to steady myself.

*This isn't your business,* my head was telling me. I remembered the words of Precious yesterday. They had their reasons for leaving Ula to her own devices. What if she was dangerous?

The animal noise came again, this time louder.

I stopped and took a deep breath then took three long strides until I was at the front of the hut. There was no way to see in through the one window at the front; there was a curtain pulled tightly across. Whoever was in there must be sweltering.

'Sadie!' Someone was calling me from below.

I stepped to the ledge and peered down where Clara was waving up at me.

'Whatcha doing up there?' she called in her West Coast accent.

'I was walking and took a wrong turn,' I lied, looking behind me at a slight pathway that led down to the hut from the other side. It could have been true. I didn't want anyone to think I was trying to cause trouble here or going against every system they had in place; however inhumane it appeared from an outsider's perspective. She waved me down and I picked my way back through the bushes and down the tiny trail until I was back on the beach. She walked up to meet me.

'What were you doing up there?' she asked again, with that same dazzling smile, a real-life American sweetheart.

'Like I said, I was taking a walk. I stumbled upon the hut there.' I pointed back up to Ula's place.

'We tend to leave Ula to her own devices. She can come to us when she wants to. None of us are trained to deal with her behaviour.'

'Her behaviour?'

'She's slightly erratic, prone to a few outbursts.'

'So when was the last time anyone saw her, spent some time with her?'

Clara thought for a moment and stared up at the hut. 'I haven't seen her for a few months now. But some of the girls have. They're the ones who take the food up to her.'

'Right. What exactly is wrong with her?' I persisted. I felt Clara would want to tell me because we were room buddies and I felt I had more of a connection with her already than I'd had with anyone else.

'She's just a bit loopy. Different things happen to different people. We can't all stay sane, can we? I'd say she had problems before she came, and something triggered her and she just . . . went a bit mad.'

'Should someone not try to get her to the mainland, get her home to her family where she can be properly looked after?'

'She won't come out; no one can reason with her. She's too far gone.' Clara shook her head.

'So she's just going to stay there?' I stared back up at the hut, imagining a woman in there all alone, hunched in a corner, rocking or talking to herself.

Clara touched my arm. 'Hey, listen, Sadie, I know how you feel. I was the same as you. I wanted to save everyone. But then I had to accept that things are different here; it's not like it is back home. Sometimes, we must accept nature as nature.' She sounded sad yet so sure of herself; she had lived here much longer than I had. I knew I needed to let things be and not worry as Clara had said but I was buzzing with questions about everything and everyone.

'Fancy another swim? Bet I can beat you back to your towel over there?' She pointed along the sand.

She took off and was practically in the water before I thought to catch up with her and try to give her a run for her money. As soon as I was in the warm turquoise waters and with the sound of Clara's voice egging me on from ahead, I almost forgot about Ula alone in the hut. Almost.

# 14
## THEN

I arrived back at the camp with Clara, euphoric from the swim, glowing from the water and sun.

I spotted Avril straight away; she was walking through to the camp from the huts looking a little more than perturbed.

'Hey,' I said when I reached her.

'Morning.' She tried to shift the frown from her face.

I fixed her with an intent look. 'Okay?' I asked.

'Yes.' She breathed out. 'Let's go to my hut.'

Avril's hut was larger than mine and Clara's. All the curtains were closed bar an inch, inviting in a soft hazy stream of light.

I fell into a beanbag.

Avril walked around the dimly lit hut, which smelt strongly of incense, until eventually she reached the beanbag I was getting swallowed by and flopped down next to me on a similar-sized one.

'These are great. Where did you get them from?'

'Picked them up from Nadi.'

'Awesome.'

'Can you get me one next time you're there?' I asked.

She nodded. She seemed indifferent today. Not the enigmatic woman who had seduced me to coming to the island a few days ago.

'Do you think you'll be happy here?' Avril asked, not looking at me. She brushed the sand from her feet. I looked towards the window, feeling the presence of the water and its expanse all around me. I thought about the question and what I had seen and felt so far. There were lots of things I still wanted to find out, but I was beginning to feel the pull of the island. Whatever it was that had made all these women stay so far had begun to embed itself in me. Yet I still wondered why Avril would ask me this so soon after arriving. Was she that confident that I would fall under the spell of Totini?

'I could certainly be happy here,' I said, not wanting to give all of my feelings away at once. I looked at Avril. 'Are you happy?' I dared to ask when I knew so little about her.

'I'm happiest where others are happy, where there is justice,' she replied bluntly. Then she looked at me and smiled. 'You know what I mean though, don't you, Sadie? That guy at the bar in Nadi.' I shuddered at the mention of Tony. 'He triggered something in you. A man has hurt you. Am I right?'

It was my turn to look down at my feet and wipe away the sand.

But I managed a nod that I hoped Avril would see.

'That is why we must all stick together, us women. That's why we're here, to protect one another, to build one another up, to thrive, without the constraints of modern society but also, without the fear of men. There are no wolf whistles, no derogatory comments, no sexism, no inequality. No fear,' she added finally and with condemnation.

'And do you think the happiness on this island is down to the lack of men?' I asked.

Avril looked at me with wide eyes. 'What do you think?' she asked candidly.

I sniffed a laugh. 'I mean, you could be expected to think that. I look around, I see women helping women, building, cooking . . . protecting.' I cast my mind back to the sheer level of bravery I'd witnessed in those women yesterday. Despite the fact it was only one man. His face came to me again, that look of hopelessness.

Avril touched her arm and I noticed for the first time that she had a long cut along it.

'Avril, is that blood? Are you cut?'

She looked down at her arm and began rubbing at it furiously. 'My foot hit a sharp rock and I went straight over into a bush of thorns.'

I thought about the combat situation; had they been chasing the man for very long?

Avril was so clear about why there were just women on this island. But I was still curious as to what Avril had experienced to want to start an all-female commune. She had seen the damage in me, and now sitting so close to her, I could sense that she too had been hurt.

'Women are warriors, and while we have survived alongside men for many years, we also thrive when we are a tribe of females.' Avril stood up and went to the other window, which overlooked the camp, and pulled back the curtain an inch. 'Have you seen us, Sadie? Have you seen what we have achieved, what we can do?'

'I have seen. It's wonderful.'

Avril walked over to me and bent down so her eyes met mine. 'You will achieve great things here, Sadie. That's why I chose you to come here. You presented great strength the way you handled that drunk at the bar in Nadi.'

I thought back to the day I met Avril, and Tony at the bar. I had been terrified. But she had seen something in me that I hadn't ever seen.

'I was scared,' I said. 'Tony, and other men like him, they frighten me.' The anger was ripe in my voice.

'But you still stood your ground. You didn't give him what he wanted or try to appease him,' Avril encouraged.

'I suppose I didn't.'

'Can you see then, what we are capable of? And there is so much more to come. I want you here, Sadie. I like you very much.' Her eyes were locked on mine. 'I can see you have had troubles, that you are in recovery from some kind of trauma. It is palpable; I can literally taste it. Here you will recover. Here you will grow. Here you will change; in many ways, you won't recognise yourself. You are a chrysalis about to evolve into a beautiful butterfly.' Avril was holding my hands now. I looked down at them and on her wrist where I clocked the charm bracelet again. I looked at all the little pendants. I saw a dog, an umbrella, the letter A, a butterfly, and a Christmas tree, and that cupcake again. I wondered who had given each one to her and for what occasion.

I felt a slight fizzle in my tummy because no one had impacted me with their words in that way before. Not a teacher, not my parents and never a boyfriend. Yet this life was all I had ever wanted. But I had allowed myself to be held back. Bruno had held me back; he had tried to prevent me from evolving into a butterfly. This was what life was all about, lifting one another up. Yet despite all the uplifting words and this feeling of sisterhood, in the back of my mind I thought of Ula and why she was excluded from it all. All I could see was an image of a faceless woman I had never met.

That night in camp there was music. This time it was guitars, and there were some small conga drums being played. I was pulled to my feet by a tall black woman, who had been introduced to me as Paula. She was French and danced me into a frenzy as if her life depended on it.

When she spun me around for the final time and I thought I was going to fall over from dizziness, Avril was at my side.

'Hey.' She smiled.

'Hey,' I said back to her.

'It is customary for the new residents to dance with everyone,' she said.

Before I had chance to speak, she had pulled me into her, so our hips and chests were touching.

I let her lead.

'That way, no one will feel jealous, as if they have been left out.'

She moved well and there was a real strength in her arms around me as we made our way about the camp. Every now and then I caught the flicker of the flames from the fire out of the corner of my eye and I could feel the beat of the drums in my chest. There was a seriousness in her face that I had not seen since we had arrived. Her grip was on my hip yet every now and again I felt her move her hand or a finger just an inch. Then, she looked down at me and smiled, more with her eyes than her lips, and I felt airy and light as though she might lift me off my feet any moment. I tried to remind myself that this was a moment, another core memory in the making.

*Feel the beat, and feel the moment, Sadie,* I reminded myself. These were the things that I would store away for eternity. Being here with these women, no restraints, no rules.

It all suddenly seemed so raw and primal. Here we were, just a handful of people existing together, with no technology and nothing but each other for company, my body pressed against that of a stranger.

Despite feeling as though I was enjoying myself on the outside, on the inside there was a fizzing in my gut, of nervous energy that just wouldn't dissolve. There was so much yet that I didn't know about everyone here. I imagined each person and the years' worth of life stories they had to say about themselves. I wanted it all now; I wanted them all to know me already, to trust me. I wanted them to like me. But other thoughts conflicted with the wants and the needs. The ifs. What if they didn't like me? What if I didn't fit in or meet their expectations? What if I too went mad like the elusive Ula? What if I were cast out?

But somehow, I knew that wasn't to be my biggest worry. I could already feel the power of Totini, the deep pull of the island, as though it already had me in its grip, and no matter what happened next, I knew it would not want to let me go easily.

Jane didn't visit me this week. There was a message on a piece of paper in her place left on the bench. She had to visit a friend in the hospital. I wondered if I had offended her last time. I hadn't answered her question about having lived in a hot country and maybe she thought that was rude. I should have given her a response. But when I heard the question, my body froze, and the words wouldn't come out. I have noticed that happening a lot lately. But I hadn't mentioned it to Dr Bhaduri. I got the feeling that he already knew things that weren't completely normal were happening to me. But he didn't push to get me to reveal them to him. He must be on a good wage and the longer he spent with me, the more he made. It seemed he wanted to drag out our session for his own benefit. Was that a terrible thing to say? Were there psychotherapists out there who genuinely wanted to do a good job and help people? I had thought that I would be pretty good at that job, especially as I was good at sitting and listening. I could do that all day. That's what I enjoyed doing with Jane: listening. But she went and spoilt it and asked me that question, and now I think I may have ruined a good relationship. Probably one of the only relationships I have these days.

I made a promise to myself that if Jane's hospital appointment was genuine and she was back on that bench next week, then I would tell her one thing. Maybe she could make some sense of it. It would make a change from talking about coffee and the weather. Because perhaps if I told her something it would make room for all the other things that were squabbling for space in the depths of my mind. They had been dormant for some time; I had to admit I wasn't even sure I had any thoughts left. But suddenly it was as if they were all waking up and fighting for space to stretch their tendrils and touch the corners of my mind, forcing the words down to the tip of my tongue where they would spill out. I would let them, I thought, because holding on to them was painful and I didn't want to be in pain anymore.

# 16

## THEN

After four days I was assigned my first task.

Kali sat down by the fire with me after breakfast and brought out a blackboard I had seen propped up in various places around the camp. It was split into sections: cooking, cleaning camp, toilets, general maintenance and fishing.

I looked at her. 'It all seems pretty basic,' I said.

'Well it is pretty basic isn't it? I mean, there are times when the workload feels heavier, when people are sick or there is a lot of extra maintenance to catch up on, but lucky for you, we just dealt with a whole load before you arrived,' she said and I felt the accusation in her voice, as though I had chosen my timing perfectly.

'I was just expecting much more I guess.' Then I looked around the camp and realised that things were simple. The life the women had made for themselves here was self-sufficient, but the island offered them everything they needed.

All the squares on the board were empty.

'Am I getting first choice here?' I asked.

'Of course,' Kali said with a smile. I couldn't work out if it was genuine.

'I don't know, maybe I should clean the dunnies first, break myself in gently.'

'I'd say all jobs are equal but fishing is definitely a skill you'll develop,' Mary said next to me and I looked at Clara. She nodded enthusiastically.

I looked at Kali hopefully.

'Okay, put me down for fishing please.'

After lunch a few of us moved to the front beach where a volleyball game began.

'Some people like to sleep after lunch, but I love this when we all spontaneously play,' Clara said grabbing my hand. 'You're on my team.' She laughed excitedly.

As I looked across at our opponents, I saw Kali staring at me. She dropped her gaze and turned to her teammates: Mary and Precious. Clara and I also had Paula who glided about the camp like a goddess in her colourful kaftans. I hoped she was better at volleyball than I was. I had a sudden desire to win at this game for the sake of knowing I had beaten Kali. So far she had not shown me as much warmth as the other campmates and I was determined to prove my worth to her.

Kali played a hard game despite the searing midday sun. I guessed she was used to this heat, whereas I was still getting used to it. Even after a month on the mainland. But somehow, between Clara, Paula and I, we managed to beat the other team. Mary and Precious came and shook our hands and I watched as Kali walked away back through the woodland, heading for camp. The other two didn't show any response to Kali's rapid departure, which I was sure was to do with me more than losing at a friendly game of volleyball. But why did she feel so threatened by me? I was here to learn to grow and surely she could see that she was the one who could help me?

Clara and I walked back to camp – sweatier, hotter versions of ourselves – and drank water from the tower that collected the rainwater. It was always warm but today I was so thirsty I gulped it down like it was ice cold. Then we sat down on the dusty track, a thick ray of sun blasting through the trees above, encouraging us to lie back and absorb the heat.

'I can't believe this is my life,' I muttered, and Clara made a noise that sounded as though she were agreeing with me. But then she was quiet and when I looked over I could see her chest rising and falling slowly and realised she had fallen asleep. That was how easy it was just to be in the moment here. We were just like wild animals, snoozing in the midday sun wherever we lay.

For dinner that night we were invited to dress up a little for Precious's birthday. I was moved to see how much effort had been put in. Someone had made paper galas, or maybe they had been left over from previous celebrations and brought out again. Either way, the colour added a vibrant feel to the evening.

Someone had cooked a spicy stew, which required plenty of kava to knock it back with.

By the end of the night I was drunk and full and feeling joyous. Someone had even managed to make a chocolate cake. Sweet treats were a rarity here, I had heard, and after we sang happy birthday to Precious, everyone indulged, and the camp had never been so quiet for a few solitary minutes. Clara and I danced until we fell over, laughing like a pair of hyenas. As the camp began to break up and women began to go back to their huts, I noticed Kali over the other side of the camp. She walked over to me as Clara went to fill our water bottles.

'What are your intentions?' she asked bluntly, holding her water bottle in front of her as though she were protecting herself, although I knew I should be the one to feel threatened after the way I had seen her deal with the male intruder.

'My intentions?' I asked her back.

She nodded expectantly.

'I don't have any.' I was aware I was slurring.

'Come on,' Kali said as though she were trying to get me on her side.

I shook my head. 'I'm just here. Avril found me on the mainland. I'm here because I want to experience this life and—'

'I don't believe you.' She lurched forward as she spoke through gritted teeth.

'I don't know why you wouldn't believe me,' I said almost laughing and then I saw Kali's face change. Where she had been perturbed before she was angry with me now.

She looked over my shoulder, and I turned to see Clara returning with our bottles.

'Maybe just think about moving on quickly,' she said and turned and walked away.

Clara arrived next to me and handed me the full water bottle.

'Okay?' she asked, seeing my shocked face.

I felt a jab of sadness. I wanted to tell Clara what Kali had just said to me. But I didn't want the night to end on a sour note for anyone else, even though it had for me.

'Yeah, I'm okay,' I said.

'Well, I'm beat. Big day tomorrow,' Clara said, referring to my first day fishing, something I had been looking forward to doing but knowing that Kali was going to be there as well, I wasn't sure anymore.

The next morning I woke and Clara was not in her bed again. It was early and my body had already gotten used to the way the sky looked at certain times of the day, so I knew it was about 5 a.m. We were fishing at 9 a.m. I tried to lie and relax but all I could think about was where Clara was and why she wasn't in her bed. Running at 5 a.m. again? The sun was only just coming up. We had only gone to bed a few hours ago; perhaps it was her new role in camp that she hadn't divulged that was taking her away so early.

I sat up, hearing raised voices coming from outside the hut. I crept to the window and peered through. I saw Clara was back, and she and Avril were standing in front of one another and just a few yards from me. Clara looked as though she had come from the woods where I had yet to go. Avril looked as though she had just got out of bed. Her hair was a mad mess on the top of her head and she was wearing only a long T-shirt. She had both hands raised in front of her and waved them up and down. Clara said a few things back and then walked past Avril. Avril shouted something after her, but I had already ducked down as I didn't want to be seen. I jumped back into bed and tried to breathe normally. I heard the creak of the door as it opened and Clara padding to her bed. I heard a few sniffs and the rustle of her sheet as she climbed under it.

# 17

## THEN

I stood on the shore next to a small boat with a little petrol engine at the back.

'So we take this boat to a sandbank just around the other side of the bay and across the reef. We use snorkels and spears. We catch enough for today and tomorrow. Then we fish again,' Mary said.

I nodded. There were five of us heading out: Mary, Kali, Precious, Clara and me. I was glad to be spending more time with Clara. I wanted to ask her about this morning and why she needed to be out running so early.

We were headed to a speck of an island in the middle of the South Pacific. Thoughts spiralled through my mind about how far and remote we already were and now, we were headed to a piece of sand that was apparently no bigger than a couple of houses in length.

As we piled into the boat, my gut tightened. I had never fished a day in my life, let alone with rudimentary tools in the ocean with women I barely knew, and I didn't want to let the team down. More so I wanted to prove to Kali that it wasn't some fad I had come for, I was here for the long term, to learn and to become part of the commune. But what if I was outed for being completely incapable?

The boat took off, and Totini Island began to get smaller, and then as we rounded the reef the island became model-sized. I held my finger and thumb up to the horizon and tried to pinch it. In the space of only a few days I had come to appreciate the safety of my surroundings and now, back in the sea, I began to feel the enormity of it, and how far I was from home. I took a few long deep breaths as the wind hit my face, and I wondered if I'd applied enough sun cream, as the strength of the sun could be deceptive amongst the sea breezes.

Finally, after a bumpy thirty or so minutes the boat pulled up at the sandbank. And it truly was just a sandbank. If I had ever imagined in my head a deserted tropical island with one palm tree on it, it was this. Minus the palm tree. The length of it could only have been about a few hundred feet. I could have run to the end and back in less than a minute.

We stepped out of the boat and made our way up onto the sand.

Mary, Clara and Precious immediately began making a shelter out of three large sticks and some tarpaulin. I stood back in awe. A job that would have set me back a good hour, they accomplished in a matter of minutes. We then sat underneath whilst Mary talked me through the dos and don'ts and how to breathe through the snorkel; I had done it once a few years ago but I let her have her moment.

Then I watched Mary, Kali and Precious run and dive into the sea, and I noticed the sense of competition was fierce between them. I hoped their passion would mean they would overlook any poor offerings from me, as I already began to regret my decision as I watched their confidence soar with every whoop and leap into the water.

'You'll be fine,' Clara said, stepping towards the water in a white swimsuit that showed off her bronzed skin. I wondered why Clara wasn't already in the sea with the others. She was just as competitive and far more athletic, but she had been withdrawn since we had left Totini, deep in her own thoughts. I had my suspicions it was due to the fight she'd had with Avril earlier this morning.

I stepped out of my shorts and tentatively followed, allowing the water to embrace me as I eased myself in and then put the snorkel over my face.

To say it was amazing would be a poor use of an adjective, as I was already imagining retelling this story and how I would explain the feeling of being so far away from everything and everyone yet being at one with nature. I knew, however, as I tried to articulate it, it would sound weak, as though all the words in the world were not enough. The water was so shallow I only had to dip a few extra feet and I was touching the bottom. I came almost face to face with a turtle and the array of colours with the coral was a spectacular show. I pushed myself as hard as the others and took myself right to the edge of the reef where it dropped off to the depths of the ocean. I held my spear in my hand but every time I came close to one of those beautiful fish, I just could not bring myself to do it. So I swam around for half an hour or so, just immersing myself in the underwater scene.

I noticed the three women had become even more competitive, racing back to the shore with their catches and whooping like excited children. Clara remained reserved, working fast yet methodically. I thought that with the rate they were catching and with how keen they were to appease themselves and one another, maybe my lack of contribution would be overlooked. Just this once. I didn't want to appear as someone who couldn't kill her dinner, as I knew this was the way of life here; there was no popping to the local supermarket to pick up a packet of frozen fish and a bag of peas. And I was glad; this was what I wanted. I would try harder next time.

I had just come up to the surface for a rest, to float on my back for a few minutes when I heard the scream. It was shrill and without anything around us to absorb its intensity, I felt it penetrate my ears and into my head. I lost my bearings with the noise and so when I finally managed to spin myself around to look directly at the sandbank, I saw the drama unfolding. Mary and Clara were clamouring to the sandbank, one holding the other up. I couldn't quite work out which one at first and then I saw it. The spear through Clara's foot. She was screaming. Blood was gushing from the wound where the spear was firmly planted.

Everything seemed to slow down. I felt as though I were watching in slow motion. Precious reached the shore and pulled her snorkel off in one swift snapping action, then jogged to where the two women were. Clara was lying on the ground, writhing around trying to grab at her foot. Mary kept pushing her hands away and dancing around her, waving her hands, not knowing what to do.

What was currently playing out as a dreamlike scenario where I was safely amongst the shallows would soon be playing out in front of me as some sort of horror show the closer I got.

Eventually, I began to move forward until I was touching the sand, then as if someone had been playing a record on the wrong speed, everything around me sped up and became louder.

Mary was shouting to Kali to get her to start the boat; Precious was running around, grabbing all the fish then pulling the shelter down.

Kali appeared next to me. She turned and looked at me with a hard stare.

'Well, come on then!'

Panic surged through me and catapulted me into action. I dropped my snorkel on the sand and hurried to the tarpaulin, which was already half off. I pulled it all off and rolled it up into a sort of ball. I took it to the boat and stuffed it under one of the seats. Precious carried the fish to the boat and even amongst the chaos of it all, I thought it interesting how she carried out her work methodically, never wavering. And I thought how amongst this tragedy, the camp would still get fed tonight, and that was still at the forefront of her mind.

Kali had started the engine and Mary was now struggling to get Clara up off the ground so I knew this was my next task, and I raced over and bent down, forcing one of Clara's arms around my neck, trying to avert my eyes from the bloody mess on the top of her foot and the mass of blood that had dyed the sand around her feet and the very spear that was still lodged in her foot.

'Sadie, hold this.' Mary grabbed my hand and placed it on the spear, so I was keeping it upright and at the angle at which it went in.

Mary began picking up the spears and snorkels. All the while I stood next to Clara saying 'shhhh' over and over and: 'It will be okay. We'll get you to the mainland. You'll be fine.'

At one point I thought she looked at me. She was foaming at the mouth, her teeth clenched, but she was probably just willing me to make the pain stop. To make it all stop. But I didn't know how. I couldn't even catch the damn fish, and now I was standing here watching a woman bleed out through a hole in her foot and, again, I didn't know what to do. I had never felt so out of my depth and whilst I recited my mantra to Clara, my mind was drifting somewhere else, thoughts of how this had come to be, how I had ended up here. And I saw Bruno's face. And I remembered he was the reason I was here. And suddenly I felt a rage build inside. He had put me in this moment, dealing with things I wasn't able to deal with.

I looked down at the sand around my feet. It was slowly changing colour from bright white to a deep red. I let out a gasp and then pushed my hand over my mouth. But Clara had already seen my expression. There was so much blood. How would one stop that much blood? Did they have the necessary medical supplies to deal with this sort of emergency?

I looked to the boat where Mary had finished packing everything on board. Was it my imagination or did she seem a little less stressed now? She was jogging back to us with a little less speed than before. Where was the sense of urgency that had been there minutes ago?

Clara was making a noise and I looked at her as she coughed and then choked out a few hurried words.

'Keep . . . away . . .'

'I can't, Clara. I have to help you to the boat. Now try and push all your weight onto your other foot.'

'That's right, Clara, listen to what Sadie is saying,' Kali said suddenly next to me. I felt a moment of exhilaration that I was doing something right.

She took the other side of Clara and just before we hauled her up, I looked down at her to see if she was going to say any more. Her lips were open as though she were about to say something else. She had a fierce look in her eyes, then her head flopped back, and she passed out.

# 18

## THEN

We pulled up on shore on Totini Island. Mary began shouting to a few people on the sand, and within a minute there were enough women at the boat helping to carry Clara ashore. She remained passed out all the way back. I held her hand even though there was no grip from her.

I spoke quietly to Kali. 'What happened?'

Kali's voice was a little shaky. 'We were standing in the shallows. I saw a fish, harpooned it, turned out her foot was in the way.'

It seemed like a mistake that could have been avoided if she had been a little more careful as I recalled how all three of them were when they took off into the water, like three overexcited children. Perhaps they had been showing off. How many times had they done this fishing trip before I arrived? Was this possibly my fault? Had my presence affected their behaviour, resulting in the accident?

Avril came out of her hut and walked over to me.

'Oh my God, are you okay? I saw Clara; it looks really nasty.'

'It's bad. What's the protocol, do you think? Will they get her to a hospital?' My words came out staggered and breathy.

'We'll let Paula take a look first.' Avril touched my shoulder. I wanted to say it felt like more of an emergency and that she needed to be seen by a proper doctor in a hospital. What did Paula know, was she a qualified doctor? But surely they'd dealt with emergencies before. I reminded myself of how efficiently they had dealt with the man.

Before I could ask anyone any more questions, Clara was getting carried through the camp to the huts and beyond. I followed after them to see they had taken a left where the main communal area ended and became dense bush and foliage. To the area where I had not yet been.

'What's that way?' I thought of the other side of the island, the place Precious had refused to elaborate on.

'The hospital.'

'Hospital?' I repeated imagining a bright sterile room where Clara would be cared for and return to full health.

'Is Paula a doctor?' I asked.

Lola appeared next to Avril and placed her arms around her waist.

'We will do what we can for her, make her comfortable,' Avril said. She gave me a smile that seemed sympathetic.

Avril turned with the young girl towards her hut and I watched them walk away, arm in arm. But just before they went in, Avril glanced back at me. She held my gaze, a softness overcoming her entire face. After what had just happened? Maybe I was just overreacting, maybe this sort of stuff happened here all the time and they were used to it.

I ran to the clearing past the camp, past the huts where I had seen the women take Clara. But I saw no path leading through the bushes. But I had seen them come this way. I was sure of it.

I turned and Mary was there.

'Don't worry too much, Sadie. We have plenty of medical supplies here; they'll be stitching her up as we speak.'

'They?' I asked. They could be a team of Oompa Loompas for all I knew. For some reason I had not seen any women who looked as though they practised medicine professionally. But then none of the women were going to be walking around with a stethoscope and glasses peering down at me. Who would help Clara? I couldn't bear to think of her in pain the way I had seen her on the sandbank.

Then an almighty roar came from the bushes where they had just gone, followed by a pitiful cry that went on until eventually, it faded to nothing. I grabbed hold of Mary's arm, and she pulled me closer. I buried my head in her hair and held back the tears.

Avril stood up after we had all eaten dinner.

'I feel I should say a few words for the sake of our newcomer.' Avril's eyes were on me.

'I'm sure you all know by now, but just so you are all aware, our campmate and fellow sister, Clara, was involved in an accident today whilst spearfishing. The spear was removed from her foot and the appropriate methods have been applied.'

'Can't she just leave the island, go to the mainland and get treatment?' I said before I realised I was speaking. Clara had been on my mind all afternoon and the stress had been building.

'Clara's passport and visa ran out several months ago; officially she should not be here. We wouldn't want to make her life even more difficult than it already is. We will keep her here where we can tend to her and make her as comfortable as possible. We have pain relief and antibiotics.'

I looked around the camp at the others. Everyone's expressions were nonchalant. Someone began to softly strum the guitar and there was some homemade beer being passed around. I shook my head in bewilderment.

'Can I see her?' I said to Avril quietly.

'We see this a lot.' Avril chewed on a piece of pineapple that had been our dessert at dinner. A tension was building in my gut that hadn't been there for a few days. Avril hadn't answered my question.

'Do *you* think she'll be okay?' I asked Avril, quieter this time. The rest of camp had moved on and were no longer listening to her.

'When she is up to it, you can go and see her.' Avril touched my arm. She held it there for a while until Lola wrapped her arms around her shoulders and whispered something to Avril that made her laugh.

'Yes, yes I would love that,' I said but Avril was barely listening anymore. I felt stupid; I felt as though I were overreacting.

I decided to accept Avril's words and the general attitude of the camp for now, but tomorrow I wanted to see Clara. And then maybe speak to Avril about charging my phone. After the chaos and horror of today, I needed to hear the familiar voice of someone from back home.

The next day I knew there would be no phone call. I had asked Avril about charging my phone and she just looked at me with sadness.

'Sadie, you can't be serious. This is a special place; phones are not allowed. I'm sorry, I should have made that clear before you came. I presumed you would have realised that was obvious.'

'I just wanted . . .' I paused to think of how to say it, but before I could finish my sentence Avril started speaking.

'You feel terrible about Clara and you wanted to speak to someone back home,' she said and I nodded. She was perceptive – I had to give her that.

Avril came closer and put her hands on my hips and looked at me. 'I'm sorry you had to see that yesterday when you've only been here a few days. I can't imagine it was pleasant.' She stroked a piece of hair away from my face and tilted her head. 'You're in recovery and the last thing you needed was more trauma.' She put her hand back on my waist and I felt her step closer to me, so her hips were almost touching mine. I could feel the warmth of her breath on my lips. I looked into her eyes and yet again it was as if she were seeing everything of me, a true understanding that I hadn't felt since . . . I tried to think when someone had last made me feel seen. I wasn't sure I had ever felt this level of understanding.

Not even from my parents.

There was a shout from behind us. I spun around to see Lola in the doorway of Avril's hut.

Avril stepped back from me and walked over to her. I watched Lola raise her hands then move her head closer, gesticulating frantically. Avril put her hand on Lola's shoulder and pulled her into her chest. Lola relaxed against her immediately, and just before they walked into the hut together Avril turned and looked at me. I looked away, ashamed I had been caught observing their intimate moment.

I sat down around the campfire and began to play out the conversation I might have had, if I'd been able to use my mobile phone.

*'And you're looking after yourself? Eating well?'* My mother's concerned tone was almost too real in my head. I would want to mention the mystery of the woman living alone in a hut and the animalistic noises I heard coming from there. I knew I would want to tell her about what had happened on the sandbank island yesterday and that someone had been seriously injured. I would want to talk of the fear I felt when I saw someone's foot impaled by a fishing spear and how it had frozen me to the spot and my gut became jittery once we were all back at the island as I watched Clara being carried away to a place I had yet to see. And how no one appeared to be at all concerned for her, considering this was a commune, a close-knit community where we all looked out for one another. But as I thought all of this I realised all I was doing was highlighting my doubts about coming here, and that maybe this was a mistake.

But I would also want to tell my family how incredibly lucky I felt and that this was a once-in-a-lifetime experience that I could never have imagined in my wildest dreams. It was pure fluke that I was here, that Avril had discovered me at the bar on the mainland. I had been given a free ticket to paradise. The incident yesterday had shaken me, but real life didn't stop happening just because I was on this island.

I finished my imagined conversation by telling my family I loved them very much and I didn't have any return dates set but that I would see them soon.

'Sorry about her; she's needy.' Avril startled me out of my daydream as she took a seat next to me. 'She doesn't like me even talking to another woman, which is tricky considering we are thirty-one women on one island.'

I smiled. 'Yeah, tricky.'

'You need to be able to surrender yourself for a piece of paradise,' she said looking away into the distance. 'You're here for a reason. Forget who you were, what you stood for in the UK, what was expected of you. This is what it's all about.'

She smiled and I tried to feel what Avril wanted me to: the dream she was selling me, had been selling me since she picked me up in the bar less than a week ago. It was early days yet; I was right at the beginning. I needed time to bed in, I reminded myself and, of course, the risk Avril had taken bringing me to this island. They wanted their anonymity and I had to respect that, and as Avril said, I just needed to let myself go, to enjoy this haven. And if that was what was needed of me, then I would do it. Because no one knows what they are truly capable of until they are tested.

But despite Avril's meaningful words, I felt a sensation growing within the depths of my gut. Something was urging me to pay attention, and I kept batting it away; I wanted to surrender myself for a piece of paradise, but I wondered exactly how much of myself I was expected to give away.

## 19
## NOW

'Sadie, we need to start moving forward. I'm going to ask you a series of questions. Hopefully I can get a few answers to them that might help me help you.'

I look at Dr Bhaduri and blink slowly. This was all getting too much anyway. The flashbacks had increased the last few days. I was worrying more about Jane coming back to see me, and the piles of paper in the wardrobe were getting out of hand. If he could do something to ease some of my worries then that would be helpful. I wasn't going to turn my nose up at that.

'Okay,' I say. 'Fire away.'

Dr Bhaduri looks at me over the top of his glasses for another moment then lets out a long sigh. He uncrosses one leg and crosses it over the other, then puts his reading glasses on and looks down at the paper in his lap.

'Okay. Let's start with the basics, shall we? When was the last time you remember seeing your friend Avril?'

The name in this room sounds alien. I try to form a whole picture of her in my mind and keep it there, but the mind is an amazing thing. If you don't see someone for a period, you very quickly stop remembering what they look like.

But I couldn't picture Avril in my mind.

Avril. Had I mentioned her name to them? When would I have told them? At the beginning when they found me in the Pacific Ocean floating like a piece of driftwood?

'I don't know who you mean,' I say eventually.

I know that is not what Dr Bhaduri wants to hear; I can tell by the way his lips part slightly that he is letting out a long breath.

He wants me to give him more. I know I should. But the words simply won't come.

# 20

## THEN

Three days passed since Clara's accident and I still hadn't seen her. I had asked, and my requests had been either ignored or brushed off until I felt stupid asking again. Despite being assured she was being looked after and that disturbing her was not going to help her recovery, I thought about her day and night. I dreamt vividly of her, and I kept replaying the incident in my mind. Each time I tried to replace the part where I was in the water alone and I heard commotion, into something more comprehensible. Putting in the missing piece of the narrative so I could see at what point Clara was injured. By Kali. Was it pure irresponsible behaviour or a total accident?

I wanted to see Clara because she was my friend, and I knew that seeing people who cared about you when you were unwell was ideal for aiding recovery. But I was being made to feel as though I didn't know enough about anything. And it wasn't anything anyone had said, just an energy they were emitting. I was wholly concerned for my friend, and they were not. I felt the very opposite. This was my new home and I had spent that time trying to get myself accustomed to the way everything worked and trying to fit in. I didn't want to stand out as someone who was incapable of adapting to this sort of lifestyle, and it did need adapting to, but I wanted to hurry the process along. I wanted to be seen as one of them and not some naive little girl who didn't understand camp life and was still fuelled by old-school ways and ideas.

I wished I was able to relax and get on their wavelength. They didn't seem to worry about anything. Yet I was panicking that no one seemed to be talking about Clara. In such a small community I didn't want to be the one to stand out despite how much my mind was on my roommate.

Avril passed through the camp that afternoon and I approached her.

'How is Clara?' I asked her.

Avril looked at me and it seemed to take her a moment to register what I was saying.

'Oh yes, she's okay. But, Sadie, she has said she doesn't want to see anyone. She hates the way she looks and feels at the moment. She knows you've been asking after her; she's such an independent thing.' Avril said the last part of the sentence as if it were an afterthought.

'But she knows I've been asking after her?'

Avril nodded firmly. 'She does. I'm guessing you won't want to go back to the fishing anytime soon, so how about we get you cooking? I know it's not on the rota for you to cook, but I don't think anyone would mind this once,' she said loud enough that the two women I knew as the mothers who were on cooking duty this week had heard. One flashed the other a look, and then they both looked at me.

'Sure,' one said and threw me a tea towel, which I caught. 'Gives me a night off.' She swaggered off out of camp.

The other woman looked at me and smiled.

'I've not started preparing anything yet, so it's all yours,' she said sweetly, and I felt her calm energy more so than her friend. The kitchen was a place where many liked to make their mark, and I imagined by now, there were certain women who thrived there. I couldn't help but feel as though I had just stood very heavily on their toes, but Avril was keen to let me have a go at cooking, I supposed, as a way to keep my mind off Clara, and I was keen to accept anything that would occupy me and deter my thoughts from the horror of what I had seen.

'Another chef is exactly what we need here,' Avril said quietly once both women were out of earshot. 'It's not that they aren't good, it's just nice to have a fresh input sometimes.' Her gaze followed where they had walked, then she turned to me and touched my cheek.

'You are a breath of fresh air, Sadie.' Avril's voice was low and husky. 'I'm so glad you're here.' She kept her hand there.

'I'm glad I'm here too,' I said, but as I said it I couldn't ignore the doubts that had begun growing within me. Had it started when Avril had lied to me about how long it would take to get here? Since then I had tried not to let my mind create a monster out of the other things that had cast a shadow over this otherwise beautiful experience. Yes, Clara had been hurt, but she would recover, and I was in a wonderful place full of beautiful women with so much to give. Without ever knowing it truly, this was the place I had always meant to end up in. And because it was never somewhere I had properly envisioned, it was going to take a while for me to fully realise it, to feel it and to relish it.

I had come from a society where everything happened instantly. Food arrived in minutes; information was at the touch of a button. Here things were slower. The culture was unfamiliar and I couldn't have been more back to basics if I tried, and yet there was this part of my brain still pulling me back to the UK, reminding me of the alternative.

'I think it would be good for me actually,' I said as Avril dropped her hand away and began tidying up the area around her feet, gathering discarded bits of wood and leaves. It was amazing to see what a difference it made to the small cooking area.

'There we go, a chef's kitchen should always be tidy. At least at the beginning.' She laughed.

'I want to be where my skills are the strongest whilst I improve at other areas,' I said. I wanted to add 'such as fishing' but I couldn't bring myself to mention the word as each time I thought of it my stomach started to tie itself in knots.

Avril kept staring as though I was the most fascinating thing she had seen.

'So, what's on the menu tonight?' I asked.

Avril released me from her gaze and looked around her. 'Eggplant, tomatoes, rice, and pineapple and mango by the looks of it.'

The one thing I would do when I was at home when I was feeling out of sorts, was cook. I loved nothing more than being in my own kitchen, running my fingertips along the rows of herbs and spices, heading to the market, and picking out fresh vegetables. There was such a calming feeling that came with this and so maybe if it didn't mean that I would step on the mothers' toes, I might be the one to take over the cooking duties from time to time. I felt it would help me transition from my life back home to here on Totini Island. Because even on the mainland, I had a daily purpose, a job, places to visit and friends to see. Here, I didn't want the monotony to catch me out; to capture me and convince me this was not for me.

I prepared the eggplants and tomatoes on a large wooden board next to the campfire. I had diced the eggplant and fried it with some herbs. The tomatoes were sliced ready and I had parboiled long beans. Once my mise en place was set up, I looked at it with pride, feeling a sense of accomplishment that I had created something, even though it was merely a few pieces of chopped veg. Something I would have previously done with my eyes shut felt trickier using unfamiliar tools and crouching and leaning on a tree stump.

Avril returned with a slab of meat wrapped in brown paper. I unwrapped it like it was a Christmas present. I looked at the dark red colour, sniffed it.

'Veal!' I exclaimed. 'Did you slaughter this here?'

I thought of the few cows I had seen who roamed freely around the island, mainly sticking to the shades of the trees where they had cylinders of water topped up regularly. I wondered which one was unfortunate enough to have lost a calf recently.

'We try to eat only meat that has been reared and slaughtered on Totini Island. It's better that way.'

I picked up the knife again. Avril took hold of my wrist.

'Here, let me. You've worked so hard slicing all the vegetables.' Avril had such a tender look in her eye and the soft way her hand had embraced my wrist made me instantly let go. I watched as she sat down cross-legged and began to slowly chop the meat into small dice shapes.

'Is this okay, Chef?' she murmured without looking at me.

'Perfect,' I said quietly. It was exactly how I would have prepared it myself to match the shape of the aubergines, with the vibrancy of the tomatoes, and the addition of the green beans would be a feast for the eyes.

Once she had finished, she stood up, and then she wiped her hands across her bare legs, leaving streaks of blood behind.

I was reminded of Ula's hut and the bloody handprints all over it, and then I knew it was real blood. But was it an animal's or her own?

Suddenly the blood, the meat, cutting and preparing in the sun, all felt so primal, the most basic and important form of who these women were, of what they were doing.

'I'm looking forward to dining with you this evening, Sadie,' she said before she walked away.

About half an hour later, everyone began to take their places around the campfire and so I tried to look cool and in control. I had started frying the meat into the eggplant, which was now simmering away in the juices. The tomatoes, which were marinated in garlic and salt, and the long beans would go in last.

There were murmurings of appreciation as senses were titillated. Avril arrived and seated herself next to me.

'It smells amazing; you're such a gourmet.' She scoffed the last part in a funny upper-class lady voice, and I leaned into her, appreciating her, thankful she was here, spending time with me. Suddenly, all the worries I'd had about Avril not being honest with me evaporated, along with my doubts and questions. It all felt like nonsense when we were all together like this, just existing with the most simple things: a fire, food and each other.

'We are in for a treat tonight, everyone. Sadie has cooked for us. It is a very special night indeed; tonight, my friends, we eat like queens,' Avril announced to the camp.

There was an uproar. Women were on their feet whooping and I had never felt so welcomed. Avril leaned forward and squeezed my arm.

'Well I can't take all the credit; Avril was a great commis chef and diced the meat,' I said loud enough so a few people on my side of the circle heard. Avril even managed to look humbled and seemed to take the compliment.

After dinner I told everyone I would wash up; it was my treat to the camp for making me feel so welcome.

'I'll give you a hand,' Avril said. 'Come on then.' She took my arm and we walked over to the kitchenette area like two old school friends. As we did, I saw Avril's girlfriend. I had now begun to call Lola that, as she always seemed to be there, next to Avril. She grabbed at Avril's arm and without even looking back, Avril yanked hers away and continued walking.

'You can go to her if you like?' I said. 'I don't mind washing up alone.'

Avril looked at me blankly.

'Your girlfriend,' I added as she seemed confused.

Avril snorted. 'I don't have a girlfriend.'

I put the plates on the table. 'Oh, Lola, I thought—'

'You thought wrong.' There was a spike to Avril's voice that I hadn't heard before.

We were both silent for a few moments.

'It's just not like that here, Sadie. We're all free here. You know?'

'Yeah, I can see,' I replied. I didn't want to pursue the Lola thing. I didn't want to say that it didn't seem to me that Lola understood the same level of freedom as Avril did and actually she seemed very set on being Avril's girlfriend.

I filled a bowl from one of the large rain tanks closest to the camp with a squirt of washing-up liquid. I began scrubbing and laying the bowls on the handmade draining board. I looked at the knots used to make the draining board and admired them. Avril arrived next to me with a towel in hand and began drying and stacking the bowls.

The chain around her wrist jingled as she dried.

'That's such a pretty bracelet. Was it a gift?'

Avril held her wrist up and looked at the charm bracelet as though it was the first time she had seen it. 'It was a gift to myself.'

I nodded. 'I love all the little charms. Do they represent something?'

'Yes, all of them.'

'I love the little cake.'

Avril looked intently at it. 'I do too,' she said it as if she had only just decided that she liked it the most.

I didn't push her to reveal more, to tell me the story behind each charm, but I could see in her demeanour that it was special to her.

'I like how you bought it as a gift to yourself.'

Avril took a plate from me and dried it with the cloth. 'We must recognise that we are worth something to ourselves, Sadie. You will learn in time,' she said.

I nodded. Avril grabbed my arm with her free hand. I looked at her.

'I mean it, Sadie. You must never let anyone make you feel a lesser version of yourself.'

I was always trying to crush feelings of Bruno. He was always in the back of my mind. I had wanted it to last; I had wanted him to love me. I let him make me feel a lesser version of myself.

Suddenly I felt the desire to open up to Avril, to tell her about Bruno, to explain why I was here, why I had run.

'His name was Bruno,' I said and the jingling on her wrist stopped as she paused drying the dishes.

'I thought he loved me. But he wanted to control me. He wanted me to be like him and his friends. And when I didn't—'

'He hurt you,' Avril finished the sentence for me.

I looked at her and she at me. Our eyes locked and, in that moment, I saw reflected in her eyes a vision of the pain that felt so familiar to me. This was why I had been brought here, so that someone like Avril could bring me back to life, give me the space and tools to become who I truly wanted and needed to be. In some way, I believed that Avril was my saviour.

Avril nodded and let out a sigh. She handed me back a plate. 'You missed a bit.'

We looked at one another and both let out a laughing snort at the same time.

There were more celebrations that night to mark some sort of milestone of one of the women. In all the bustle of having a garland placed around my neck, and kava getting passed at a rate I had never yet experienced in Fiji, I missed what the occasion was. Each of the women came and kissed the woman who I think was called Rachel. But I noticed that Kali was the only one who didn't do this, as she had immersed herself in getting the old cassette player set up ready for the music, which when she pressed play was loud and fierce.

Avril was the first to grab me and dance. The music was an R & B track I recognised from back home, and my body overflowed with euphoria and nostalgia as my muscle memory kicked in and the moves from my youth came back to me. Avril's hands were all over my waist, as she danced around me. Then she was back in front of me, an intense look in her eye as she held me and pressed her groin against mine, grinding it against me in time with the music. Her hair was loose tonight and she flung her head back. When she retracted it, she had a wild look in her eye. Then when the track finished she was gone, leaving me feeling out of breath and slightly bereft. I watched her move over to another girl and then finally to Lola, who had been waiting to welcome her.

I knew I wanted to walk tonight and so I slipped away to the beach, where I intended to dip my toes in the sea.

I headed past women who were spilling out from camp and were almost on the beach themselves. Contemplating walking, but getting caught up in last-minute chatter. It still amazed me how relaxed this place was. Besides the no phones rule, there were no rules. Everyone just got on with what needed to be done and for most of the day and evening there was this general sense of contentment, that people were happy with the simplicity that they had created for themselves and that intrigued me. The mornings were the best here for me; every day I woke and couldn't believe how lucky I was to be here. The sound of the cockerels first thing, the simple sounds of the camp coming to life, the smell of the fire pit, the scent of warm skin all around me. It was paradise. There was no other way to describe it.

But despite all of those wonderful things there was an underlying buzz of discontentment, a flurry in my tummy, as my parents used to call it when I was little and I sat up late at night worrying about things that I couldn't control. I couldn't stop thinking about Clara. About where she was and how she was. It had been too long. I wanted more than anything to go and find out for myself.

I stopped walking and turned suddenly. I had heard the sound of a twig breaking just behind me. Had it come from the foliage around me? The sky was now pitch-black but full of stars and a bright moon lit the pathway and guided me towards the beach. I turned back around and carried on walking. I had been jumpy at the sounds of the forest around me before. I had nothing to fear here; it was probably a cow moving about or a hen that had lost its way back to the pen at dusk. But the snapping came again, and I swung round faster and as I did, this time I caught sight of a small figure just before it disappeared into the bushes.

# 21
## THEN

My blood ran cold for a second, then I reminded myself that I was on an island with many other women and I could shout at any moment, and someone would come running. I had nothing to fear. This was probably one of the children who had escaped the clutches of their mother at bedtime and was now trying to prank me.

'Okay, come on out little one.' I held my cool, the kava in my system giving me confidence.

'I know you're in there. Please come out.'

I heard a rustle then another twig snapping then a small bare foot appeared. Next, a small torso and then a head. Of what appeared to be a small boy of about five or six. I had only seen the one boy here before and the girl. This child also had dark hair and piercing dark eyes to match. Who was he and why hadn't I seen him before now?

'Hello,' I spoke. 'I'm Sadie. What's your name?'

He just smiled inanely.

'Are you lost?' I asked.

The little boy looked at me, sniggered and then scuttled back into the bushes again.

I stood there looking at the empty spot where he had just been and wondered if I had imagined the whole thing. The kava was well and truly doing its job; my veins tingled, and I felt small bursts of euphoria and so I laughed out loud at the absurdity of it. How had I not yet seen this boy already? He must have stayed hidden away; maybe he was more feral than the others. He certainly seemed it the way he jumped into that bush like a gazelle. I turned back to the path to the beach and kept walking until my feet were no longer on dusty earth, but pure white sand, and the sound of the waves were immediately lulling me into a meditative state. I really didn't need anything else but this.

I wondered how long I could be happy here for and live with so many unanswered questions. I had my reservations – that was for sure. There was happiness and contentedness here, but there was something else, lingering in between each sunrise and sunset. I could align it to the general lack of interest over Clara's injury for example, or the way Kali looked at me, and refused to hug me like all the women had, or maybe even the absence of men. I had seen no hysteria over Clara's injury, instead an acceptance for what it was. Kali didn't stand around the fire and tell her tale to the group, revelling in the drama and attention. No one spoke of it or questioned it the next day and no one had mentioned it since. It was only because I had asked that I was given an update. Perhaps their emotions had numbed, but it felt too pragmatic to me. Maybe it was one I would adopt over time and I wasn't sure I wanted that.

There was a sense that they had all slid into a state of obscurity here and that they had, whether consciously or unconsciously, adopted a new set of life rules. Some might feel threatened by it, scared even. I wasn't sure how I felt yet, but I was aware of it.

The next morning I took my usual route from the cabin to the front beach to listen to the sounds of the waves greeting me and I sat and absorbed the negative ions, to set me up for the day. It was the last thing I had heard last night and the first thing I would hear this morning. It was usually the two mothers I saw when I woke as they were already up with their youngsters. No sign of the little boy from last night though. Had I imagined him?

I approached the first mother first. Her name was Star. She told me that wasn't the name her parents had given her at birth, but when she came to Totini she gave herself a new name and everyone had called her that for years. It backed up my theory about them having their own set of rules here, and how anything was possible.

'Morning,' I said as I approached her.

'How are you today?' She smiled. I wasn't sure what her accent was. It sounded a mix of South African and Australian, and I guessed she was the sort of woman who had travelled a lot in her time. She was still young-looking. A rash of freckles adorned her cheeks and nose, but I would have said she was older than me by seven or eight years.

'I'm well, thank you. Hey, I was walking last night, and I stumbled across a young boy.' I was sure I saw Star's lips pursed suddenly and momentarily. 'Anyway, I wasn't sure if I was imagining him what with the tiredness and kava—'

'You didn't imagine him,' Star said seriously. 'He lives here, mainly in the forest areas. We leave food out for him to collect. He drinks from one of the rain barrels.'

'But whose son is he?' I pressed.

'His name is Adi. His mother abandoned him.'

'Adi. That's so sad.'

Star nodded. 'He won't let any one of us near him. Hester and I, we've tried to mother him, make him one of our own, but he has problems, learning behaviours, social issues.'

'Neurodivergent,' I said recognising her descriptions.

Star shrugged. 'Who knows. There's no one here to diagnose him and he never lets any one of us near him for long enough. How was he when you saw him? I haven't seen him for a few days.'

'He was sweet. He stood in front of me and smiled. Then ran away.'

'He smiled? Wow, that's more than I've ever got out of him. He must have liked you.'

I felt a warm feeling wash over me, and then the same feeling I'd had when Avril had prepped the dinner with me and praised me for my culinary skills. Just like Ula, he was an outcast of sorts. Maybe I could be the one to help him? I would definitely be on the lookout for him again.

I carried on walking down to the front beach and looked at the risen sun and wondered what the day would bring. Each one here seemed to offer something new, yet the framework was the same. Get up, eat breakfast, do chores, eat lunch, rest, or play, prepare dinner, eat dinner, sometimes sing and dance, then bed. It was a very basic existence when you broke it down to that.

I got back to camp just as breakfast was being served. A sweet coconut rice pudding with cinnamon and slices of papaya. I took a seat and began to eat as a few more women meandered into the main camp area.

I saw Avril rise from her hut. She saw me and made a beeline for me.

'I wanted to see you before breakfast.'

I was holding my bowl in one hand and a spoon in the other. I had taken one mouthful. She crouched down next to me, and I felt her arm brush against mine. She smelled sweaty from the night before. I could hear her breathing.

'I wanted to let you know that Clara passed away in the night.'

My body suddenly felt weightless, and my arms went limp. The bowl and spoon almost slipped from my grip.

'Dead?' I said to clarify that passing away did mean the same thing here.

'Yes, dead.'

I looked down at my lap at the breakfast that had been so enticing a few moments ago, which was now unappetising.

'But. She got harpooned in the foot, I . . . I don't understand why she would die?' My voice was shaky and high. I wanted to cry but no one seemed to show any emotion like that here. I already knew that a death was not something that would devastate anyone.

'I know this is hard to digest this early in the morning. We didn't think she would make the end of day yesterday, but I didn't want to spoil your evening as you were in your element cooking.'

I glanced at Avril. There it was again, that nonchalant approach to something so serious.

'No, Avril, you should have told me.' I saw a flicker in Avril's eyes as my firm voice seemed to penetrate.

'A spear in her foot, how did she die from a spear in her foot?' I said. My voice was beginning to get louder and I felt the stares of some of the other campmates. Did they know she had died?

'I'm afraid Clara refused her antibiotics and became very ill very quickly.'

'But you said she was fine and doing well.' I knew I was crying now and I couldn't stop my tears and nor should I, because Clara was my friend. I tried to take a few deep breaths.

'I didn't want to worry you. We all hoped she would pull through without the aid of medicine.'

I sat for a moment, trying to take it all in. Suddenly an image of Clara and Avril outside my hut that first day here resurfaced. She had been distraught. Avril had comforted her. I thought about the moment I had walked in on her in the hut, where she had tried to conceal something and also her emotions, but it was clear she had been crying. Now she was dead.

My mind was reeling. Avril crouched next to me, patiently waiting for me to speak again or to answer another question. But I remained quiet until she finally got up, touched my shoulder briefly and walked away. As I sat, unable to find the words to say how I felt, I saw a cup of kava that had been left out from last night. I picked it up and drank. Images of Adi, the little mute boy, and Ula, the faceless woman from the shack, were now fresh in my mind, where before they had been hiding in the shadows. And now I could add the face of Clara, and I felt their silences echo my own.

# 22
## NOW

I know my name is Sadie. That I am very sure of. Yet everyone keeps trying to remind me. I have been told repeatedly that I speak often of Avril and I together in Fiji and came home without her. I had dreams about her, Avril. But her face in the dream was not one I recognised nor remembered. I felt the dreams came from the sessions I had with Dr Bhaduri. I felt he had imprinted those thoughts into my mind, and I had begun dreaming them. When I really think about it, I don't remember a lot about anything. But I feel okay. I don't feel worried or anxious. I feel fine.

I believe it is harder for everyone else to accept it. They are the ones who feel all the emotions. It's hard even to trust or believe anything that anyone says when your own mind is telling you something completely different or even nothing at all.

They tell me I have disassociated amnesia. I'm not exactly sure what that is. But I come here and speak with Dr Bhaduri every week. He hopes he will begin to bring more information out of me.

I have been hiding the images I have been drawing in the wardrobe because I am terrified of them. But it could be time to tell. It could be time to hand them over. For a professional to look at them and tell me what they mean and tell me if I am well and truly mental and that yes, I have been a part of some terrible crimes.

# 23
## THEN

Everything changed. The doubts I had in my mind, instead of pushing them away in favour of the tranquillity and beauty of Totini, I let them fester, toying with each conversation and contradiction. I began to look at the camp differently. It was no longer just a place of sanctuary and escape where people came to be their most authentic selves without the constraints of everyday society amongst a paradise backdrop. It was now a place where people died. It was a place where people were alive one minute and then dead the next. It could have happened to any one of us. It could happen to me. It could happen to Avril. None of us were immune from death, and with the lack of laws and protection and access to proper medical help, any of us could be next.

The campmates went on about their days, and as I moved into my second and then third week on the island, I felt a hardening develop. Where I had been affected so much by things like Ula living alone and then Clara being carried away in the woods – to die alone – I now felt as though I had lost a fraction of empathy, and in its place, I had grown a thicker piece of skin. Was that the piece of myself that I had to lose to enjoy the paradise that Avril had talked of? It didn't feel wrong; that was for sure. I understood that was how people had to be here to have some existence. If they were constantly pent up with daily frustrations, emotions and worries, what was the point? Life wasn't perfect anywhere, I had now come to understand; it was how you chose to live it regardless of whatever else was going on around you.

Surrender a piece of yourself for paradise. That was the mantra. I could do that.

The hardening was also showing on the outside too. My hair was dry and was beginning to mat at the ends. I hadn't brought any conditioner with me and I was considering not washing it for a few weeks and allowing the natural oils to seep through. My fingernails were dirty, my skin a little burnt and crispy; my feet were hardening where I was walking bare-foot every day.

But still within me, a softness lay for the things I missed, like my family and the few friends I cared enough about. And I missed Clara. I had longed for her company when she had been convalescing. Now I understood that Avril and the others all knew the wound was eventually going to kill her and they took her away somewhere quietly to do so. But I was haunted by images of Clara in her last days and hours. How had she been feeling? What had she been thinking? She had no one there with her in the end and I felt a weight of responsibility for that.

I should have pushed harder to see her, to be with her, even if it was only to hold her hand.

But somehow the very act of death felt less apparent here. It went hand in hand with the way of life because there was so very little else to worry or care about; it seemed less significant. It was as though, in the UK, we were so consumed with so many other irrelevant things from food to shopping to work to clothes, and fashion and celebrity, that when a death occurred it became amplified, as though we were glad of the distraction from all the other bullshit. We relished it; we absorbed ourselves within it. Here on Totini, we were animals. A member of our pack had died, and we were all carrying on. I was trying to carry on, and I knew I would have to hide my sadness because there was little room for it here.

Because apparently my cooking had been such a hit I had been allocated the role of camp cook three times a week. But I knew this was Avril's way of distracting me from Clara. It fulfilled my need to produce something for the camp, but not so much that I became frustrated by having to do it all the time. Others liked to cook too and especially when meat was involved. There wasn't a lot of meat to eat on the island, but also adopting a more plant-based lifestyle seemed appropriate for somewhere like Totini, and there was a lack of cold areas to contain the slaughtered meat. But when we did eat it, it felt like a special occasion. Everyone seemed to revel in eating it as though it were something sacred. Which I appreciated as that was how it should be. Mass meat farming and consumption disgusted me now. I had almost begun to lose track of the days, and time was also not something I thought about often. Mealtimes were not taken on the hour but whenever food was ready or when people began to gather around the camp or the gong was sounded.

If I just continued the way I was, memories of Clara might eventually fade. I wanted to talk about Clara eventually, but even thinking her name brought tears to my eyes. However, I wasn't going to just give up and ask to return home. I felt I had so much to prove to Avril, Kali, the rest of the camp and myself.

Avril found me after breakfast one morning, a few weeks after Clara's death. I had been spending a lot of time on my own and admittedly kept my distance from her. Words kept coming at me, half-formed sentences, fuelled by an anger I didn't want to feel here. The two were incompatible: utopia and this rage that was bubbling up within me. I didn't want it to become something more, something so fierce that it erupted. That kind of anger was the worst, the hardest to clear up and to make excuses for. I knew, I had been the recipient once. I wondered if Avril was about to become the recipient because I was so frustrated with her, yet she had already done so much for me. Gave me this opportunity, which I knew wasn't given to just anyone.

I was struggling with the emotions I was feeling. One minute I longed for the attention that Avril gave me, the way she made me think that I was strong and capable and reminded me that the reason I was here was to grow. The next minute that rage was there, simmering. I knew it could only be because of Clara's death. But maybe it was all the other little things, like the way Avril had lied to me about how far away the island was. Exactly how remote it was and cut-off from civilisation I was going to be. Although I had formed bonds with most of the women here, it was Clara I had gelled with the most. I just couldn't let it go the way the rest of the women had. I wasn't there yet.

'Are you okay?' Avril asked. She had been asking me this often and I appreciated her checking in with me.

I nodded. I didn't want to be the only one who showed any signs of distress over Clara.

'Why don't you and I have a picnic tonight? On our own. On the beach.'

I felt my spirit lift. I had been feeling the familiarity of each day and with the nagging thoughts of Clara, I would do anything to forget for a while.

We left the camp just before sunset with a basket of food plus a small amount of kava. I had taken to drinking it more often since the morning that Avril broke the news about Clara's death. It helped to tone down any sudden emotions. There seemed to be an abundance of it anyway, so why not use it to my advantage? It helped me sleep during the very hot nights as well.

The sun was lowering and we would need to hurry if we were going to make the sun setting.

'You look lovely,' I said as we walked. I wanted to appease Avril, to make up for my absence in mind and negative vibes of the last few weeks.

'Thanks.' She smiled.

Avril had pinned her hair to one side and had put a pink flower in it. She was wearing her green sarong and a turquoise bikini top. I was wearing shorts and a bikini top. 'I should have made more of an effort,' I said looking down at my attire.

'I hope you understand I've been in shock these last few weeks.'

'Over Clara – of course, Sadie. Why wouldn't you be? Clara was your room buddy and I know you two got on well.'

'I just didn't expect anything like that to happen here.'

'We're not immortals, Sadie,' Avril said. 'We've lost people in the time we've been here.'

I immediately wanted to ask who and I thought of Ula alone on the cliff. Had she lost someone?

We began the walk to the beach.

'And I need to apologise too, Sadie. I've been a little absent in mind and body since you got here. A lot has been going on. Things have been . . . evolving. And the women, they look to me to resolve everything, and sometimes, I can't, you know.'

'Things are a little different to how I imagined them to be.' I had an image of Clara in my mind, her smiling face already a blur and fading.

'I can see that,' Avril responded.

'I mean it's beautiful. I'm just intrigued . . .' I spoke slowly, trying to choose the right words '. . . how differently people react, like to Clara for example. I was horrified; I won't lie. But everyone took it in their stride.' I looked at Avril. 'As though it happened every day.' I laughed uncomfortably. I thought it was almost as though they were desensitised to it. But I didn't say those words, because I was scared to even think them. Because how could I truly exist somewhere where death was ignored?

'It is a very different way of life here and most women have seen a lot in their lives, which is why they have chosen this exist-ence, something pure, no dramas. You know. They just want to live in the moment, most of the time.'

I nodded, but I was thinking about how things might evolve from here. Would I stop being my complete self? Would I stop feeling sorrow, horror and anger because I was now an inhabitant of this island? They were all valid emotions. To suppress them would be to stop being who I was. Or to be human. I know I wanted to change and grow, become stronger away from Bruno, but I didn't want this as well.

We didn't speak then for the rest of the journey except to comment on the excursion, dimming light, or how we were both hungry and ready to eat.

We reached the beach as the sky turned a brilliant orange and pink.

'I don't think I will ever get used to this,' I said but I wasn't expecting a response because of course it was too spectacular for words and I had already said too much when no words needed to be spoken at all. I laid all the food out on the blanket, and we began picking and talking about the camp life, and Avril asked if I had intentions to go back out spearfishing again. I stopped swallowing. A tomato sat in my throat as I felt it swelling up. No one had expected me to start spearfishing again, since Clara. Avril was talking about me getting back out there as though the incident had never happened.

I swallowed hard and the tomato began making its way down my oesophagus.

I went to answer her question the best way I could, then stopped myself.

But a scream, loud and piercing, carried across the beach towards us.

Avril was on her feet and looking up and down the beach.

'Was that an animal?' I asked. 'It sounded like an animal.'

'It wasn't an animal.' Avril sounded adamant.

'Human then?'

'The child.'

'Adi?' I asked.

Avril looked at me.

'You've seen him too?' I asked, for I knew it couldn't have been the other boy who never strayed too far from his mothers' sides.

Avril sat back down on the sand, but she seemed agitated. The sound had obviously bothered her.

'Should we try and see if he is okay?' I asked.

Then when it came again, louder this time, Avril was up and running along the beach. I found I was following her instinctively. She was right to run. What if the child was hurt or in trouble?

The moon provided us with enough light if we needed it, but we relied on our ears to work out where the sound came from and where it would lead us.

We ran up the beach for what felt like a long time before we came across the remains of a fire. Someone had poured water over it. There was no smoke but there was the scent in the air. Avril stood with her hands on her hips, looking up and down the beach. Eventually, we heard a rustle from the bushes in front of us. I tentatively took a step forward and Avril grabbed my hand.

'Sadie, wait.'

I looked at her. 'There's nothing to worry about,' I said. I knew it would probably be Adi, the little boy I had met walking to the beach, and he had been perfectly sweet. I hadn't seen him since, which was a bit strange. You could walk around the entire island in two hours, but the shrubbery and trees in the middle of the island were dense and it would be perfectly easy to live or get lost amongst those and not be seen for a long time.

I took another step forward, reaching out with my hands to part the foliage.

'Sadie, I really think you should be careful. You don't know—'

Before she could finish what she was saying a pair of hands shot out of the bushes and grabbed both of mine. I screeched loudly and went to step back, trying to pull away as I did, but the hands were latched on tight. I looked down at them, long bony fingers, which looked as if they belonged to a female, and even with only the soft lighting I could tell the hands were covered with blood. Horrified, I pulled harder, writhing both my arms until the grip was finally loosed and my arms were free. I looked down at my hands and from the little light that was left I could see dark shades in streaks.

'Oh God, oh God.' And then I looked up. The hands had gone and in their place was the face of a woman. A young woman, blood smeared across both of her cheeks, but it was her eyes that spoke to me first, intensely staring into mine. Then her mouth opened. It was barely a whisper, but the one-syllable word was easy for me to hear and understand.

'Run.'

# 24

## THEN

'You're shaking.' Avril bent down to wash my hands of the blood in the shallows of the sea.

'She gave me a scare,' I said, my teeth chattering so hard they were clattering against one another, despite the heat of the evening.

'I tried to warn you,' Avril said.

I carried on washing the blood from my skin, using the natural sea exfoliation to feel clean.

'Was that Ula?' I asked.

'Yes.' Avril sniffed nonchalantly. 'I don't know why she's out of her hut. She rarely leaves her hut. Especially at night.'

I stood up and dried my hands on my shorts.

'But why does she live there? Why has she chosen to live alone?'

'Because men are bastards,' Avril snapped.

I was shocked into silence.

'Don't you see, Sadie, it's always the men. It was too late to save Ula, but it's not too late for you. Think of Bruno, think of Tony. They can't be the only ones who treated you like shit, am I right? We have to take a stand.' She stopped and panted. 'We have to take a stand,' she said quieter, her shoulders hunched, and I thought for a moment she was crying.

Then she pulled her self upright.

'Sadie, mental health problems still exist even in Totini. Ula is unwell in her mind and there is no one who can help her. We do what we can for her, accommodate her . . . ways – and that is that.'

We tried to finish our picnic after that, but I could almost taste the blood on my hands. We gave up and walked back to the camp. As we walked Avril talked about the meals she wanted me to try next week as she has access to some new types of vegetable. I was barely listening. I was thinking about how angry Avril was, about the men. I thought of Bruno and Tony, and I understood it wasn't right how women had to suffer daily, whether it was a misogynistic comment or gender-based violence. I wanted things to change, I wanted women to be safe and to know equality. Yet I didn't feel as angry as Avril was in this moment, as though she carried her anger like a cloak she was never able to shake off. Tony, Bruno, all the other men, they weren't here; it was a wasted emotion to feel that about someone who was so far away from me now. Any anger that still simmered away within me, was at Avril for how Clara had been dealt with, and how I wasn't allowed to see her. But I suppressed it as much as I could.

But why did Avril still have all this pent-up rage for men when we lived in an all-female commune? Wasn't that the whole point – to live freely? We had rid ourselves of them. It didn't feel that Avril was living free of them; it felt that they were still wrapped around her neck; whoever had done whatever to her to make her dislike men so much had created this incessant hatred of all men.

We stopped outside Avril's hut. It was late now and I could see a few women in the distance making their way to their cabins.

'You must learn not to worry about so much, Sadie,' she said and then she leaned forward and pressed her lips against mine. Only for a mere second, then she pulled away and walked into her hut without looking back. Leaving me standing there again, the way she had after the dancing on my first week, with a cocktail of emotions I was unsure how to deal with.

I slept fitfully that night, fuelled by enigmatic dreams about the kava, my strange encounter with Ula, and my frustrations with Avril. In my dream, I found Avril's face among a small crowd. A man had a guitar. He was strumming a song I recognised. I smiled at her. She smiled back, a wide toothy grin. She came over to me and pulled me up from my space, where I had been sitting on the sand.

'Come and dance. Come and dance.' She pulled me to standing. We weaved our way to a space away from the others. I felt awkward, and people were looking at us. *But they don't care,* I tried to tell myself; even in my dream, I found some confidence.

I took her in my arms and swung her around; she threw her head back and laughed, and the people on the table looked up and smiled. Then I was swinging her so fast, a power was coming out of me that I didn't know existed. Then she lifted off the floor and flew. Initially she had a smile on her face, a half-stoned look, but then it changed. She realised she was going too fast; she was going to hit the rock on the sand.

And then she did. Blood splattered where her head had hit it. She looked at me, an expression of betrayal and confusion. Then she stood up and began to walk away. Quickly at first, then slowly. She turned and she looked down at her feet. They had blood all over them; she had blood all over her hands. Then she started running towards the sea and was out of sight quickly. I ran after her but she was gone. But I could still hear her. Her voice whispered my name. *Sadie, Sadie,* over and over until I woke up.

I had been lying in bed, listening to the rumble of thunder in the distance. I had seen one strong storm on the mainland, but this was going to be a very different experience. I had heard the cockerel, I was sure of it, which meant it must be after 4 a.m. The thunder came, louder this time. I thought about the sky and how the air was desperate to be cleared, like my runaway thoughts. Maybe once the storm was over, my mind would be calmer.

I pulled on my rain mac over my shorts and vest and headed out to stand near the beach so I could get a front-seat view of the storm when it arrived. It was still dark. The sun would rise soon, but we wouldn't get much light today.

Out of my peripheral vision, I saw a figure moving through the camp. I turned suddenly and saw it was Kali. She was moving swiftly, pulling on and moving and retying ropes attached to a large tarpaulin cover tied between several trees. It fell gracefully down on three sides to create a shelter. Kari had arranged it so it now covered a vast area of the camp, including over the fire and seating area. We would have somewhere dry to sit later other than the kitchen area or our cabins.

'Hey, Kali,' I called.

'Storm's coming,' she said without looking at me. I had felt the chill from the rain and now from Kali, but this wasn't unusual. I had come to accept that not everyone could like everyone, even if we were living in one of the most beautiful places in the world.

I hadn't thought much about storms since I had been here, only the white sands and glorious endless sunny days. But I guessed it had to break eventually. I felt a pang of worry. What if the storm turned bad? What if the shelter wasn't sufficient? What if there was a tsunami?

Kali turned to me as if sensing my energy. 'It's a small one. It will only last a day.'

'A day?' I said hardly able to believe what she had said.

Kali didn't respond; she just continued to tug at the ropes to secure the tarpaulin.

I moved closer, a way of offering my services but knowing I had nothing to offer here. Kali was tying knots that made me wish I had concentrated harder in Girl Guides.

'Hey, could you teach me how to tie some knots later?'

She had almost finished up. She looked at me suspiciously.

'I mean, weather's going to be bad all day, a way to pass the time maybe?' I continued.

She gave a short, sharp nod. *That will do,* I thought.

I gave her a thumbs-up, looked into the distance and waited for the storm to come.

Despite Kali's words earlier, the storm was fierce. It was loud, it was strong, and it was relentless. Everyone seemed to go about their day unaffected by the noise and rain, except Avril. She had appeared for breakfast when the first rumbles began and then became more agitated with every passing hour. At one point I clocked her and Mary under the kitchen gazebo. They seemed to be having a heated discussion because Mary went to walk away towards the woods, but Avril grabbed her arm, said something to her and she stopped.

I was not one to be able to sit still and so I sought out Kali after lunch and pinned her down to teach me some knots. She invited me into her cabin, albeit reluctantly. Mary was sitting in a chair in the corner sewing.

'Sadie,' she said warmly. Their cabin was slightly larger than mine. I felt sad at the prospect of the cabin only belonging to me now; I no longer had a buddy. They had two beds made up on the floor, a little more rudimentary than my own bed, which at least had legs. There was a small table in the corner and a chair where Mary sat with her clothes and sewing kit.

Kali brought in lots of rope and laid it out on the floor.

'Right, let's start with a basic. Reef knot.'

'So what do you usually do with your time when things are wet like this?' I heard a crack of thunder overhead and flinched. Kali glanced up at me.

'There's always something to do.' She moved her hands slowly to show me the knot.

On my third attempt, I did it.

I let her show me a few more knots and we worked silently, as I copied each one. Then I asked, 'Where did they bury Clara?'

I heard Mary move in her chair. Despite the rain lifting some of the heat, I felt a sudden oppression amongst the three of us and in the room.

'They burned her body, Sadie,' Mary said quietly.

'Oh.' My heart sped up. It felt as though it were in my throat. A lot of burning went on this island, usually where they were taking down foliage or the odd tree to make room for another building; they always planted more though, which was a good thing. But why hadn't I known? I had seen smoke from the other side of the island a few times over the last few weeks. I had presumed it was trees. That could have been Clara then. An acidic taste was in my mouth, which I had to ignore as Kali was now in full swing, and in her element it seemed.

Kali demonstrated a more difficult knot twice more and then handed the rope to me. I stumbled at first, but Kali set me right. Then, to finish off, I tied a reef knot three times, feeling a sense of accomplishment.

'Would you like some tea, Sadie?' Mary asked as she put water on a small gas hob. It looked and felt so homely in here and I suddenly I felt Clara's absence more fiercely again. As though what Kali and Mary had here was what Clara and I should have had.

'I think I need some fresh air; it's jolly hot in here.' The reality was I wanted to throw up and I didn't want to have to do it in Kali and Mary's cosy shack. I stood up. 'We must do some more soon.'

I took myself out of the cabin and walked across the way to my own hut.

The rain pelted at my face, and the sound of the storm above my head whirred like a helicopter.

I tried to suck in as much air as I could on the way to try and settle my gut. I knew I should rest and do what everyone else was doing, which was pretty much nothing, but I had a desire to see where they had burnt Clara. Perhaps it would bring me some closure. I glanced around to see if anyone was watching me before I headed off through the trees to the back beach.

I found myself looking out to the Pacific Ocean as the storm raged on around me. I had a sudden desire for a primal scream, but it would only attract attention so I kicked furiously at the sand, picked up some stones and threw them as hard as I could into the ocean; however, it would not shift the feeling that was creeping through my veins. Rage was not the sort of feeling I knew how to deal with, let alone when I was on a small remote island with people I had only known for a few weeks. Most things about Totini were pretty good. Why couldn't I just focus on them? I couldn't risk losing my mind, not this soon. I knew I would need to find a way to release my anger and the frustration that was slowly building up inside me. Or I could do something that I might regret.

## 26
### NOW

'You understand why you are here, don't you, Sadie?' Dr Bhaduri asks. The question sounds familiar. Had he asked me that before?

I try to work out what I am supposed to say.

'Is this how we open each of our sessions?' I ask him. 'With you asking me if I know why I am here.'

Dr Bhaduri nods earnestly. I almost felt the need to smile, as though I am a schoolgirl being told off for something I shouldn't have done. I just want to giggle my way right out of this room, but I also know that there is a very serious undertone to these sessions and that there is a very specific reason I am here with a psychiatrist every week. They want to know what happened. And I want to know what they thought had happened.

'Okay.' Dr Bhaduri sighs, and I feel as though I know what is coming. 'Let's start at the beginning.' He looks at me. 'Again,' he adds. I am not sure if it is for comedy value for himself, or he genuinely has had enough of sitting here with me for the last few weeks.

'You were picked up in the middle of the South Pacific Ocean on a small power boat, drifting. You were rescued by a group of Fijian fishermen. Who knows where you could have ended up if they hadn't found you when they had? You claim you had been on an island called Totini for the last six weeks and then you passed out on the boat. When you woke, you couldn't remember anything, not the last thing you had said to the fishermen, nor why you were there, not even your name. The only thing you could remember was that you had a friend. Your friend Avril. Your passport was with your belongings, and you were first taken to a hospital where you had some basic health checks done before you were taken to the British High Commission in Fiji, and then shortly afterward you were flown home here to Britain.'

Dr Bhaduri looks up at me briefly to make sure I am still listening. I am. Intently, the way I was sure I did most days because to me it was a fascinating story, not one that had happened to me, but something I might read about in a newspaper or magazine. He looks back down at his papers, although I am sure he must know this verbatim by now if it was something that he told me each time we met. 'You were greeted at the airport by your parents who took you home to their house for a short while.'

Dr Bhaduri stops speaking and looks at me again.

A loud bell sounds. Is that the end of our session? The sound is familiar. Have I heard that before? If feel as though I have heard it in my sleep for weeks, waking me up.

'The bell,' I say out loud.

He nods and looks happy that I said that. He quickly scribbles something on the paperwork in front of him.

'You looked pleased,' I say.

He keeps smiling. 'Yes, I am. I feel we have made some progress here. You recognised the sound of the bell. It rings at this time every day. That is the visitors' bell.'

I screw my face up. He has not spoken this way before . . .

'Some patients like to receive visitors here.'

I waited for him to elaborate.

'Visitors come here, to The Forestry.' He shifted in his chair, uncrossed and re-crossed his other leg. Then he looked directly at me.

'Sadie, you are in a psychiatric unit, and you have been here under our care for the last three weeks.'

# 27

## THEN

I left the front beach, making my way through the clearing, and edged my way through camp, trying to appear as inconspicuous as possible, and then found my way to the path that led to the back beach. The rain lashed against my face, the thunder rolled on, and then, occasionally a flash of lightning. I imagined it would look just as spectacular from the back beach, but I wasn't going to watch a thunderstorm; I was on a mission to find something else. Even though they had burned Clara, surely they must have left some sort of grave for her? It was only right that when someone died they were given a proper burial and a grave. Clara had parents, maybe sisters and brothers; there would be people who needed to know where her final resting place was.

I thought about my own family and my last conversation with them. I would need to speak to them again soon. But already I felt different to the person who had left the mainland a few weeks ago. I felt this island had made its mark on me in some way and that trying to put myself mentally back into a world that was so far removed from this one would be impossible right now. Yet the doubts about why I had come here and whether I should be staying consumed me just as much. I had not considered the effect the island would have on me, that it would get into my skin the way it had. And I hadn't thought that I would feel compelled to see it out despite my reservations. And I certainly hadn't imagined just a few weeks into being here I would be looking for the grave of a friend.

If I could have seen into the future, would I still have come?

I pushed on through the terrain. The path always became thinner towards the end before it suddenly opened up again to the vast white beach. Except I was seeing it through sepia today. The whole island had lost its vibrancy and colour, washed out by the almost black clouds and torrential rain.

Once on the beach, I wasn't sure which way to turn. If I went right, I would eventually end up by the foot of the highest peak, past Ula's shack. Or I could go into the depths of the forest where I had never been before. The foliage was so dense, I was sure I would get lost. I knew I was being silly and, of course, I would find my way out eventually, but I was still nervous around the island, of her tendrils taking hold of me and pulling me in.

I took a walk along the beach to the right. Ula's cabin was perched up on the ledge and would be visible in a few minutes. I hadn't ventured past it before. I hadn't even walked the circumference of the island yet. There was no time like the present, so why not choose to walk around the island when the weather was the worst since I arrived here? After walking for a few minutes with the wind and the rain in my face I looked up to my right and saw Ula's hut. I wondered what she would be doing in there, how she must feel alone. And then, as I heard the word she had spoken to me through the bush that night, it was as if the wind had just whispered it back at me to remind me.

Run.

I didn't feel as if I was in any immediate danger. I was perturbed about the attitude of the campmates, and yes Clara's death had shocked me. Still shocked me. Then the way the campmates reacted to things that I would have thought would have affected them more. The way no one spoke of Ula, the woman who lived alone in the shack on the hill. And a young woman at that. When I had heard of her, I had presumed she would have been elderly and out of her mind with dementia or something.

I took a sharp left, leaving the sanctuary of the beach behind me, knowing I was venturing further into the woods where the trees grew thick and dense to see if there was any other sign of a path. And then I spotted it. A very slight indent amongst the foliage, as though someone walked there occasionally, but it hadn't yet evolved into a path. I wondered if this was where Ula walked or where Adi hid out.

The rain pelted relentlessly at my face. I kept wiping my hand across my eyes, but it made little difference; my vision was a watery haze.

I pushed through the first part of the bush, expecting it to open up immediately, but the plants stayed close to my arms, the sound of them scraping across my rain mac as I walked. I felt my heart thump in my chest as I thought about trying to find my way back. The woods and forest here were wider than where we were at the camp – to get to the other side of the island from here would take me at least thirty minutes, maybe more in this weather. Or so I had been told when I asked the questions when I first arrived. There were so many questions, yet I was too terrified to go and find out for myself. I had stayed where I felt secure within the camp area. But now the time had come and my curiosity had got the better of me. I wanted to work out exactly what I was surrounded by.

Clara had been burned here somewhere; there had to be another clearing around where they could have done that safely without risking burning other trees or foliage. I walked on. My face was drenched, and I had stopped wiping it a long time ago; now I just let the rain fall over it. Eventually, I saw ahead the path began to open up into something more substantial, and I almost yelped with relief. This could be it; this could be where they left the remains of Clara. But even if it wasn't, I reminded myself, it was a milestone for me; I had made another break from camp and ventured out alone.

I stopped among the clearing, the rain pouring through the trees. I could see a small path opposite, so I headed straight for it, not before making a note of where I had come from. I picked up a rock and placed it next to the entrance I had come through, as I could now see several indents within the outer foliage.

I looked around, took in my surroundings. All around was just trees, foliage, and nothing else. What was I doing coming here in this weather, soaked through only to stand in the middle of a clearing getting even more drenched? I scanned the area once more, and my eyes landed on the mark I had left, a large rock. Yet what was that? Before my gaze landed there, I had seen something in my peripheral sight. I turned an inch and there it was. I had missed it because I had been looking everywhere except right under my nose. Three rocks, each the size of my palm. Not a coincidence that they had all ended up there together in a small circle. They had been placed there. Was this the final resting place of Clara? They must have burnt her up on the beach and buried any remains here. I was thankful that they had done this. I couldn't imagine her just left somewhere or tossed into the sea.

I took two steps to my right and bent down next to the shrubbery. Three small rocks perfectly placed on top of a small mound. I leaned closer. The rain was beginning to blur my vision, and I had nothing dry left to wipe my face with. The droplets kept falling as I bent to look closer. I could see one of the rocks had marks across it. I crouched, almost touching it, and then I could see there was writing. It had been scratched on the rock with a knife or another sharp piece of rock. It spelt out one word. A name. D E N Y.

Deny. I said the name out loud, and then a recollection hit me hard: I had heard that name before. The little girl on the beach, her doll had been called Deny.

I had come looking for the final resting place of Clara and instead I had found some sort of memorial path. I cast my mind back to the beach and the rudimentary wooden doll with the locks of bright blonde human hair glued to the head. Someone else had died here too. I wondered how she, if it was she, Deny, had died and if she had been in another accident. I thought about the mothers telling me Adi's mother had deserted him. Was Deny Adi's mother? Had she gone, or was she another victim of something gone wrong? Another accident?

Leaves shook behind me, and my heart rate sped up. As I turned, I thought I saw a flash of bright colour amongst the forest's green, but my eyesight was so blurry now that it was impossible to tell for sure.

I took one last look at the memorial spot and headed forward towards the tiny path. Not knowing where it was about to take me, but then realising that I hadn't really known much about where anything was taking me since I got on the boats and helicopter with Avril three weeks ago. As I walked, I thought about what Deny would have looked like. Would she have been tall and fearless or scared like I was? Did she come alone? Did she die alone?

The thoughts kept moving around my head and I forgot that I was still moving forward. Did I imagine the trees and shrubbery around me becoming thicker and denser? The rain was slick, falling down my face and clinging to my skin. I thought about dipping further into the woods and finding shelter for a while. I started to breathe faster, and realised I was crying although my tears were mixed with rainwater. I felt all the anger and sadness surge through. I suddenly wanted to be back at the camp.

My ears began to tune in to a sound, a loud braying. I was approaching the area where the cows and goats were kept. I was sure of it. I understood why this area was kept so far away from the main camp, because of the level of noise, even with the storm so loud overhead. I could hear the definitive sound of cattle.

Finally, the path seemed to open up. Trees swayed on either side of me; a wind hissed, thrusting in my face. This area had less protection from the storm and so I was exposed to the elements, rain now hitting me from all sides.

As the path opened up further, I began to see something through the foliage. As I allowed my eyes to adjust through the flurry of wind and rain, I eventually worked out that they were panels of wood standing upright. The wood became more prevalent with each step I took until finally I was able to see it was a cage. I saw a breed of bird I didn't recognise. From where it was perched it looked as though it were in the cage. Maybe this was an aviary, although I'd never heard anyone mention one. I could imagine Avril wanting something so beautiful like that here. But the bird leapt from where it was perched and flew up and over the cage. Of course it wasn't trapped in there. Caged birds went against everything Totini stood for. So maybe this was where the animals were kept, more chickens and the goats, yet I had seen cattle grazing freely around the island.

The closer I got to the cage, the more my gut began to protest. A tightening began there and expanded right through into my chest. Fear clamped in my stomach the way it did when I was unsure. An instinct told me to turn back, yet a yearning to know forced me forward.

I eventually found myself in a clearing, with the cage now directly in front of me. It was about ten foot high. I could estimate this accurately because the wall around the flat I had in the UK was ten foot. I had looked at that wall endless times, and now I was looking at a cage that represented that exact same height. Within the cage was a small hut, almost like something I had seen on a pig farm. I stared and stared at that cage, waiting to see the pig, or something that made sense in my mind. Then as I continued to stare at the cage in front of me, I saw it, the thing that my gut had been preparing me for. I saw a pair of legs, then the torso they were connected to. A slick, sweaty, tanned body with the head of a man attached. He was lying on his side, as though he were sleeping, but the rain was dripping into the cage and onto him.

A sound took my attention from him and I swung my head to my right. Another cage, this time, another man. It was impossible to tell his age. I would have guessed anywhere in his twenties or thirties. He was wearing a thin pair of trousers soaked to his skin, and he was clinging onto the thick wooden bars of the cage.

He was mouthing something, then the sound came again, the one that had brought my attention to him in the first place. The animal sound I had heard, except now I knew that animal was human.

'Help us,' I heard, and I swung around again to my left, to an older man with greying hair and a skinny, tanned torso. Beyond him, in a separate cage, I glimpsed a face, and I had a flash of recognition. It was the same man that I had seen in the clearing when I had first arrived, the one who had been marched off by Precious and Kali. The look of hopelessness was still on his face as though it were permanently etched.

I looked again at the sleeping man in front of me and then again to the man who was calling out to me, then my eyes roamed beyond and as far as I could see was cage upon cage, each one containing a man.

# 28
## THEN

I didn't dare move in case I disturbed something or set off an alarm, or that somehow if they all saw me, they could come charging for me, despite being behind what appeared to be sturdy gates. I didn't want to even think of the word *prison*, but it was obvious to me that this was what this was. An image of the man from the first day came back to me, how efficiently he had been dealt with, as though they had done it before. These men had to have gotten here somehow, and Avril must have been instrumental in all of this. I looked again at the man I had presumed to be a pirate. She never did tell me that he wasn't.

'I've not seen you help us?' the man to my left shouted across the noise of his storm. 'You're new,' he called. His voice was husky as though he had talked or shouted a lot. I looked around and beyond at the other cages, at a rough quick count I made it fifteen cages. Fifteen cages, each with one man inside. The men were in various positions of sitting and lying. Most displayed a demeanour that suggested they had given up somehow. That they were just letting the rain do its thing as though surrendering to the elements. A few of them were half in half out of the small hut, which was just big enough to take a full body.

'Come over here.' The man had a South African accent; I could hear that clearly enough. He was the only one who was standing up.

'I've seen them all. You are new,' he called again. 'Come here.'

I took a tentative step forward. He was behind bars. He couldn't get to me.

I was a few feet away from him when he spoke again.

'Come closer. I'm not dangerous.'

'Stand back, Sadie!' I jumped at the sound of Avril's voice, loud and shrill behind me. It made some of the other men stir, a muscle reflex to the sound of her voice. A few even dragged themselves inside their huts as though her voice elicited a dreaded fear in them.

'Don't listen to him, Sadie. Move back.' I turned to my side and saw that Avril was right there.

'Get behind me.'

I did as she said. She was carrying a rifle again, something I had only ever seen her carry when a man was around. 'These men are dangerous. Just like all men. That's why they need to be here. That's why you are on this side and they are on that side, Sadie. Don't you forget it. Don't you forget Bruno, Sadie, what he did to you.'

My body tensed at the way Avril had brought Bruno back to life, as though he were suddenly here on the island.

Avril began walking over to the cage. She stood next to the guy who had spoken. He had a slick chest, a shaved head, three tattoos on each arm. They were the wavy kind that meant something in Maui or something. But then further down his arm something caught my eye, because I had seen it so many times since I had been here. There on his arm, not as professionally done as the other tattoos, was a cupcake.

As we walked back to camp, the storm began to subside, only slowly but enough so we didn't need to shout. Avril walked with intention; the rifle slung over her shoulder. She looked so casual with it now, as opposed to how she looked five minutes ago: fierce and ready to aim it right at that guy's head.

'Obviously, I have a lot of questions.'

'Okay, I will answer all of them,' Avril said with conviction. We walked at a pace.

'How did you know where I was?' I asked.

'I followed you.'

'Who are all the men?'

Avril paused for a second. 'They are men who were brought here because of crimes against women.'

'What sorts of crimes?' I asked.

'Any kind. Inequality. Sexism a lot of the time, but sexism that has been harmful to the life of a woman. To her career. Actual bodily harm, domestic abuse.' I flinched at her words. An image of Bruno was clear in my mind. The punch, the hole in the wall. Avril also looked across at me, knowing that those words would have the most impact on me.

'Who brought them here?'

'I had them brought here.'

I stopped and Avril stopped too. We looked at one another.

'What is going on here?' I felt the rage bubble up inside me. Was it all just because of the sight of these men or was it also to do with Clara? I had been angry at Avril for some time now.

'Did you coerce them here?'

'We did what we needed to do. Each situation was unique. Each woman's voice was and is unique.'

'And what happens to them? Are they serving some kind of sentence?'

'No. I don't know. I haven't thought that far ahead.' Avril sounded stressed, the first time she had sounded that way. She started walking again, and I followed.

'How long have they been here?' I persisted.

Avril was quiet for a moment. 'The longest, five years.'

Five years? For five years, this island had held men captive. I had been swept up in the idea that I was living in paradise, when all the time I had been sharing my surroundings with criminals.

'And that was the purpose of coming here?' I probed Avril further.

'Not initially. I had the idea of a commune. In the end, I knew I couldn't afford it. Until I met someone. They needed somewhere to home a male prisoner; I needed an island for my all-female commune and we made an agreement. All the women who live here needed somewhere to live, away from society. Away from their past. And then every time I went to the mainland, there was another man, who was . . . handsy, inappropriate, and wouldn't take no for an answer. It turns out when you do a little digging, you can find out quite a lot about these men, about what they do with their spare time. And who they are with. Where they lie about, waiting to commit their next act.'

'But are they actual proper criminals?' I asked, and heard the stress in my voice. So did Avril. She stopped walking and grabbed me with both arms.

'Sadie, these are men who would otherwise be going around committing crimes and getting away with it.' Her eyes were desperate and pleading for me to understand. 'The women on this island understand that they need somewhere to live, and they have accepted it. It's not that hard to get your head around.' She rubbed her hand across her face. 'Besides . . .' we continued walking; the rain had eased up more but it was still dripping on my face '. . . you don't think I get this island for nothing?'

'I didn't know. So each woman is running from the same thing? Like me?' I stopped us walking again by placing my hand on Avril's arm. 'Like you?'

Avril looked at me. 'That's why I brought you here, because I could see in your eyes that day at the bar, how that guy made you feel. Tony. He's on our radar by the way. And I can see your wounds even though you don't think you are displaying them.'

Avril hadn't answered my question, but I was getting a good picture of what was going on here. Avril had started off by incarcerating one man in return for some free time on the island. She utilised the space to bring more men, and the women who come here have many things in common, the most important being they have all experienced some kind of injustice from men.

We stopped at a clearing, and I recognised it as the place where I had seen the stones with Deny's name carved into them. I looked down and sought them out. 'I need a second woman, someone to assist me,' Avril said. 'All the girls here came specifically for the commune, to exist, to just be, but I can see there is something more in you. I've been watching you these last three weeks. You rise early every day, you struggle to relax, you are not sure how to just be, which is fine. But that is exactly what I need in a woman here. I wasn't sure if you'd be up for the job, but now after seeing you here, I think you'll be perfect.'

She breathed out loudly as though she had been holding in her breath all this time. 'I need you to help me with the men. Together we can do this, Sadie.' She grabbed my face in her hands. 'And I think you need this too.'

# 29
## THEN

That night, Avril let me cook, even though it wasn't my turn. The camp was a washout, and Mary, Precious and a couple of other women helped restore it. Branches and leaves were cleared away, a fresh fire was built, and before long, the place looked like its old self.

I prepared fish in silence, despite the company of women around me, mulling over everything I had heard from Avril that afternoon.

I couldn't quite get my head around what I had seen and heard that afternoon. Whenever I thought of the men caged up, skinny and tired and all with that look of hopelessness that I had seen in the one man that first week, I felt sick. I managed to smile and make small talk but their faces would not leave my mind.

I tried to take in the enormity of the situation. The reality of where I was living and who I was now sharing the island with, but it just felt too big for me. I wasn't sure I was going to be able to stay let alone assist Avril with prison duties. What exactly had Avril seen in me? Was it merely that I was wearing what I presumed were invisible wounds and that she could see them? Did the abuse I suffered at the hands of my boyfriend make me an ideal candidate for prison duties?

I looked around me and realised I had forgotten to grab the spices I was going to use in the fish curry. Some good ones had come in recently and I thought I would spice things up; the more I poured myself into cooking the less impact the caged men had on my mind. But I knew it was only going to be temporary and the second I had stopped distracting myself, they would be back at the forefront of my mind.

In the larder, I felt her presence even before I turned around. It was Kali.

'Ah my favourite chef,' she said.

My hand reached for a bag of herbs. My heart was thumping a little faster than normal and then out of nowhere, an image of the spear through Clara's foot came at me fast. I grabbed awkwardly at the bag, nearly knocking a neighbouring bag off the shelf.

'Oh be careful, Sadie, these are expensive. We can't go wasting precious stock.' Kali reached for the teetering bag of saffron and pushed it back.

I looked at Kali for a moment, wishing Clara were here, but she was not. As the weeks passed, I realised that the shock of seeing Clara with that spear through her foot had prevented me from ever really asking some serious questions.

'What happened on the beach, Kali?'

Kali recoiled, her expression set hard, and she began to bite her lower lip.

Then her eyes narrowed.

'You need to watch yourself,' she hissed. I realised our time together in her hut making knots had been a one-off. She still had something against me.

'Why, because I might end up with a spear through my foot?' I snapped back.

'I am famished,' Precious announced as she appeared next to us. I took a step back from Kali and smiled at Precious.

'So what's on the menu tonight?' Kali said, her voice as light as air.

'A fish curry, with rice, and sweet potato and tomato salad.' I played along.

'You're quite the gourmet, aren't you? But I knew you would have talents,' Kali replied.

'She is,' Precious agreed as she took down some bread from the shelf. 'I won't let it ruin my appetite.' She smiled sweetly and skipped away.

Kali watched, and once Precious was far enough away, she swung her head back to me.

'Don't think because Avril has asked you to assist her that you are something special . . .' Kali's voice had lost the lightness it had a moment ago.

I let out a sigh.

'And now you know our little secret. I hope you'll behave and play by the rules.'

I snapped my head at her. 'What do you mean, Kali?' I said, a tide of aggression growing in my voice.

Kali looked stunned. She hadn't expected me to respond that way.

'Those men, they're not here for our entertainment.'

I shook my head. 'I have no idea what you mean, Kali. All I know is that I'm aware of what is going on now. I didn't know before, but now Avril has told me all about the men.'

'Okay, I'm sure she did,' she said, the tone of her voice revealing she was determined to try and find fault with me, in order not to like me. I got it; I was the new girl. Not all women were comfortable with someone stepping into their arena. Perhaps Kali had been lining herself up to be Avril's right-hand woman. Another image of Clara, the spear through her foot. Had Clara been in Kali's way? Is that why she ended up hurt? I edged away from the shelves. Was I headed the same way? Is that what happened to people here when they crossed an invisible line? I headed back to the fire to continue cooking. But this time, along with Clara's face was Ula's and a faceless woman. Deny.

*You need to surrender yourself for a piece of paradise.*

What if that piece meant that you never got your whole self back, or worse, you didn't make it out alive?

I left the food simmering on the stove and went to fetch some water. The tank was situated at the back of the kitchen and stores. I pressed the tap down and began filling my water bottle.

Something hit me on the back. I jumped up and swung around, doing a full 360-degree turn. The water was spilling out everywhere.

'Shit, shit.' I turned it off, already so conscious of waste.

What the hell was that?

Then I heard it, a loud giggle. I turned to my right and saw his face in amongst the foliage. He was smiling. Laughing. He was laughing at me. Adi, the little feral child, was laughing at me.

'Hi, Adi,' I shouted over the rain, hoping he would come forward. I didn't want him to fear me anymore. In some ways, I needed him more than ever. That pure innocence of a child could help me heal and distract me from all the things I had yet to understand or process.

I wasn't sure if he understood a word I said but he turned and scooted off into the depths of the woods. I wondered once again why no one spoke of Adi. I thought often of who his mother might be and if he was receiving enough care. I wished he would stay around longer and I contemplated how I might coax him to me next time.

I returned to my cooking in silence, images of the men now infused in the cocktail of images in my mind along with Adi, Ula, Clara and Deny.

In such a short space of time, Totini Island had revealed so much to me. The tropical paradise I had arrived on was now a myriad of death, depression and captivity.

How was I expected to thrive amongst that? It was the very opposite of what Totini appeared to offer when I first arrived. Yet twenty-nine other women seemed to be doing it, even though I could see and feel their anger. Was that because the men were so close to us?

I knew I could not be both – someone who condoned the captivity of men who had apparently not stood trial for their apparent crimes and someone who was living in the moment and healing from her past. Avril seemed to have some almighty faith in my capabilities, but I could already see beyond all of her words and praise. I could feel something much more intense and real. I could sense danger.

# 30
## NOW

I have begun to repeat to myself over and over that I am in a psychiatric unit. It had been written down several times for me, but now, the chanting in my mind has begun. It is becoming part of a daily mantra. I am in a psychiatric unit.

They must know all about the pictures I have drawn and what they mean. Maybe we've had that conversation already, and I just can't remember. I can see the images in my mind, the wardrobe stacked with drawings.

By the time I am due to have my next session with Dr Bhaduri, I am terrified this is it. I am going to be arrested for my crimes. I have gotten away with it for too long.

I sit down on my usual chair, slightly to the right of Dr Bhaduri's, and wait for him to begin. Each week it is different. Today I can tell he has something important he needs to say. Why don't I get rid of all the drawings? Why did I stack them in the wardrobe? That was not the right thing to have done. I look around the room in case someone else had slipped in unnoticed and they are about to arrest me. But the atmosphere is as calm as it is each time I have been here.

Dr Bhaduri clears his throat and begins speaking.

'Following on from last week's session where we explained to you, again, where you were, there have been some uncoverings regarding your friend.'

I feel my heart thud in my chest. It is all over, my time here, nestled amongst others who had forgotten, who are lost in their minds. This was the beginning of the end for me. I couldn't have done something so terrible and remained living in such comfortable conditions.

'Sadie, while in the care of your parents, you spoke of nothing except your missing friend, Avril. Your parents had never met Avril before. So there have been several checks run on one Avril Quinn, and several checks run under different variations of the name. We haven't been able to link her to any social media accounts. You claim you had been living on an island with this woman. We've assisted the investigation into this woman who you claim was the leader of a commune, and we can conclude it has come back unsuccessful. There is no record of any woman, meaning that your friend, whom you say you were living with and were very close with, may never have even existed.'

# 31
## THEN

The storm had turned the whole island inside out. We had managed to sort the camp but everywhere else I looked evidence of the force of the weather was all around. Avril was up and around me early the next morning after the big revelation of the male prisoners.

'Are you okay?' she asked tentatively.

'I'm fine,' I said, trying to add some colour to my voice. Trying not to let a note of doubt slip from my lips. I needed time to think, to assess what was going on here, and I didn't want to alarm Avril. I didn't need her to think I had doubts. I also didn't want to end up with my name on a stone or burned and forgotten about.

Maybe every other woman here had nothing left to return to, and so living alongside these men in this way was something they could just forget about, pretend it wasn't happening. But it wouldn't sit right with me; I couldn't make it right in my mind. And so for now, I would smile and be cooperative.

'I didn't want to shock you. You needed time to settle in. And as I said to you yesterday, I think you are the perfect one for the role, to help me with Camp Z.'

'Camp Z?' I repeated.

'That's what we call the camp with the men in it.'

I swallowed slowly. It had a name and it sounded post-apocalyptic.

'It's a prison though isn't it?' I said my mouth drying up.

Avril looked exasperated. 'Yes I suppose, if you want to look at it like that.'

How else did she expect me to look at it I thought, as I poured water into the huge kettle ready to start heating for morning tea.

Avril gently touched my arm.

'Sadie, you've had such a terrible time; this will be good for you. It will help with your healing. I can't bring your ex here, but I can show you that we do not allow men to get away with treating women like shit.'

Images of a now blurry Bruno swirled in my mind. I was far enough away that I could begin to forget him and everything he had done. But now there was a whole camp full of men supposedly here for similar crimes. I scratched at my neck and tried to calm my thoughts. Avril saw something in me, a strength I didn't know I had. Maybe the way to finally be rid of Bruno was to face the men every day. So I was no longer scared of Bruno or any other man who could do the same to me. It was safe enough with them all behind bars. They couldn't get to me. This was how she wanted me to see it. This is what she wanted me to do. All I could think was what might happen if I didn't go along, if I wasn't the person she thought I was.

'Let's talk more later,' Avril said softly, and she walked away.

Yet again, I was unable to put one emotion at the forefront of my mind and hold it there. I looked around at the peace and serenity of the island all around me. I looked at the women existing around me. They had managed to file away what was happening on the other side of the island. Should I try and do the same?

There was already music playing this morning from a speaker. That hadn't been the case when I first arrived. Was the music for me? A distraction from Camp Z? Even thinking the words made me shudder.

Two women were now in camp preparing breakfast. The air was beginning to heat up and after the force of the storm yesterday it was as though the sun had been missing for weeks and not just twenty-four hours. I left them to it and walked to clear my head. I had barely slept, as the rain had come and gone all night, interrupting sleep that did not come easily and dreams that were full of men in cages.

Without realising it I had found my way to Ula's hut and as though she was there in front of me saying the word again, I could hear it. 'Run.'

Was that what she had said, and was it because of the men? Or had Ula rebelled against Avril and had she been segregated for it?

I looked up at it and again wondered what she did in there all day. I thought of her most days. Was she scared?

But general day-to-day life on Totini had a way of holding you in a gentle hug, so any slight frustrations or worries seemed to come and go in spurts and disperse as quickly as they emerged. As soon as thoughts of prisons and Clara's death and Ula living here alone began contaminating my mind, I would be pulled back to the present, the heat, the smells of the campfire, the roosters calling, the sound of a fallen coconut hitting the tin roof of the rain tower. And the peace and the quiet. There was so much time to think, and maybe all I had to do was learn how to turn those thoughts towards things that would benefit me and to try and just exist and live in the moment as these women did. We had all run from the same thing. And even though there were men locked up half an hour away, I had witnessed that it was entirely possible to forget about them.

Ula was apparently mad, mute; she was to be left alone. I thought about the words of the campmates and how they had spoken of her. But I needed to know for myself. Maybe Ula was the one who could help straighten this all out in my mind, help me make sense of it. And maybe I would get some clarity on her own life story. I took the path I had walked up the first time and found myself at the side of the hut. The red handprints had faded after yesterday's storm. I walked around the side of the hut and arrived at the front where the one window and door were. The window was heavily curtained still. I thought of the impossible heat inside the hut and wondered how Ula managed to stay there for a few minutes, let alone days at a time. The only thing I could think was that the trees provided enough shelter from the daily sun to keep the cabin relatively cool.

Where was she, I wondered? Apart from that one encounter with her on the beach through the foliage, I hadn't ever seen her out of her hut.

I stood in front of the door, took a deep breath and knocked firmly.

'Ula,' I called. Did she even know her name? Was that even her real name or one that the camp had assigned to her?

I knocked again, this time three times in a row.

'Ula, you don't know me, I'm Sadie. I have been on the island a few weeks and I would like to speak with you.'

I looked around and then down at the beach in case Ula was there, but more importantly in case I had been followed and someone was watching me. I was now more wary of stepping out of line than ever, getting things wrong and going against the grain. Systems had been set in place and I had already tested them. I was never one to just accept what I was told without good enough evidence.

'Ula,' I called again without knocking this time.

I placed my hand on the door and, with it, a tiny bit of my weight, and as I did, the door gave way and opened an inch. I felt my heart begin to skip. All I needed to find out now: was she was inside or not?

I shoved the door another couple of inches, edging my way across the threshold as I did. A few more nudges and the door was half open and I stepped fully into the cabin. The now open doorway cast a pathway of light through the centre of the dark room. Immediately, I was surprised to see the level of tidiness inside the hut. There was a curious array of objects lined up along a table and around the edges of the room, things that looked as though they had been washed in from the sea, a clue that Ula did spend time outside, or maybe she once did. And of course she was not in the hut now. I could see every corner from where I stood.

There was a very basic roll-out mattress on the floor with a thin cover, a small pile of books next to the bed. This surprised me more. Did Ula sit and read? I dared to step closer and saw there were few classics: *Wuthering Heights*, *Pride and Prejudice*, and *Life Between the Tides: In Search of Rock Pools and Other Adventures Along the Shore*. This made me feel a little sad. Ula had been or still was someone who had a keen interest in marine life. Then my eyes were drawn to the final one, *A Rough Guide to Fiji* and there on the front cover, a perfect paradise island with white sandy beaches and a turquoise reef. I imagined an Ula in another life heading to her local bookshop to pick up a copy, thinking she would be taught everything she needed to know. Did it say in the foreword anything about giving away a part of yourself for a piece of paradise? The Ula who bought that book would have not had any clue of what lay ahead for her, a life stuffed away in a shack on a ledge, living alone, cast away from the group. What terrible thing could she have possibly done to warrant this treatment? I stood in the centre of the room; I was surprised it wasn't hotter. I had expected to walk into a room that felt like a sauna, but it was surprisingly cool.

Then it seemed my very thoughts had summoned her. I heard footsteps scuffing against the dusty pathway and then heavy breathing. Then a long shadow was cast across the threshold as a tall female figure now stood there looking in at me.

I felt my stomach drop and my mouth became dry. If Ula was as unhinged as everyone said she was, then I was a trapped animal. I had nowhere to go. I thought about the books just to my right by my feet. The rough guide to Fiji was almost brick-like and could be a good weapon should I need to fling anything at Ula so I could get out of her shack and to safety. I stood waiting, to see what she would do. Would she scream at me, or would she give me instructions to run again?

She walked through into the cabin. Her height both astounded and unnerved me; I hadn't imagined her to be so tall. She almost had to crouch to come in through the doorway. I noticed the blood on the crotch of her trousers. And now I knew that the handprints on the outside had been made with her menstrual blood. Ula was someone who bled freely. Another reason her campmates didn't want to come near her maybe. Her long light blonde hair was tied back in a very loose ponytail. Even though she had blocked most of the light out with curtains, I could see her eyes lacked sparkle, her expression, dull and lifeless, seemed to match the ambience of the room.

Then she spoke. Her voice was low and husky, which surprised me initially, then the words she uttered startled me even more.

'Well, this is a nice surprise. I was wondering when you were going to stop by.'

# 32

## THEN

I was still trying to figure out what I was supposed to do when Ula stepped right into the room and pushed me firmly, so I fell back into a small hardbacked chair next to the bed.

'Guests must sit when they come.' There was an edge to her voice. I could now see that she was twitching slightly, maybe some sort of tick.

'I'll make tea.' She shuffled to the table where there was a small gas stove. She began trying to light it, but it appeared not to be working. Perhaps it hadn't been working for some time and Ula was just going through the motions, doing what she thought she was supposed to do when a guest arrived at her home. I gave her one minute of trying to get the gas stove to work and then I cleared my throat.

'Ula, it's fine. I didn't come here for tea.'

She turned at the sound of my voice and for the first time I was able to get a good look at her in full view. She had on what looked to be harem pants that perhaps had once been turquoise or blue, with a very faded gold pattern crawling up the leg. What I could see was how utterly filthy they were.

'I, I came to see you, because I was told you lived here. Alone.'

Ula scratched at her head, her ponytail looking as though it might fall loose any minute. I imagined she didn't wash her hair, and now she was stationary I could see it had begun to mat in several places as though it were trying to form dreadlocks.

'I do live here. Alone,' she repeated.

I looked around the shack again, searching for something to focus on for inspiration so we could start a conversation.

'You have lots of lovely things. Did you collect them all yourself?' I asked her.

Ula looked at me again. I pointed to the shells and such on the table just behind her.

'The shells and driftwood. Did you collect it all yourself?'

She turned and gently put her hand on one of the pieces of driftwood. A small piece, grey and knotted. She looked thoughtfully at it, and I wasn't sure she was going to reply, or if she might freak out or cry, perhaps I had touched a raw nerve.

'Someone collected them. For me.'

I nodded. 'Nice.'

I had so many questions for her, but where was I supposed to start?

'Ula, I wanted to ask you if you were okay.'

She pulled her face into a frown. The she turned back to the gas stove, attempted to light it again.

'Do you want some tea?' she called over her shoulder.

I let out a long breath. 'Sure, let's have some tea,' I said.

Was Ula pretending she didn't understand my question? It was hard to know what her true state of mind was. But I could tell that a piece of Ula was missing. Was this the obligatory piece that we all came with but had to forsake for our time here in paradise? If it was it seemed to me that Ula had got the raw end of the deal. I did not know her or who she was before she came here, but she seemed to be someone who had lost a part of herself somewhere along the way. I wanted to help Ula. I wanted her to trust me.

Ula gave up trying to get the gas hob to work and turned around. For a second she seemed shocked to see me there, as though she had forgotten I had been sat behind her.

I smiled so she wouldn't feel any sort of threat from me.

'Thanks for letting me come and see you. Would you mind if I visited again?' I got up from the chair, my foot brushing against something that was half tucked under the rolled-out mattress. It was a notebook of some sort.

'It's such a lovely day isn't it?' I pointed to the door and Ula looked that way as I quickly bent down and scooped up the notebook, stuffing it into the back of my trousers. Ula turned back around and I didn't think that she had seen me swipe her property. I would just look at the book, see what it contained and then return it. My stomach lurched as I thought about what might happen if Ula caught me. But something had made me pick up the book and maybe it would give me some answers about what had happened to Ula and why she was here. I had an inkling that it was a diary of sorts. Either way, I would find out tonight. Then I would bring it back the next time I visited her. I walked to the doorway, hoping she would let me out. Again, her height intimidated me; she could easily knock me down. I smiled at her, not letting my eyes rest on her.

She didn't move from where she was standing, still by the table of collectibles and the small camping gas hob.

I stepped outside the door and relief washed over me, alerting me to how tense I had been in the hut.

I waited to see if she would say anything more, if I could work out anything from just being here with her. I could feel the presence of the notebook tucked into my trousers and I knew there must be some answers here.

'What's a nice girl like you doing here? She'll get you mixed up in all sorts,' Ula said. I presumed she was referring to Avril.

'Is that why you told me to run the other night?' I asked, and waited for Ula's response, knowing it might not come. 'I'm here to help. In any way I can. Including you, Ula. If you need help, just ask. I'll help you,' I said, and then we locked eyes for a second before all the light seemed to vanish from her eyes as though she had fallen asleep with her eyes open.

'I'll come back,' I said as I stepped away from the door.

As light as it was, I could feel the notebook pressing against my skin, urging me to open it yet also taunting me with the notion that I had done a terrible act taking it from Ula. It might offer nothing but a bunch of blank pages or some seriously bad poetry or prose, perhaps the beginnings of a novel. 'Bye Ula.'

As I arrived closer to camp, an unusual sound drifted towards me. For a moment I thought someone had acquired a TV and was playing it very loudly. But as I approached the clearing, I could hear shouting. Two women's voices, high-pitched and both clearly enraged. I dared to walk into camp not knowing what I was about to come across and I was not surprised when I saw Avril standing in front of a woman, their heads almost touching. Avril seemed ready to launch herself at the other woman whom I recognised as one of the other mothers, not Star; this woman was known as Hester. I hadn't had much to do with either of the mothers; maybe if I was a lot more maternal myself, then I might have got to know them better. They seemed to have their own little clan and were quite content as they were with the two children.

I stayed back for a moment just to gauge the extent of the argument, to try and ascertain who was blaming whom for what before I stepped in.

It took me a moment to try and break down what it was they were saying, shouting, at one another and then put it in some sort of context.

'He took my stuff and I want it back.' Hester sounded petulant.

'Why would he take it? Why? And even if he did, which I highly doubt, why would that give you the right to act that way towards him? Like some savage beast? Is that how you treat one of your own, is it? How would you like it if someone were to threaten your daughter that way?' Avril was practically seething as she spat her words at Hester.

'I have used discipline on my own daughter when it is needed, but that boy is feral. He is an animal and deserves to be treated like one.' Hester was still shouting.

'You're an animal and deserve to be treated like one. How dare you treat an innocent boy like that!'

Hester let out a loud, fake laugh. 'Innocent boy, you don't know shit. You don't notice anything. You've been so wrapped up in Lola and now Sadie. And you think you know everything. I've been here. I know. That boy needs discipline and there isn't no one here to give it to him but me.' Hester was pushing her luck by all accounts. A few inches shorter than Avril, I was sure she would be the one to come out worse, but then I wasn't sure what had happened. I presumed they were talking about Adi who had obviously stepped over some invisible line and Avril was there to stand up for him. I would stand up for him too, if I only knew what he had done.

'Hey,' I called before I had properly thought about what I was going to say. Both women and the small crowd that had formed around them looked over at me. I saw Avril's body language change. She seemed to recoil slightly, and Hester sensed her backing down and relaxed her stance.

'What's the lad done that's got you all riled up like this?'

Hester spoke up first. 'Stole a freshly baked sourdough loaf.'

I nodded as though I understood. Then I took a few steps closer.

'And it isn't the first time he's done it neither,' Hester went on. 'He was at it last week with the sugar buns, and he took my favourite scarf.'

'And does he do this a lot?' I quizzed. I could sense Avril shuffling uncomfortably next to me. I wasn't sure if she was okay with me stepping in, but if she wanted me as her new assistant, maybe this was a good way to show her I was willing, even if it was just so she didn't see through me straight away. Anyway, I wanted to stand up for Adi. He was a sweet child.

Hester snarled as though she were already defeated. 'No. Only recently.'

'Well maybe he feels threatened?' I suggested.

'I feel threatened! We give him plenty. He has enough food, and he still takes more. It's only him who eats it. He chooses not to live among us. I don't feel safe,' she cried.

It was Avril's turn to laugh loudly this time. 'Ha! He's a six-year-old boy. What have you to feel scared of?'

Hester kissed her teeth, making a lip-smacking sound.

I was practically between the two women now.

'I don't think we should be showing any anger towards a small boy whatever his crimes. This is not the Dark Ages. We may live in a place where we make our own rules, but this is one area where I suggest we tread very carefully,' I said, realising that all eyes were on me.

Hester looked at me and squinted her eyes. ''ang on a minute, you've been here for five minutes and now you're trying to tell me what to do!'

I cleared my throat and glanced at Avril. She was looking at me with wide, encouraging eyes.

'I'm not telling you what to do, I'm offering some sound advice. It's easy to become locked in your own rant and train of thought but there is a solution. He's wanting more food. He's a growing boy, so instead of trying to fight him and everyone else on the matter, just make more food. When you make sourdough, make two loaves, when you're making the sugar buns, make extra. It's a simple solution. There is usually a reason behind a behaviour. I'm sure he isn't doing it to upset you.'

Hester was quiet and Avril nodded and smiled.

'She's right,' Avril said. 'If the boy needs more food, we make more food. That will solve this little problem, for it is a little problem.'

Hester took a deep breath and let it out in one angry yet defeated sigh before she stepped away and back to her hut, where the little girl who had the doll on the beach climbed into her lap.

Avril turned to me and grinned.

'See, this is why I need you. There are so many mixed emotions and dynamics all the time. And then with Camp Z on top, knowing you can be there to take care of any . . .' Avril paused '. . . issues, is a weight off my back.'

'What will I be expected to do over there?' I asked tentatively, the assertiveness I had felt moments earlier now fading away as the looks on the faces of the men came flooding back.

'Just be there really. Not all the time, but once or twice a day, check on them, feed them, and make sure they have water. Check none of them have died,' she added nonchalantly.

I sucked in a breath. 'And have they, any of them? Died?'

Avril shook her head but it didn't feel real. Surely I wasn't equipped to deal with any more death on the island.

'You'll be fine.' She winked at me. 'Look how you deal with situations. Sadie, start believing in yourself.' She squeezed my arm, her little trademark power touch. I knew why she did it, to reinforce her words. But they were powerful enough to be believed.

We watched the mothers as they began talking animatedly, obviously discussing me and what had just happened.

'Is she always like that?' I asked. 'I feel kind of bad now.'

'Well, she shouldn't be threatening little kids like that. And yes, she can be a pain in the rear end sometimes. She tried to hit him with a stick!' Avril said her voice tight and strained.

'What? That's not good.'

'Thank you for remaining so calm. Hester takes her baking very seriously.' There was a hint of laughter in her voice. 'Anyway, I'm glad that's sorted. We'll meet after lunch, right?'

'Okay.' I felt a swell of dread. But I kept up the inane grin so that Avril would think I was keen and willing.

'Oh, and later, you'll have your first assignment,' Avril called as she wandered off, leaving me wondering what it could be.

Hester glared over my way; Star gave me a sympathetic smile. So Hester was the feistier of the two. I smiled back.

I could still feel the pressure of the notebook against my back under my T-shirt. I walked quickly back to my cabin and closed the door. I took my backpack and added it to my one pillow for extra back support, then sat on my bed. I laid the book out in front of me and could see for the first time, the words *travel journal* very faintly written on the front.

Oh my God, for the first time in weeks I felt a genuine tingle of excitement. This was Ula's travel journal, the woman who had been living alone for a long enough time that her hair had begun to turn to dreads and she no longer knew how to have a proper conversation. Somewhere within these pages was her story, if not all of it then some of it. I would finally be able to get some answers to some basic questions.

I opened the first page and there, on a brittle-looking page with writing that had begun to fade were the first words.

*We arrived! We absolutely did it!*

# 33
## NOW

I take myself off to the bench for one final time. Jane is sitting in the usual place. She has the coffee and pours it out for both of us.

'I'm leaving tomorrow,' I say. I can feel Jane nodding.

'We've had some good chats these last few weeks, haven't we?' I say and I am smiling.

'We have,' Jane says. 'And you know, we can carry on the chats, if you like.' She smiles. 'I feel as if there is a lot more you want to talk to me about. Even though they say you don't need to be here anymore, I think you and I should carry on, see if we can work it all out between us. You'll be right, Sadie?' She looked down at her lap. 'You always are.'

I began to analyse her face a little closer. There was some sadness there for sure; maybe it was the amount of time we had spent together recently, and she was the only person I had been speaking to on a regular basis beside Dr Bhaduri.

An image sliced through my mind, gone before I had time to hold on to it for long enough to properly see it, but it was an image of two young girls sitting by water, perhaps a pond, or a lake.

I looked more closely at Jane, and she looked at me and smiled.

'You know who I am, don't you, Sadie?' she said softly. She delivered the line in such a way that I knew she didn't just mean from the last few weeks.

Jane's hand was on mine again; her face was brighter.

'I know you and you know me. Very well.' She was almost giggling now. I felt as if she wanted to stand up and dance around me. I could sense her excitement. 'It's me, Sadie. I've been here all this time. I'm your big sister Jane.'

# 34
## THEN

*Journal entry*
*We've arrived on the lovely Island of Kenco. It's so quiet here. I cannot believe how quiet it is here. Maybe it's too quiet, but then I have been used to the louder life. I like distractions. There aren't so many here. There are a few families living here and a bit of a community. I'm not sure how long we'll stay.*

*I like the kava, we've drunk it nearly every day. Is that bad? It makes me really relaxed. It comes out most nights. Although sometimes we have drunk homemade beer, which made a nice difference, I am craving a nice, sweet wine or a cocktail. I wonder if someone could pick up some rum from the mainland and we could make pina coladas. There are enough coconuts here to sink the Titanic. Hey, if all else fails we just live on coconuts, ha ha!*

*Things seem to work here, and I am really happy we came. I have wanted to travel for so long and now I am doing it. There's this guy, Deny. He keeps eyeing us up, like he has never seen a woman before. I'll see if he wants to join us for drinks later. Every one here does seem to be very . . . what is the word I am looking for? Sedated? I don't know if that is the word, but they seem to be very unaffected. Numbed even. Is that the right way to describe it? I guess that is a good thing but if I am being honest – and if you can't be honest in your own journal then where can you be – I find it a bit unnerving. I know I shouldn't and that is just the Western side of me still coming out. I just need to get used to the idea that people can live somewhere on the planet and not be affected by the stresses of the world and life.*

*People on Kenco Island are not living by modern standards here, it's like I've stepped back in time. I know I should feel wholly comfortable with that but there's a small part of me that doesn't.*

*But island life has captured me. And I could stay here forever.*

## 35

### THEN

I was just getting into the second chapter of the journal when an ear-piercing scream rang through the camp and into the cabin. I stuffed the journal under my pillow. I didn't know what to expect when I got outside but the scene that was unfolding in front of me was not one that I would have imagined.

Dancing around the fireplace, with just a loose piece of material wrapped around her chest that barely covered her buttocks and threatened to fall off any moment, was Ula. In her hand was a large dead fish. It looked like a baby shark, and red gunge and guts was falling out of the fish from the belly where it had been sliced through the middle.

'Jesus,' Avril said and began walking towards Ula. The women were standing around and it was Star, one of the mothers, who was screaming the loudest. I turned and saw Hester, who was approaching Ula with a big machete in her hand. My

God, Hester had some pent-up frustration. Something I had only seen from Kali until now. I knew Mary and some of the others were off spearfishing and so it was Precious of all people in the end who made it to Ula first, intercepting Hester and Avril on the way. Hester looked taken back as Precious easily wrestled the machete off her. Ula must not have put up any fight because she was taller and broader than any woman. I had felt her strength from that one push in her hut earlier.

'She needs to know who the boss is around here; she can't keep showing up uninvited like this and trying to freak us all out with her weird ways,' Precious said to anyone who could hear.

Ula let out a loud manic laugh and I shuddered at the noise.

Precious looked across the camp as Kali, Mary and a few others returned from spearfishing. The women walked briskly across the camp and were next to Precious. Between them, they began to try to manhandle Ula up and away from the camp. But now suddenly, she began to demonstrate her strength. She was like a sturdy Amazonian giant, and so a messy and undignified struggle ensued.

I had to turn my head away at one point as the piece of material that was tied under Ula's shoulders rose up right around her waist and exposed the entire bottom half of her naked body.

'Christ the Lord,' came Hester's voice. 'That woman needs putting down.'

'So much for the sisterhood,' I shouted over to Hester, and I was sure she understood my dig as she shot me a wry smile.

I looked back over at Ula as she was carried away, kicking and screaming, but just before they made it out of the camp and onto the beach, presumably to deposit her back at her shack, Ula looked at me, her eyes brightened, and she grinned at me. I let out a small laugh. Was that smile aimed at me? It had to be, but why? Was she trying to tell me something? It was as though a secret coded message had just slipped between us that no one else had picked up on. I couldn't for the life of me work out what it was that she was trying to convey in that smile. But it felt good. Reading her journal, I felt as though I was going to get to know a lot more about Ula. And I would slip it back into her hut before she had noticed it was even missing.

I glanced around self-consciously, wondering if anyone else had spotted it, or maybe they thought the smile was part of her madness. But I didn't think that. It was something in the way she looked directly at me and the subtlety of the smile. It wasn't the smile of a crazy woman; it also had knowledge hidden behind it. It told me that she knew something. Once the camp had gotten over her outburst maybe I would make my way over there again, see what the whole thing was about and maybe she would be a bit more coherent this time. Maybe she had been overwhelmed by my presence last time. Perhaps she was so shocked to have seen someone in her cabin that she forgot how to act.

But for now, I would go back to the cabin, hibernate for a little while and get back to reading the notebook.

Hester was perched outside her cabin as I passed. The young girl was cuddled up on her lap, the little boy next to her feet playing with the doll. A flash of the doll's blonde hair caught my eye, and I felt a tug in my gut. I'd had an image of a woman in my mind, but reading Ula's journal just now, could it be a coincidence that she had referred to a man called Deny? I shook the infectious thought away because it could only trigger worse thoughts. Thoughts of people dying on this island. An island where people should be thriving. Somewhere I was trying to thrive.

I managed a friendly smile, but it wasn't reciprocated by Hester. My opinions on Adi and now Ula had hit a nerve. It was interesting how I had expected the island to be full of well-rounded folk with nourished souls who would welcome the likes of Adi and Ula no matter the circumstances.

I left the camp and arrived back at my cabin.

As I went to walk up the steps to the hut, the first thing I noticed was the door was ajar. Had I left in such a hurry that I'd forgotten to close it? My thoughts turned to the notebook next. I already felt it had some sacred value and as I took the final steps towards the pillow, I already knew what I would discover as I lifted it up. I pulled the pillow to one side and looked at the empty space. I instantly fell to my knees and scoured around by the bed and under it as well, but it was gone. There was nowhere else in the room it could have been, and as I knew, the last place I had put it was under the pillow. I knew it had to have been taken.

Who had seen me come back with the journal? It couldn't have been Ula; she wouldn't have had time. Whoever it was had taken an opportunity when I had run outside, and whoever had taken it had been watching me.

I took myself out to the communal area; someone had started lunch, and there was a charred smell in the air, the sweet smell of onions frying. Kali was sat near the campfire. She looked at me and I wondered if there was a message in her eyes for me. Had she been the one in my hut just now? She had been the one to drag Ula away; and that wouldn't have left her much time to get in and out of my hut without me noticing.

Now, I was in Hester's bad books, and with Kali's looks never ceasing, I was starting to feel I was being judged – not only judged but watched as well.

# 36

## THEN

As soon as the coast was clear, I stood up and walked right up to Avril's cabin. I had seen her around the camp during Ula's performance, and then I hadn't seen her again and now had the urge to dispel the suspicion that maybe Avril had been the one in my hut. I knew standing around at the bottom of the steps would only make me think too long about it and eventually back out, so I took the steps two at a time, until I was on the small veranda where she would stand and take in the camp like the lioness of the pack every morning.

I pushed the door, and of course, like all the other doors here, it wasn't locked.

I wasn't sure what I was expecting, but it didn't surprise me that the inside of Avril's cabin was heavily furnished. She had a simple roll-out double mattress, but the blanket was a mass of rustic oranges and golds and turquoise. There were planks of wood balancing on bricks, which made shelves around the cabin and ornaments and books adorned them. There was a heavy scent of incense.

I knew it was a long shot, but maybe there was something inside that notebook that Avril didn't want me to see. I bent down, gently lifted the mattress, and felt under it all the same. Nothing.

I stood up. I was next to a small table where an array of what appeared to be ancient tribal tools sat. They were all similar-looking, like long statues about six inches in length, some longer, with splayed ends that formed four spikes. There were different styles, and some were made of different materials or finished with a different colour. I picked one up and held it; it felt like some sort of weapon. I felt my stomach tighten and twist at the thought of Avril ever having used this, and if so, what for? They looked more like trinkets sat there for show rather than for practical uses.

I began to feel uncomfortable being here, and I knew there was nothing here that would give me any more information about Ula or Deny or anything else that had been bothering me these last few weeks, nor would I find the notebook.

I slipped from the hut, looking around to make sure no one could have spotted me. I decided to wander down to the beach.

But as I began my approach to the beach, I saw that a boat had arrived. A few of the campmates were on board as well as two people I didn't recognise.

When I squinted, I could see that they were men.

'What the—?' I whispered.

I looked around for Avril so that I could speak with her and ask her why two men had just arrived. Were they new prisoners?

They didn't look to be with their pristine clothes, slick hair and bright white smiles.

I moved along the beach until I was next to Mary, who was standing watching as the men jumped out of the boat and onto the sand. They looked around and I could see the excitement in their eyes, the way they saw everything for the first time. A spike of fear ran through my veins. Avril had said that tonight I would be assigned my first task as her assistant, and now I was looking at two men who looked like a pair of children on Christmas morning. I knew somehow that my task involved them. I knew it wouldn't be something I felt entirely comfortable with.

Avril was suddenly next to me.

'I need you at Camp Z immediately,' she commanded.

I furrowed my brow and stared at her, unease seeping through me. 'What am I supposed to do?'

'Something is going on and I need you to find out what it is and deal with it immediately,' she seethed and then turned back to the men, her arms open wide. She took two flower garlands from a pile on the sand, sashayed over to them and placed one around each of their necks. I watched for a minute, unable to gauge what I was seeing. Was Avril welcoming men to Totini? Had I missed something? Avril swung her head around momentarily and shot me a glare that made me turn and head away.

I filled my canister with water and began the walk through the forest towards Camp Z knowing that I needed to appease Avril for now. But I was nervous. How was I supposed to interact with all the men? I had no idea how to speak to prisoners.

I was certain the men would want to speak with me, engage me in conversation the way the man had been trying to do when I discovered them by accident. Of course they would be desperate to escape and tell me whatever I needed to hear but I had a good radar for bullshit, especially from the opposite sex. Although I had only done the journey once, I felt driven by the destination and what lay ahead. I had been transfixed by what I saw when I was there last time: the men in cages, with pig huts for their comfort. And that tattoo. The cupcake. Was it a coincidence that Avril also had a cupcake charm on her bracelet?

When I reached Camp Z, I wasn't sure what I was supposed to be doing. Avril had seemed distracted by the male guests. The thought of it sent a shiver down my spine. From what I understood, men had been brought here to Totini for one reason: to be incarcerated. Why was Avril making a fuss of them?

I heard a scream as I approached the camp and it was getting louder as I got closer.

When I could finally see into the camp I saw the back of a small body, pressed against the cage. The screams were coming from him. It was Adi. He was being held there, by the man with the cupcake tattoo, who had been trying to communicate with me last time.

I raced down the rough terrain that led into the camp, almost falling over on my ankle on the way, and took hold of Adi. He spun around and looked shocked for a moment, then his face softened as he turned back towards the man. A look in his eyes told me he was trying to show me that he was in danger and that I was the one who must help him. We had only two interactions since I arrived here, but I sensed that Adi trusted me more than many on the island. And right now, he was looking for help.

'Take your hand off him,' I asserted. The man looked frustrated. He knew I was new; he had established that already when I was here before.

'Avril sent me. Take your hands off him,' I said a little louder this time. I had no gun. No weapon to speak of. The man looked at Adi, then me, then let go of Adi's arm. Adi made a squeal like a small animal, rubbed at his arm, then he bore his teeth at me like a dog smiling at its owner. I reached out to touch him, to comfort him after his ordeal, but he danced around from one foot to the other before finally darting out into the forest.

'You'll need a long leash and a ton of treats to train that one. He's like a dog,' the man said.

'And is that what you were trying to do?' I asked, wondering if he had escape in mind and that by training Adi he could get him to do what he needed to get out of there.

'Wow, you're on to me. She got inside you already has she?'

I clocked the man in the cage behind, the man who had managed to escape somehow. He looked at me and nodded, sagely. He had that same look of hopelessness.

I walked closer to the cage in front of me, feeling a little braver. The prisons were constructed very well and were very sturdy. I wondered how the man behind had managed to get out of his.

'I saw an older man hurting a young child and I intervened,' I said to the prisoner in front of me.

The guy looked solemn for a moment and stepped back from the rails. He began biting the skin around his thumbnail; even from where I stood, I could see that it was red and sore.

'That looks like it needs some attention.' I pointed at his hand. The man pulled his mouth down almost in disgust.

'That doesn't happen around here.'

'Why did you have hold of little Adi just then?' I moved an inch closer to the cage.

The man moved his arm and began to scratch his head. 'That's between us.'

'It's not when it alerts us. Avril sent me.'

'Avril sent me,' the man said in a higher-pitched voice. He sang my words back at me, and I narrowed my eyes at him.

'What's your name?' I asked.

'Right there,' he said and pointed to the rudimentary tattoo on his lower arm.

'That's a cupcake?' I said questioningly.

He widened his eyes, pulled his lips tightly together. 'Yep.'

'Is that some sort of prison name?' I asked.

'I didn't put that tattoo there if that's what you're asking.'

'I guessed that,' I said, looking at the other more detailed professional tattoos on his arm, which had that faded look as though they had been done many years ago. This one looked amateurish.

'So that's your name? Cupcake?'

The man gave a pained expression again. 'Just call me that. Everyone does here.' He motioned to the other cells where I noticed men had begun to edge forwards out of curiosity. I felt their presence as they found their way to the bars and began whistling and coughing to get my attention. Fear gripped me like a vice, but I continued to stay looking and sounding calm and in control.

'So, Cupcake, what did you do to find yourself here?'

He sucked in a long breath. 'I could ask you the same. Nice girl like you. You don't seem the type to get mixed up in something like this.'

I realised that Ula had said something similar to me.

'I came here to escape for a while.' I didn't mention that I hadn't been aware of Camp Z. I thought it might somehow make me appear weaker that I had been fooled. Besides, these men had no clue when I had been told about them.

'This ain't no great selling point is it?' He motioned to the other cages.

'Well, we don't really see or hear you where we are,' I said, and he looked down at his feet. Guilt swept through me. 'Sorry, that was insensitive,' I said, and he looked at me, brighter this time and with intrigue.

'You're not like them, are you?' he asked.

I shook my head defensibly, realising I had let my guard down and I was supposed to be here doing a job. 'I don't know what you mean.'

Cupcake laughed and looked away. 'You're not like them. I can see it. I can feel it.'

A wave of nausea swept through my body. I didn't like the way I was suddenly being watched by all the men as though I were the one in a cage.

Yet there was something undeniably intriguing about this man. Despite the situation he found himself in, he had a twinkle in his eye. A glimmer of a past personality that he hadn't shaken. He was emitting something that resembled . . . I wanted to say lustfulness. He was looking longingly at me, as though I was the first female he had seen in a long time.

'And so back to you, you're here because?' he asked.

'Why don't you tell me why you're here first?' I retorted and eyed his ribs, the way they protruded from out of his torso.

'Let's start with your name, shall we?'

I knew there was no harm in telling him my name. How could he use it against me when he was trapped behind bars and I was on the other side?

'Sadie,' I said after a beat.

The man crouched down and relaxed his legs so they fell across one another. He leaned his arms back behind him.

'Sadie. That is a very nice name. I can't say I've ever met a Sadie before.'

I felt as though he were enticing me into a conversation, but I didn't have anywhere else to be and I had been sent here to find out what the hullabaloo was. Avril had assigned me the role of her right-hand woman and I guess that was what she thought I was now. Even if none of this sat right with me.

'Do you have a cigarette, Sadie?' he asked. There was a pained tone in his voice, as though he were trying very hard to speak. He didn't want to sound as though he were begging, I realised. It was beneath him. This was a man who was in a position of power once. I looked around at the other men, and wondered what it was they did before they had arrived here.

'I don't.'

'That's a shame. I didn't actually smoke much. Well, you can't maintain many habits under these circumstances. Hey, I don't suppose you fancy getting me out of here today do you? Be a gal! I won't tell a soul. I'll be gone before you know it.' His voice had a forced hope, as though he had said this a few times before I came along.

'I wouldn't know how to do that.' I looked at the cage's complex locking system and wondered how deep it went into the ground. It must be pretty far or these men would have dug themselves out with their bare hands by now.

'Besides, I don't know anything about your situation, why you're here, what you did. I discovered you just now trying to hurt a small boy.'

'I wasn't trying to hurt him. I was . . . it doesn't matter anyway. It was pure fluke I managed to get him that close to me. He won't come within ten metres of me ever again. That's a fact.'

I sat down. 'Do you want to tell me why you're here then?'

Cupcake shook his head.

I took in a deep breath, feeling the presence of the other men around us – a few were calling, whistling and whooping louder now. I would get to them all eventually. But the task felt monumental as I saw how they were all looking and waiting.

'Avril asked me to come here and sort out what was going on.' I looked to the edge of the forest to check that Adi had definitely gone. That he hadn't just crept back in when I wasn't looking. 'I've done that now,' I said quietly. Cupcake edged himself closer so he was holding onto the bars of the cage.

'How old are you?'

I paused again, always wondering how much information to give away. I thought of Bruno, how much of myself I gave to him and where that left me. I thought of men like Tony on the mainland who I knew thrived on information they could extract from you. Was this what was happening here?

'I'm twenty-nine,' I said.

'I'm thirty-five. I think,' he said straight away and I felt relief that he offered some information about himself straight back, that a fair and equal exchange was happening between us.

'You think?' I quizzed.

'Yeah. I've been here a while. Can't you tell?'

Was he the one who had been here for five years?

'Were you the first inmate?'

'Inmate,' Cupcake scoffed. 'The second.'

I nodded. He could have been here a while, but I didn't want to quiz him about it.

I couldn't tell. Apart from the protruding ribs and the ingrained dirt on his skin, which, from a distance, looked like a tan, I now realised was a combination.

'Your accent?' I moved the conversation away from incarceration.

'South African.'

I nodded. I was going to say as much.

'You're not like them though. Are you. The others? Avril?'

'I'm new. This wasn't what I expected when Avril invited me out here. I didn't expect there to be only women. I discovered you by accident,' I suddenly found myself admitting. I still had the upper hand, I reminded myself. I was on this side of the bars; they were on the other.

'I know. I saw the look of horror on your face.' Cupcake laughed. 'It's not every day you discover a prison on a paradise island.'

Of course, I remembered how I had discovered this place and knew my emotions would have been written all over my face.

'I was just getting over the magnificence of the place.'

'Marred it slightly.'

'It's not quite out of sight out of mind enough. I must accept the ugliness of what this is before I can truly embrace the beauty.'

Cupcake's expression was dull and flat.

'Sorry.'

'Oh don't worry, I appreciate the beauty. I see it every day, albeit from the same spot. It's all I have now.'

I had so many questions bubbling on my lips that I wanted to ask Cupcake. Like why he was called Cupcake for a start and what he had done to be here. But this all felt so impertinent already, like I was betraying Avril. She had tasked me with coming here to sort out the noise. Whilst she was with the new male arrivals. Luring them in. Those were the words that I heard in my mind. But I didn't want to think it. I didn't want it to be true.

'I need to get back.' I suddenly needed to see what was happening at the main camp. Cupcake stepped back from the bars.

'Will you come again?' he asked. 'It's nice to have company. I haven't had any for a while. Clara, she used to come,' he added quietly.

'Oh.' Hearing her name mentioned was like a small stab in my chest. 'She used to visit you?'

Suddenly I remembered the job that Clara had that she didn't reveal to me, one that took her away early in the morning. This was where she had been coming?

My face must have given away what I was thinking.

'She's not here anymore,' he said without question. 'I get it. Her visa ran out. She needed to go home,' he said wistfully. 'She didn't say goodbye . . .' He trailed off.

My heart sped up, and my mouth went dry. He didn't know. Someone had lied to him. But why, I wondered, would they tell him a lie to protect him? Why not tell him the truth, as it would hurt more?

'I have to go,' I said; his mouth fell into a boyish, lopsided grin.

'But you'll come back, no?'

I walked away, already with a feeling that there was more to this man. Clara had spent time with him, were our intuitions right? Was this man not dangerous?

Cupcake had somehow drawn me in, and I knew I would be back and not just under the role Avril had assigned to me. 'I'll see you again. I'll bring a cigarette,' I said.

# 37

## THEN

Back in camp the men were getting treated like kings, lured in one hour at a time. That had to be what was happening. Because how could it be anything else? How could I be tending to Camp Z whilst Avril had fun with the men? I could almost hear the clock ticking as their time ran out.

After reporting back to Avril and sitting on the sidelines as a spectator for long enough that no one would suspect I was not really participating, I hiked up to Ula's cabin, knocked hard on her door, and then, when she didn't answer – not that I expected her to – I walked straight in. It was empty. I had a few hours before dinner and a small amount of vegetable prep to do. If I got lost in the depths of the forest for a while, I would be fine. But this time I looked upward instead of across. The hike to the top of the hill, I would take it carefully and slowly so that I didn't fall once I got higher. Perhaps I might find Adi up there to check he was okay. If I was discovered, I could say I was checking on him after the incident at Camp Z. Avril seemed protective of him and so I was sure she wouldn't see it as anything other than what it was.

From Ula's hut I looked at the surrounding shrubbery and trees that formed part of the small mountain that Totini boasted. I couldn't see any obvious pathway and so I got closer to the foliage and there I could see where the branches had slightly parted over time and had formed a gap that was just big enough for a small skinny boy to slip through. I pushed through and found the space, continuing up the mountain for some time. This had to be one of Adi's secret pathways. I felt a shiver of excitement at my discovery.

The terrain was rough and wild, and the incline was steep, but I kept going. It had been on my list of things I wanted to do when I first saw the mountain – if you could call it that – it was just a big rocky hill, really, but it was a challenge, and I liked a challenge. Besides, it seemed that Ula and Adi had places that they hid around the island, and I knew I wanted to become as familiar with these places as they were. The hill hadn't looked that high from Ula's hut and I had always looked up at it and thought that I would be able to get up there fairly easily. But my breath had become laboured and the sweat was slick along my back and forming around my temples, threatening to drip into my eyes.

Time passed and the tension on my calf muscles slackened. I was on even ground again. The trees and foliage made way for dusty ground and rocks. Lots of rocks. They ran right up to the edge where I now found myself looking down to my right. I could just about glimpse the sand, then I looked straight ahead and all I could see was the ocean. Some of the surrounding islands were visible but very far away and the sandbank I had been to once, where Clara had her accident, was a mere speck.

I shuddered at the sight of it now having not seen it since that day. I felt an overwhelming sense of sadness that the spearfishing day had been Clara's last expedition. She had been a lover of life and adventure and, even though I'd only known her a short while, I missed her.

I stepped back from the ledge. I had felt a flutter of fear at how close I had come to it, how just a few more inches could have seen me teetering over the edge, how a further inch would have had me falling down over the rough terrain, probably smashing my skull and breaking my back.

The path expanded around, and I followed the dusty track until I hit rock. There was no way of getting any higher. Even though the rock went up another few feet, I wasn't going to try and mount that for the sake of it. I was almost about to head back down, admitting defeat on this leg of the journey at having not discovered anything, but satisfied I had finally made it up, when the breeze blew a large section of foliage that was nestled against the rocks in front of me. The breeze moved some of the twigs a few inches and I caught a glimpse of something dark that looked like a gap, or a hole. I edged closer cautiously, in case it was an animal hole, and something might jump out at me. Although I wasn't sure what it could be; the only animals on the island were cows, pigs and hens. But maybe there were some marsupials or reptiles living up here. I was still open to being surprised by this island. It seemed to have a lot more to offer, more than I knew right now.

I manually moved the bush this time and pushed it as far back as I could and there, just a few inches behind, was an opening into a rock. Large enough for a slim body to climb through.

I had come all this way; I wasn't about to ignore it and just head off back down the cliff. I had to find out if anyone was or had been in there; maybe they were in there now.

'Hello,' I called into the hole.

My voice echoed back at me. There was some space in there. I wasted no time and clambered in. I had to remain on my hands and knees for a few feet. The walls above and either side of me were inches from my skin. I was surprised at how dry the rock smelt, and how cool it was in here.

After a few strides on all fours the space opened into a wonderful cave, something out of a child's storybook. The sides of the walls had small nooks and were crammed with shells, dried seaweed, and pieces of driftwood. In one corner was a collection of shiny objects, bottle tops and pieces of shimmery wrappers presumably washed up on the shore. On one side were several blankets bunched up. I sat on my knees and looked around and saw what appeared to be a space a child would inhabit. Immediately the face of Adi came to me with his infectious smile.

Of course this was where he would live. It was dry, and cool and out of the way of the camp.

It felt very homely in here and I wished I could have stayed. But I knew I would need to start preparing dinner soon. Judging by the empty cave, I could for now presume it was Adi's and that he was off somewhere around the island.

But just as I went to turn on my knees to clamber back out of the cave, I spotted a flash of faded pink in one of the nooks. I edged closer and saw that a large pile of shells was on top of a notebook. The notebook I had been reading that had disappeared from the cabin. I snatched the book and a couple of shells fell onto the ground.

*Damn it, Adi.*

But how could I really be angry with him? There was no real malice behind taking it, judging by how much stuff was in here. It was like a magpie's nest.

I went to scoop up the shells but spotted a shiny object amongst them.

I picked it up and saw it was a cupcake pendant.

Perhaps Adi had found it and collected it as a treasure, or more likely he had taken it like he had the other things – like the bread. I took one last look around the small space, feeling glad that Adi had somewhere he could come and he could feel safe and protected from the elements. But what I still hadn't been able to work out yet was why Adi had been segregated in the first place. Even if his mother had abandoned him, why had he not been embraced by the other two mothers? Star had said that they had tried with him; they had made out he was untameable. I looked again around at the cosiness of the place, how this was clearly somewhere where Adi lived now. But only now it occurred to me that perhaps it was Adi's own choice and that there was a reason he didn't want to stay in camp. Adi was here because he was staying away.

# 38
## NOW

I trace the pattern on the fabric of the sofa with my hand. I try to conjure an image of Avril. Her face is not entirely clear in my mind. Maybe I imagined the whole thing. It is always like that when you haven't seen someone for a long time; eventually, their features become distorted in your mind, and you can no longer imagine them in full HD as you once could. Their face is a mere smudge of what it once had been and all you have left is the idea of what you thought they looked like.

Or maybe it was the dissociative amnesia, the condition I had been told I was suffering with. But all the while I was in the unit I saw so many vivid images. Apparently I had made some progress and that was why I was now here, at my parents' house in Dorset. All this I knew. My parents talked regularly about things that they thought I would need a refresher on, like who had married who and who was living where. I would one day remember, they said. But when they said that, a cold sweat came over me. I thought about the tens of images I had drawn that I had stuffed in my wardrobe at the unit. I had managed to tear each one into tiny pieces and then add them to a pile of rubbish I cleared out of my bedroom before I left. Images of men in cages, of the blood on the beach.

'Tea?' A voice filters through my thoughts and brings me back into the room. I look at my hand on the sofa. The woman who was asking if I would like tea had introduced herself to me as my mother yesterday and as it did with my sister, Jane, my mind is slowly opening doors to forgotten memories.

I look at the photos of me above the fireplace and running up the staircase, which I can see from where I sit. It's like watching a weird, surreal film. Was this all just a dream, and would I wake up and feel more whole and complete?

I look up at my mother and accept the tea. It seems to create a sense of calm and unity in the room. There is even a plaque that reads, *Where there is tea, there is hope,* so I am investing in that for now.

My dad is reading the newspaper, occasionally filling me in with what is happening around the world. I don't tell him that his words are making my head spin.

The tea tastes fine, but my mind buzzes with flavours I expect my senses to experience. But they don't come. So I drink the tea with the milk and sugar the way I have been told I like it. My mother perches on the sofa at the other end of me, trying not to watch me, but I can feel the flickers of stares. She is waiting for me to get better as though that might happen with this first sip of tea, and I will suddenly stand up and shout, 'I'm fine now,' and she could then go on to tell the story years later of how one sip of a brew made by my mother was all it took to cure me.

I understand her frustrations because I imagine if I had carried and birthed a baby and then twenty-nine years later they looked at me blankly and barely spoke, I would be wanting and waiting for a miracle. But I sip the tea and say nothing. The door to the living room opens and there stands Jane and suddenly I feel a little brighter because we spent all that time together in the unit. I am so pleased to see her, my big sister looking out for me and protecting me. But for a long time I had blocked out the memory of who she was. I was told that was part of the recovery process; the brain needs to focus on getting well, so it blocks out anything else to concentrate on that task.

The prospect of staying here with my parents – these people who have so many memories of me running through their minds and scattered around the house – is disconcerting. How am I supposed to act? At the psychiatric unit, I didn't need to think about who I was supposed to be related to or whose feelings I might be hurting with my apparent aloofness.

My name is Sadie. I went to Fiji. I did something terrible, and the only friend I had ever really known is dead. But I can't tell them that, and I can't tell them all the other terrible things I have done because I will be locked away. So I stay mute, nodding in the right places but making out that I don't remember anything.

They gave my condition a name. But it doesn't matter.

Because I remember it all. How could I possibly forget?

# 39
## THEN

Avril presented the meat to me an hour or so after I returned from the cliff. The two men were seated around the campfire, their garlands still hanging around their necks, although looking a little dishevelled, their faces easy with kava.

Avril began slicing it and placing it in the pan. 'It's sacred, Sadie,' she would say each time. We ate it so rarely. I had become to accustomed to the ritual.

We were only at the end of month one. I was sure Avril would begin to entrust the preparing and cooking of the meat to me at some point, but for now, she liked to revel in the moment of it all – the catch, the kill, the slicing and dicing, and even placing it in the pan.

I continued to look enthusiastic; I kept playing the role, knowing that I was thinking and feeling differently to everyone else here, that the doubts were growing stronger, but I also knew I was being watched now. If I didn't comply would I end up like Deny and Clara?

I focused my mind on the field to fork. Our food was reared just metres away. That was what life here on the island meant, and being self-sufficient was exactly what Totini was about: living off the resources available. It was how it should be. And that I was thankful for. It was something during a time of such uncertainty.

I had managed to read one more page of the notebook before I realised it was time to start preparing dinner. And I didn't want to be late, not once. So, I took a shower and began prepping the vegetables. I didn't want Avril to sense my hesitation at being around camp tonight with the men, as I had avoided her for most of the afternoon – Avril had yet to confide in me about what was going on. But I was desperate to get back to Ula's diary; I needed to read it chronologically so I didn't miss any key information that could have been inserted in those first few passages.

Avril finished the meat in the pan and then stood up, brushed herself down, and scooched past me. Her hands grazed my hips as she looked at me. I looked at her, and she smiled softly. I felt a wave of relief that things were good between us, that she hadn't sensed a change in my behaviour. I wasn't sure what vibes I was emitting.

Camp began to fill up as the smells from the meat filled the air. Avril took herself to her cabin and stood on the veranda. Precious was draped over one of the men, and the other had about three women all over him. They both sat down close to where I was serving. One of them looked at me; our eyes locked for a second. I wanted to say something to them, to warn them of the danger they were in. I could do that now, change the course of their life. If I stayed silent, I was about to be instrumental in their incarceration. Because why else would Avril have brought them here? My stomach was churning and I couldn't let it overwhelm me and ruin my appetite. Would Avril begin to question me, see that I was not totally on board?

The men were her little mice to toy with first. They were young guys. Not much into their twenties. They probably had mothers at home waiting for them to call and a pang of sadness grabbed my gut. I wondered what their crimes were in the eyes of Avril, as it seemed she was the one who was instrumental in bringing men here. The kava came out again after dinner and so by the end of the meal I felt as though this was just an ordinary day anywhere in the world where men and women were existing side by side.

I was at the pot wash as most of the other women were preoccupied, still drinking with the men. One of the guys approached. He seemed a little inebriated, but he held his hands out.

'Can I help?'

He was offering to wash the dishes and already had his hands dunked in the soapy water.

'No,' I almost yelped. I didn't want to engage in any normal behaviour with this man.

'Oh, okay,' he said in a British accent. There hadn't been many of them here and so instantly I felt a pang for home and a familiarity with him.

'My mum had me doing the dishes from age four, so it's a skill that's been hardened into me; even flying halfway around the world won't keep me away from a dishcloth.'

I wanted to scream. To run away. I looked at his soft skin and eyes. I imagined his mother. What the hell had Avril done? Why had she brought him here?

'That's very admirable.' Not wanting to look at him, I began to scrape some of the debris from the plates into the food bin.

'I'm James,' he said.

*I don't care I don't care,* I sang over and over in my mind. *Please go away. Please just go away.*

He immediately held out his soapy hand. He was looking at me, questioningly, waiting.

'Sadie.' I shook the tip of one of his fingers and he laughed.

'Great name,' he said.

I felt my insides begin to wobble. I thought I might cry.

'Thanks, I like it. I'm thinking of keeping it,' I said and wished I had never said a word and just ignored him.

I looked around before I spoke to make sure no one was nearby and listening.

'So how did you find out about Totini?' I asked in hushed tone.

'Well, I was on the mainland, and I got chatting to this girl in this bar; she told me about it, how to get here, or at least to, what was it, Kenco Island? And that was it. I have always fancied this sort of experience.'

'And your friend? What about him? There were two of you weren't there?'

'Oh, yeah, he's not my friend. He'd been in Nadi as well. We ended up travelling together, though, so yeah, I guess we are mates now. So, what's the deal here? Is it all it's cracked up to be? It's an all-female camp?' James looked and sounded like a small child mad with excitement and anticipation for what was to come. And although I didn't exactly know what was to come, I think I had a better idea than he did.

'It takes a bit of getting used to, but the general vibe is pretty relaxed. It's beautiful and it's exactly what I need right now. It sure has an addictive quality. But forever? Who knows?'

'I know what you mean. I can feel those vibes already from being here for a few hours. It's something different isn't it – tick it off the bucket list. I lived as part of a commune in the South Pacific. Tick.' He laughed. 'One to tell the grandchildren that's for sure.'

My heart thumped hard in my chest. *Just warn him, Sadie. Just tell him.* Why couldn't I do that? An image of Avril crept into my mind, the responsibility she had given me, what she saw in me. Is that what she saw in Clara? I couldn't be seen to be failing. And poor Clara. Here one minute, gone the next. I had to consider what may happen if I didn't go along with what they expected of me, or if they had a heavy premonition that something might happen if I tried to upset the proceedings, if I didn't do as I was asked. You had to give a piece of yourself for a slice of paradise. Nothing this good in life came for free, I now realised.

I carried on washing the dishes and wondered when James would leave. We carried on chatting asking one another about our lives. But half of my mind was on our conversation, answering all the usual questions one has for someone they have just met, on autopilot, and the other half of my brain was in perpetual waiting mode. Whatever Avril had planned, I didn't know how I could help them, because if I suggested they were in danger, then in their drunken state, they might repeat it back to the others, and I would be ostracised and at the worst . . . I couldn't think of the worst. I just knew I couldn't endure the madness anymore.

I was desperate to get away from James, and the journal kept playing on my mind. I wanted to find out what had happened to Ula before I arrived. She had arrived here as a normal functioning woman, and something had happened, and I was sure I would be able to find out by finishing the notebook.

I had an overwhelming desire, as I did most evenings, to be by the shore. Tonight, it was to calm my nerves. I needed to take some deep breaths, get away from everyone for a while.

I noticed James had been smoking earlier.

'Hey, I couldn't bum a fag off you, could I?'

James grinned and handed one over.

I picked up a packet of matches from the larder. Before I let myself think too much about it, I began walking towards Camp Z, feeling the cigarette between my fingers and trying not to think too hard about its significance.

# 40
## NOW

'There is someone who would like to see you, Sadie.' It was Jane speaking.

I had been at home for three days. It was around three o'clock in the afternoon. Mum had made a cake to try and stimulate my senses and evoke some memories. I still couldn't tell them, and the longer it went on, the harder it was to stop all of this and admit to them that I remembered everything that had happened on that island, I had just managed to block out everything else out about myself and my real life as a result.

'I don't know if you want to see him, but I thought it might be a good opportunity to increase some memory flow. This is someone you knew very well.'

I search my mind, for whom Jane could be referring to.

'Can I invite him in?' Jane asks sheepishly, looking between me and our mother.

I nod and Jane walks out of the sitting room closing the door behind her. I feel my mother shift about on the end of the sofa and I feel my guts twist as I imagine who Jane might be seeing through to the sitting room.

'You'll be fine, love,' my mum whispers and I am not sure why she is talking in a hushed tone. I feel as though it should be me reassuring my mother.

The door opens again, and Jane appears with an edgy smile. She seems to be harbouring all the feelings I should have felt as well as her own.

She stands aside and a man steps from behind her and walks into the room, so he is now standing in front of her.

'Hello, Sadie.' His voice bears a quiver that sets off a pulse inside my gut.

I look at Jane. She had stepped closer to me and is looking at me expectantly as though she is trying to suggest without words that she is here if I need her.

I look back at the man again. He is smiling. My response to his expression comes suddenly and without warning. It's visceral, because I don't need to think too long about who this is. The memories of my life before Totini returned hard and fast after Jane.

My time is up now. They can all see the expression forming on my face.

I open my mouth but I am too scared to say his name.

Finally, my mouth forms the word and as it leaves my lips I hear collective sighs around me.

# 41

## NOW

'Bruno.' I say his name and his face breaks into a huge smile. Jane joins me on the sofa, takes my hand and squeezes it hard.

'Darling, you remember.'

Feelings and emotions hurl themselves at me. Of feeling alone, powerless, and scared. He looks nervous, like he is gulping a lot. Is he actually crying?

After some more hand squeezing and watching my parents shift about the room uncomfortably, Bruno finally walks towards me.

Then he falls to his knees and pulls me into him. The familiar smell of him makes me want to retch.

'I should never have let you go,' he whispers into my ear. Then he clears his throat and lets me go. I look at Bruno and then at Jane.

Bruno stands up and so does Jane. Bruno takes his place on the sofa next to me and I am mesmerised by this man. It's like I am seeing him brand new but also as if I have seen him every day for the last few months because he has never really left my mind. I shift in my seat and Jane gives me a quick smile. She hadn't known what Bruno was like. None of them had. I had left so quickly after he attacked me that I never had a chance to explain it all to them. I had always worried that they would be disappointed in me, for letting the relationship end. I was too scared to tell them I had let him treat me so badly for so long. I was too scared to shatter their illusion of Bruno.

'There is so much to talk about,' he says through a snotty laugh and Jane hands him a tissue. I wonder how he has managed to make himself cry that way. I have never seen Bruno cry. He blows his nose. A loud trumpeting sound echoes through the room and there is a smattering of laughter from everyone.

'When you say you shouldn't have let me go, what do you mean?' I ask loudly, with little expression to my voice that I can see has startled my mother as she begins wringing her hands. Jane shifts on the sofa. Another throat clearing and a rattling of the newspaper from my dad this time.

'Darling. You've had quite the adventure, haven't you? I imagine you need a lot of rest.' Bruno looks at Jane for confirmation. 'She probably needs a lot of rest.'

Jane nods firmly. 'Doctors' orders.'

I feel my whole body tense up listening to Bruno talk. The sound of his voice makes my jaw tense.

'You did not let me go,' I say quietly at first, and when no one seems to notice me I say it louder.

'You did not let me go,' I say again, this time attracting the attention of everyone. And then I am back there again on that day, the smashed wall, the red face, the enraged look in his eyes, the fear quickly replaced by pure relief that I was alive. That I had made it. But then the fear again, because I knew I might not next time. And then I remember vividly, that it was I who walked away from Bruno.

I must have shown signs of distress because Bruno was up and Jane took his place, holding a glass of water. I can hear Bruno's voice in the background as he mutters something to my father who grunts in agreement. Then I feel like I am wrapped in a tornado of voices and images from the past.

It is Fiji. It is Totini. There are so many women, and the men, they are caged. They are shouting and screaming; there is a fire. More screams. Then the roundabout begins to slow down, but the images of flawless white beaches are distorted because where I had only seen light colours before, I can now see a darkness amongst the golden beach, the colour of red blood as it runs in streaks across the perfect white sands.

# 42
## THEN

*Journal entry*
*Things were pretty okay before I got here weren't they? I'm not saying I'm going to go home or that I'm even considering leaving, I was just contemplating the time I was at home, and what drove me to come here. I took hold of the idea and began to roll with it. Soon it became my reality too and when we found the island, well then it was easy. We just booked the flights and found our way here. But life is very different here but there was no one at home who is missing me. I had to get away from all the anger, all the fighting.*

*I am happy here; it just takes some getting used to, and I am still adjusting to their way of life. But I can be honest here, can't I? This is my journal; these are my words. No one will read them but me. This thing that happened, it happened to me. I was drunk on kava. I don't remember consenting. And now I feel as though my body is trying to tell me things, and if I don't speak about them, I might go mad. But I am scared to write the word because then that makes it real, and then I will have to admit it, and then I will have to face it and deal with it. And that's not easy here when life is so insular, and there are only chickens and coconuts to talk to. There really is nowhere to escape. There is no discussion about life outside of the island and I am really quite desperate to talk to someone about things.*

*But it's been several weeks. I just need to suck it up, right? It will be like one of those TV reality shows where they get dropped off on a remote island for twelve weeks and have to do insane challenges. I should just see it like that. Except for the thing that happened. That guy, that wasn't supposed to happen was it? But I had drunk way too much that night and I wasn't sure what I was doing, so I suppose I am partly to blame. Aren't I?*

# 43
## THEN

Even in the dark I could see Cupcake's eyes had lit up when I produced the cigarette and the matches.

He held his hands out with glee.

'I need to light it for you. I can't really give you an entire box of matches,' I said, putting the cigarette to my lips. It had been a long time since I had smoked a cigarette.

I heard a rustle behind the bars of Cupcake's prison. I looked through the gaps and saw a man had pushed himself right against the bars of his own cage. He had made himself a bed on some leaves. He was looking down in his lap. I felt sorry for him.

'Hey,' I called to him. He nodded back at me. I was happy just talking to Cupcake for now. It was easy discourse.

When it was lit, I handed the cigarette through the bars to Cupcake. He sucked it and held the smoke inside, a satisfied smile creeping across his lips until his whole face was full of joy. I heard groans of protests coming from some of the other cages.

'Tell them I'll bring more tomorrow,' I said to Cupcake. He nodded but continued to smoke the cigarette. I didn't speak to him for five minutes as he smoked it down to the nub. I found a spot on the ground next to the cage.

Cupcake shoved the butt into the earth.

'Thank you.'

'So what did you do? To find yourself here.'

Cupcake shook his head. 'What did any of us do? No trial, no justice. Just this. Locked up.'

'Avril said . . .' I started.

Cupcake looked serious. 'We all know what Avril says. But do you believe her?' He jerked his chin out and widened his eyes.

I looked shamefully at my feet. I was here tonight because I was too scared to stand up to Avril, and I didn't know the answers or the truth. I only knew what she had told me. But here were fifteen men all locked up. What was I to think?

Cupcake sat down close to the edge of the bars.

'I've had a lot of time to think in here and sometimes . . .' he grabbed the bar with his hand '. . . I get very angry. But what can I do?' He looked up at me with pleading eyes.

'I don't know what to say,' I said pathetically 'I'm sorry. I . . .'

'I get it – you're scared,' Cupcake said.

I felt my hackles rise. I had been scared of Bruno, but I had got away. If I was brave enough to do that, I was surely brave enough to face this scenario head-on. Avril had lied to me from the beginning, about where I was headed, about Clara, about who I was sharing the island with.

'So what will you do, Sadie?' Cupcake's voice filtered through. 'You've been given a job now, no? Look after us, poor silly men.'

'I have been assigned the task of checking in on you regularly.'

'But not sitting here and chatting with me.'

'Probably might be frowned upon.'

'By Avril, your boss? And you do everything she says?'

'No,' I said quickly.

'I can hear a faraway beat. Another party tonight?' Cupcake looked into the distance as though he might be able to see what he could just about hear.

I didn't mention the men arriving or the way the girls had been draped over them when I left, or my fear for James and his companion.

'Yes, they like to party.'

'And you? You're not a party animal?'

'Oh, I've been known to throw a few shapes from time to time.'

Cupcake laughed then, and I wondered how it felt to be locked up and not able to go anywhere for years. Yet still be able to laugh that way. I thought about Clara then and how she would have made him feel. Did she give him the hope that he needed to get through a day? When I glanced around at the other men, they all had a glassy look in their eyes. Some were just lying there, not moving. I felt a stab of sadness in my gut, and it rose up into my chest.

'We used to sing. When we first arrived. Quite the camaraderie here,' Cupcake joked. But a bitter tone to his voice gave away his true feelings. This man hadn't given up; he was pissed off. He wanted to be free.

I wandered into camp the next morning. Mary clocked me first, and then Precious and Kali. The mothers looked at me and the feeling seemed to spread until there was a moment when every person in the camp turned and acknowledged me. But not with a smile or a hand raise – they looked at me as though I were an outsider. And I felt it. Not only in the brief, nothing looks, but it was in the air. It was all around us. I knew that something had shifted. My lack of time in the camp had been noted.

I remembered how Clara used to disappear so often in the mornings, and the argument she had with Avril. Avril must have known she had got close to Cupcake, and I could already see how that had happened. Had she been planning on setting him free? Had Avril got wind of this? I couldn't think the thought, let alone consider putting any sort of plan into action. I had to consider my own safety. And not this uncomfortable feeling in camp; maybe it was time I considered a way to get myself out of there.

'I hope you'll be playing by the rules.' Kali's words came back to me. I was supposed to keep an eye on things down there. Not get cosy with them. But already I could see what Clara had seen, why she had wanted to spend so much time in Camp Z. Cupcake was an alluring character. And the more I considered him and the situation, the more doubts I had about why he was there.

'Missed you last night,' Avril said, a hint of something in her voice that didn't sound as though I had been in her thoughts in a good way.

'I was tired.'

'Have you been to Camp Z?'

'I checked on them again last night.'

'You only need to go once a day. Give them their food and water rations,' she said as though I should know all this information.

'Right okay, I'll start that as of today.'

She looked thoughtful. 'And Adi, he . . .' I hadn't mentioned to Avril that Cupcake had been holding on to Adi when I had arrived the day before yesterday. Already I knew I didn't want to make things worse for him.

I told her he had been caught in the mimosa bush.

'Did you see him?' Avril sounded concerned.

'I didn't,' I said and she seemed okay with this.

'We should get those cut back a bit maybe.' She looked thoughtful. 'If it's worth it,' she mumbled afterwards, and I didn't ask her what she meant by that.

I wanted to get away, to get up to Camp Z, and as it was first thing my duties were to feed and water them. After a fitful night's sleep I knew I needed some straight answers. Someone had to tell me the truth, and I had a feeling it could be Cupcake.

I ate breakfast with the camp. James and his friend weren't anywhere to be seen and I presumed they were still sleeping. I hoped they were still sleeping. There was a sullen feeling over breakfast, and it seeped into my veins. I didn't like it, and I was glad when I could excuse myself and go back to my cabin and open another page of the journal before heading to Camp Z.

*Journal entry*
*I am feeling sad. I am feeling sick. I know what is wrong with me, but I can't talk about it with anyone. I heard there is a witch*

*doctor on the next island; they help with all sorts of problems, and maybe they could help me with my problem. Maybe they could make it go away for good and then I can carry on with island life as if nothing ever happened. I just need to find the confidence to go. It's a short trip of about an hour, but what if something went wrong? What if I didn't come back? I couldn't risk my life. I can't even call home, I can only imagine what they will have to say. I wish I could just talk to someone about this. I am held here by the ties I have. I will forever be bound by this one act.*

# 44

## THEN

Ula had a child. Was that why she had been banished? It made no sense when there were two mothers on the island. And where was Ula's child now?

Hester had told me that Adi had been abandoned by his mother. Had Ula abandoned Adi?

It was so sad that the two of them were separated, that both were missing out on parenting and being parented. Was it the pregnancy and birth that had driven her mad?

I took time to check on every man in Camp Z later that morning. I gave them water from the rain canister and gave them the rations I had been sent with. It was measly and pathetic. Some fruit and bread. But I took time to try and talk to each man. It wasn't unpleasant, but I didn't enjoy it. I passed them their food through the small hatch and enough water to get them through the day. Some of them spoke to me with pleasantries; others barely raised their heads, their spirits crushed.

I began to notice a similarity to the men. Firstly in age. They were all between twenty-five and forty. And the way they looked. Despite the weathered outer coat of their skin and the way their hair was matted, a few of them had teeth missing now, but it was easy enough for me to see that if they received a good scrub and a haircut, most of them would be pretty easy on the eye. They were all roughly the same height, with a similar shade of light-coloured hair. And I couldn't deny that Cupcake had a certain look about him too. Is that why the men were here, because of the way they had looked? Did they all remind Avril of a certain man who had hurt her? It seemed as though the answers were all offering themselves to me but I would need some confirmation from Cupcake.

'I don't know what to think about all of this, but I have some doubts.'

Cupcake looked intrigued as I passed him the bread, fruit and water.

'Okay, doubts about who?'

'Avril,' I said quietly in case someone was lurking in the bushes and might report back what they had heard.

'So talk me through it,' he said, putting a piece of bread into his mouth.

'It started at the beginning; there were things she didn't tell me, and this camp being the biggest thing.' I thought again about Clara, but I couldn't do that to Cupcake, not when he had clearly something going on with her. 'I just get this vibe, that she . . . that what she tells me isn't the truth.'

Cupcake remained silent as he ate.

'And there are men here, in our camp.'

He stopped eating and looked at me. 'Men?'

'Yes.' I cast my mind back to last night and the way they had looked. I could see a similarity again. Same height and build. The build Cupcake could have been a few years ago.

'You need to tell them, warn them,' he said. A panic rose in his voice. Where he had been calm each time I had spoken with him, he was now clearly alarmed.

'I, I don't know what to say.'

'Tell them to get off the island right away.'

'But everyone will know it was me who told them. My life is in danger,' I said and as I spoke those words I finally knew. I was scared, I was trapped and I had no one to help me.

# 45

## THEN

When I sat down to eat dinner with the camp that evening, the atmosphere had an edge that I could almost taste in the food.

James and his friend, whose name I still didn't know, were seated and seemed to be enjoying themselves as much as they were last night. I even began to doubt that anything was going to happen and maybe they might just be put back on a boat tomorrow and taken back to the mainland.

But Avril couldn't just let men arrive here and then leave and not be sure they wouldn't tell others who could then arrive uninvited. I was sure that these men would never leave Totini.

Avril prepared and cooked all the dinner this evening and that was interesting. She had never cooked and served before.

When the kava came around I passed and when I looked up Avril was watching me. I was curious as to why we were drinking it so often now. There was usually a break between evenings; it gave everyone a chance to recover if they'd had too much the previous night. But there was a lot of deviation just recently.

I was itching to get back to the diary – Ula deserved for me to get to the end of the book to discover what had happened to her.

I forced myself to make polite conversation with Star, the mother who was more relaxed than Hester. But right now I didn't trust any of them. All it would take would be for me to have a drink of kava and my true thoughts would surface and I might say them out loud. When my bowl of food arrived my mouth was filled with saliva and not in a good way. I was worried I was going to be sick, as the thoughts began to spiral through my mind. Then I began to worry that I wouldn't be able to eat the food, and everyone would be looking at me and wondering why I wasn't eating. I looked down at the bowl in my lap and tried to keep my face bright and the conversation flowing.

The kava came around and I refused again. Avril was up and still speaking to the group, but I had stopped hearing her words; I was suddenly thinking of home and what I would be doing if I was hanging out for a whole evening with my parents, which I did once a month. I wanted to speak to them more than ever. I felt a small lump form in my throat and I swallowed it down with a mouthful of food. Avril's words eventually faded to nothing, and I was grateful that she had finally ceased speaking but no sooner had I found myself grateful for that than a low murmuring began. I couldn't work out what it was at first. I thought it was thunder and then I looked around the camp circle and I could see everyone's lips moving, and the murmuring became louder until it was obvious they were repeating sounds over and over, turning into a chant, some sort of mantra. It seemed foreign to me, but it became louder and more primal until I realised everyone was making this sound, everyone except me and the two men. Were they mad? Had they drunk too much kava?

'I'm feeling really tired so I'm going to get an early night.' I had to shout for Star to hear me because the chanting had got really loud and I wasn't sure if she was listening, but by now Avril was on her feet and stamping her foot into the dry dusty ground and suddenly everyone was up and dancing on the spot.

I slipped away from the crowd and retreated towards the cabins. I walked past all of them, only looking back once before I reached the pathway that would lead me to the beach, and as I did I saw the whole camp up and dancing around the campfire. From where I stood I had never felt more like an outsider. Memories of Clara and the men in the prison. No matter how much Avril tried to make out that this was a haven, I just couldn't get it out of my head that this is where she and the rest of the camp had incarcerated many men.

I ran up the first part of the pathway and the moon guided me all the way to the beach. I turned left and headed towards Ula's hut. Out of everyone, she was the one I needed to be with. Despite how everyone called her mad, I felt drawn to her in a way that I couldn't explain. Avril had brought me here to show me my strengths, and now I needed to use those strengths to my own advantage.

At the foot of the hill that led to the hut I looked upwards; and there stood Ula, illuminated by the torch she was holding.

# 46

## NOW

Bruno. Why was he here? Did he think that I would have forgotten what he did, that he could just creep back into my life and use my amnesia to hoodwink me into thinking that things hadn't been as bad as they had been between us?

'I don't think Sadie is ready to hear all of this right now, Bruno,' Jane says with concern in her voice. 'I think she has heard so much already and what with seeing you and all those memories, she must be exhausted.' She looks at me. 'Are you exhausted, Sadie?'

I look at Jane but I am through with words.

Bruno is now up and pacing the room.

I am tired of everyone looking at me like I am a delicate little flower that would break if handled too much. The initial memory loss of my family was hard, but as I have begun to come back to myself, I'm now mostly terrified to tell them anything about the island or Bruno.

'I am sure things will start to come back to you soon, my love, and when they do we can put all this behind us and move on with our lives. We can plan our wedding.' He takes a chance and leans in and kisses me lightly on my cheek. 'Sorry, I've been wanting to do that for so long, I've missed you, Sadie, so much.'

'Bruno,' I say suddenly, clearly and loud enough that everyone can hear.

Bruno looks at me, a mixture of bewilderment and something else. Recognition. He can see what he saw in me before. When I decided I wasn't going to take any more.

'I would appreciate it very much if you would leave and never come back.'

I stand and listen to the commotion around me, cries of disbelief from Bruno and apologies from my mum.

Jane reads the signs and is already ushering Bruno out of the room. He says his goodbyes and then Jane takes me to my bedroom. It is not actually my bedroom anymore, but the room I'd had before I moved out a few years ago.

Once Jane has left me, closing the door behind her, I fall onto the bed and cry a mixture of tears of relief and anger. I had forgotten the strength I had within me. Avril had used my vulnerabilities to dupe me to go to Totini. It had all been a trap from the outset. But it was I who was instrumental in everything that happened in the end.

# 47

## THEN

I walked up the hill and joined Ula outside her hut.

'Hey,' I said to her, but she didn't look at me straight away; she continued looking ahead towards the sea. From here, I could hear the chanting, which must have gotten louder since I had left the camp.

I listened to see if I could make out any words, but it was as inaudible as it had been when I had been standing right next to them.

'How are you?' I asked Ula but I wasn't expecting a response. She and I had yet to converse in any way that made sense to me. I knew today wouldn't be any different. But I needed to hear something from Ula; I needed her to help me.

After a few seconds' silence I turned to her.

'Ula, I think . . . I'm feeling uncomfortable. Avril has asked me to tend to the men in the prison. It doesn't feel right if I'm honest. What do you think? And these new men that have arrived. Avril has them in camp tonight. I have a really bad feeling.'

'Listen.' Ula's voice punctured my ramblings. I looked up and beyond the sound of the swishing waves. I heard the constant thrum of the chanting.

I looked at Ula. 'I hear it,' I said. 'What does it mean?'

Ula shook her head. 'It is too late now. There is no time left. You must accept this.' Then she glanced back at her hut. 'The way I have.'

I felt my throat tighten and my guts suddenly felt loose. I swallowed but it felt painful and dry.

'What do you mean, it's too late. What does that mean, Ula?'

Damn this woman. Could she not just speak one coherent sentence? Just fucking one. I was half tempted to shake her, to see if that would bring her out of this permanent daze she seemed to be in. 'Ula, what do you mean it is too late?'

She turned so she was looking at me full-on. 'You must see for yourself.'

And then she was off with her torch in her hand. I ran to catch up with her, and we were back on the beach. She was striding off ahead towards the camp. Christ, what was going on? I had just come from there and I had no desire to go back there again tonight. Especially not with Ula in tow. What would the camp think? I could be turned on; they could hurt Ula. I ran to catch up with her, but she was tall and strong and her stride was twice as long as mine.

'Ula, stop, please, I don't want to go back there. Please, stop.' I grabbed at her arm, but she just shook me off.

'You must see for yourself. Then you will know.'

I carried on trotting next to her, trying to keep up with her pace.

'Okay, but when we get there, please can we hide, can we not be seen? I don't want them to see me or you?'

Ula glanced at me and then carried on looking ahead. I had no choice, I could follow her and find out what the hell she was ranting on about or I could stay here on the beach alone, worrying about Ula and if she was safe. I had done this walk a hundred or so times these last few weeks but today it felt particularly long and arduous as the ground rose and fell again. Once we were on easier terrain I knew we weren't far from the camp now, that and the fact that the chanting had increased in volume. I could see the strain in Ula's eyes, as she concentrated on walking at a pace.

Then suddenly she dropped to a steadier walk as I began to see the light from the camp in the distance. Ula took us to the right through the bushes and I knew what she was doing. We would be hidden here; we could observe whatever the hell was going on and no one would see us.

We moved stealthily through the bushes until we reached the very edge, not that we needed to. The noise from the camp was now more of a consistent roar and would have drowned out any sound from us scuttling around.

Ula crouched down in the long grass and then motioned for me to sidle up next to her, which I did. I wanted to block my ears from all the noise but at the same time, I was trying to tune in to hearing anything they were saying; if I could maybe catch the odd word, it might make sense. My heart thudded in my ears almost in time with the drum, which was now sounding out across the camp.

I looked across at the camp. We were well hidden in the grass and Ula had turned off her torch, so we were crouched in the dark. Everyone was up and moving around. The sound of the drum was now echoing in my chest, and I wanted it to stop, for all of this to just stop, but somehow I knew it wouldn't. Somehow this suddenly felt much bigger than me and I knew it was unstoppable. It felt as though whatever was happening had been brewing for some time.

I tried to focus on a few of the faces as the fire seemed to be growing in size as well, the light from it illuminating the crowd. Everyone was there: the mothers, Kali, Mary and every other woman who made up the thirty-or-so-strong camp. And standing at the head of the camp was Avril. She was moving slightly but was focused on something to her left. I hadn't noticed it before with all the commotion, but there was now a chair where there had never been one before. Someone was seated on the chair, but I couldn't tell who. I did another quick scan of the camp and saw the other man sitting on another chair close by.

'That's James sitting in that chair,' I whispered to Ula, but she didn't respond. She didn't know who James was. 'He arrived yesterday. His friend is there.'

Nothing from Ula.

'What is going on?' I hissed.

The chanting and drumming ended with one loud final thump. I was sure I had been heard. Ula looked at me. I thought she was about to tell me off, or shush me or something, but she just looked at me and her whole face had changed. A terrible sadness had washed over her.

Avril had mounted James. Precious was on top of the other man. Both men looked elated; this was what they had come here for. To be surrounded by goddesses on a tropical island, far away from society.

I shivered and wished I were somewhere else, not watching this, but this was what Ula wanted me to see.

'Ula, is this usual? Do they do this often?'

She looked at me and nodded.

'Look, as erotic as this is, I don't feel happy watching from the bushes,' I said. I was sure Avril would have wanted me to have been a part of this evening, but I didn't feel comfortable with that either. The girls made quite a show for a few minutes, but it was all too much for poor James and his travelling pal, who climaxed and then began laughing hysterically.

Ula looked at me again. The energy had shifted in the air. Out of the corner of my eye, I saw a glint of something against the light of the moon. By the time I had turned, I had just caught the end of a fast and vicious swipe as a blade came across each of the men's necks.

# 48

## THEN

The men lay limp. I looked at Ula but I noticed she had already begun to crawl away. She stood up, fully visible to the entire camp, but she didn't seem to care. I stayed where I was for longer than I should have done, thinking and watching the camp return to normality. The bodies were removed and the merriment continued with kava continuing to be passed around. I couldn't move; I was frozen to the spot. If I moved they would see me. I would be caught and they would kill me, was all I could think.

Eventually I began moving back very slowly. And once I was away past the clearing, I ran as fast as I could, stopping every now and then to vomit foamy bile on to the ground. Ula was long gone.

Once I was on the beach, I took off along the sand, a pain in my gut pulling me forward and making me retch even more. I could no longer ignore the stitches that were trying to slow me down and I eventually stopped and lay on the sand, feeling the safety of some bushes that encased me so I was barely visible. I covered my head with my hands and cried angry, frustrated tears.

I was not safe. I needed to get away. But I was trapped. With these women. With Avril. I could feel my heart racing and panic struck me. I couldn't breathe.

I must have passed out because I opened my eyes not knowing how long I'd had them shut for. I stood up, blood rushing to my head, and I threw up again.

I thought of the cave, of Adi up there alone. I needed to be there tonight. I started making my way up the incline past Ula's house and into the small clearing that was not really a path. I felt my way in the dark with just my hands and the small amount of light from the moon to help me. My fingertips brushed against the tops of the grass and plants, and I took it as comfort. It was like a gentle stroke on my hand. In my head I began to chant:

*It's going to be okay. You're going to be okay.*

But I was lying to myself. I was never going to be okay again.

As the incline grew I began to worry how I would feel once I reached the top and whether I would end up too close to the edge, but already my muscle memory had kicked in, and as the grass opened up onto the clearing at the top of the hill, I could see the rock face and recognised the shrubbery in front of me that covered the gap to the hole. I pushed back the grass and put my head into the hole. There was light coming from inside.

'Adi, it's me, Sadie. I'm coming in.' My voice was a shaky mess as my body convulsed and spikes of terror hit me one after another like electric shocks.

As I climbed in further I could see the light was coming from a small fire in the middle of the cave. I looked up and saw there was a small slit in the top where the starlit sky was peeking through, and the smoke was escaping. I pulled my body through into the clearing. And crouched down on all fours although I could have stood there was enough headroom.

I recognised everything as it had been before except this time, Adi was here. He was at the far end of the cave on the blankets, but he wasn't alone. He was wrapped up in the arms of another and before I'd had the chance to think it, I was saying her name.

'Avril.'

# 49
## THEN

'Sadie,' Avril croaked.

I saw on the blankets next to Adi's leg, which was entwined around Avril's, the faded pink journal.

I leaned forward and took it. Adi went to try and snatch it off me, but Avril made a sound through her teeth as if she were training a dog, and Adi stopped dead then moved back into the crook of her arm. I watched the two of them for a second, wondering what it was I was witnessing here, but unable to fully take it in as my mind replayed the images from the camp over and over. The soft sound of the drums was still in my ears even though I was sure they had ended already.

'This book, I have been trying to read it, trying to get answers.' I was crying and spilling tears on the cover, as finally the shock wore off and I was able to release some of the emotion.

Avril moved from the bed and got closer to me. She put a blanket around my shoulders and then handed me something to drink that was not kava but was alcohol.

'Why is this in here?' I asked.

'Adi brought it to me; he loves paper and stationery. You really shouldn't have this journal, Sadie. But you have it now. So go on, read it.'

I tried to imagine Avril as the girl I had met in the café a month ago, but now all I could see was a killer.

'You killed James. Both of them. They're dead.'

'Yes,' she spat. 'Because they are monsters, just like all of them.'

Again I found it difficult to believe that the nice young man I had spoken with at the wash-up was a monster.

'But why didn't you lock them up in Camp Z?'

'Do you see any more jails?' Avril's words punched me. But I didn't care. I needed to know the truth.

'I know you've been having doubts about staying here. It's written all over your face. I don't see the girl I met in the café. I see someone who is terrified.'

I looked at Avril and I knew I wanted to be as far away from her as possible.

I skidded and slipped back down the mountain until I was back on the beach under the bush I had passed out in earlier. Still clutching the journal I held it out under the light of the moon and continued to read. I knew the answers would be in here somewhere.

# 50
## THEN

*Journal entry*
*I was an easy target, lost, wandering. Fertile. Now I am pregnant and ready to burst. I can see that now. I feel stronger. Stronger and more powerful than I have ever felt. And that was why Deny had to go.*

*Ula does not understand. I tried to ask him to leave, but he wouldn't – he just wouldn't listen.*

*Even after what he did to me.*

*Luring me in. Taking advantage.*

*I still have flashbacks, the way he had been calling me Cupcake down on the beach all night. The way I had tried to walk back to my cabin, and he had followed me. The way he pinned me down to the ground, told me he would kill me if I screamed.*

*But in the end it was he who screamed.*

*I didn't want to be a mother, but I have been burdened with this task. I will do the best I can. But I was not shown how. I have called him Adi. I will do what I can.*

*Ula is not doing so well. She had fallen in love with Deny but in the end, she didn't understand.*

I stopped reading and stared at the words. This was not Ula's journal I was reading. This was Avril's.

*We need to move on and quickly, there is a job on a neighbouring island. Ula is not doing well. She has agreed to come with me. But it is like a switch has just gone off, and I don't think I will ever get her back again.*

I was too scared to go back to my hut and too scared to go back up the mountain. So I made my way back up to Ula's place. She opened the door as soon as I approached it as though she had been waiting for me. I stepped inside and fell onto the mattress, leaving a gap on the other side so that Ula could lie down too.

'What will happen to me?' I whispered into the dark.

'You're like me now. If you try to leave, she will kill you.'

# 51

## THEN

I woke thinking of Avril and Adi curled into one another, my mind racing with questions.

Avril and Adi.

Ula and Deny.

Ula and Deny had been a couple. Deny was Adi's father. Deny was dead.

I remembered what the mothers had said, that Adi had been abandoned and how they talked of Avril spending weeks away at a time. She had never wanted Adi; she had never wanted to be a mother.

If it was Deny who had committed the crime against Avril, what did Cupcake do? I hadn't thought about the other men. I had been so consumed in Cupcake but suddenly I needed to see the rest of them. I crept from Ula's bed, hearing her stir slightly as I did, then I almost ran all the way to Camp Z. It was still early. The sun had risen and most of the men were in their huts. I took a stick and began running it along the cages, shouting for them all to get up. Men began to emerge bleary-eyed and confused. I went to the furthest cage and a young man stood there staring at me as though I were mad.

'Hold out your arm,' I commanded. He looked bewildered and a little scared but eventually he lifted his left arm and held it close to the bars. I grabbed his wrist and pulled it closer to me, and there on the bottom was the same branding: a cupcake.

I dropped his arm and moved on to the next cage, demanding the man push his arm through the bars. Again, the same rudimentary cupcake on his arm. I checked another three or four until eventually I raced round to Cupcake's cage.

'You all have them,' I said. 'She gave you all the cupcake tattoo.'

Cupcake nodded.

'What is your name?' I exhaled.

'Kai.'

'What was your crime, Kai?'

He looked at me, his eyes bleary from the morning light. 'Nothing,' he said.

It wasn't just the men who were prisoners; I, too, like Ula, was a prisoner. She had not been complicit in Avril's plan. She must have loved Deny and had never gotten over what Avril did. Maybe she had known what he had done to Avril, and that too made it impossible to come to terms with.

Avril. She was punishing every man for the crime that had been committed against her. And now with no more cages left, she was simply sacrificing them. And according to Ula, had been for some time. Kai had told me to warn James and his friend, but I had not done it; I was too late. It was my fault they were dead.

I ran and ran back through the woods until I neared camp and ran straight into Avril.

'Sadie.' Her voice was low and husky. Her eyes bored into mine. 'You're up early,' she said as though nothing had happened last night.

'Yes, up doing my job, checking on the prisoners. I'm going to bring them their daily rations.' I tried to keep my voice calm and steady.

Avril looked at me conspiratorially then she rubbed her head. She looked tired.

'I'm sorry you had to find out about everything through that stupid diary I wrote,' she said yielding to my lies. 'I was not well. After everything that happened to me.' She pulled her arms around herself. 'He was feral from the day he was born. I didn't know how to maintain that, how to be a good mother. Only this last year has he allowed me to become close to him, as he has pushed more for his freedom, he still returns to me. I know he is safe up there. He's not like the other children, is he? He's different. That's the curse. The curse that was put on me when he had his way with me.'

I didn't dare utter Deny's name.

I didn't try and discuss how each and every man who was locked up here was innocent of any crime.

'You understand that things are changing?' She moved in closer to me. 'The job I was set here to do, to be a pig farmer.' She laughed.

I have managed many years here, no one has ever come. A long as I delivered them a dead pig every now and then, they left me alone. It's all coming to an end, Sadie. They are coming to reclaim it. And we need to get out,' she whispered. 'I have an island full of men. They all need to go. And you need to help me.'

# 52
## THEN

I turned straight back around, and ran to the beach. I lay on the sand and took in a gasp of air as though I had stopped breathing. My heart thumped hard in my chest. I had barely slept in Ula's cabin. I couldn't bear to be around Avril, after I saw her early this morning. I was even more repulsed by what she suggested we were to do and I had taken myself to the beach to try and sleep.

I looked at the sun now high in the sky. I lay there, willing it to burn me, maybe to death, then this nightmare would end.

My body felt as though it didn't belong to me anymore, as though a part of me had been lost last night. The beach was empty and the noise that had been pounding for hours in my ears had finally ceased, but I was sure I could still hear echoes of it as the memory of last night played tricks with my tired mind. I could hear the waves but they did little to soothe me as they usually did. All I could do was wonder what was coming next. Nothing, it seemed, except the desperate quietness that echoed of the night it had left behind.

Now I was lost. I didn't know what to do next. Part of me was ready to start swimming; the other part of me knew I had to go back and face whatever it was back at camp. A new dawn had broken and it brought a whole new dynamic that was completely alien. Surely I was in a dream. How was I to go back and live amongst these people, have a conversation over breakfast? Would anyone mention it? Would they mention where I had been? Was I now expected to play my part in this sadistic nightmare?

I couldn't lie here on the beach all day, but the thought of returning to camp and discovering the aftermath was not an option I was considering either. But I knew it had to be done. Every part of my body ached and I felt weak with lack of food and water. I stood up and began to put one foot in front of the other, each step reminding me what I was heading toward. I tried to believe I had imagined it all and that I would wander back to camp and everything would be as though it hadn't happened.

The walk took me twice as long as it usually did and so when I finally saw the clearing, I was ready to flop again. But I needed to remain strong and focused.

As I entered camp I could have been fooled into thinking that nothing had occurred, that all was well. The camp was the cleanest I had ever seen it. The fire was still smoking ready to be stoked for breakfast. Any remnants from last night were gone. The chairs the men had been sitting in were gone. I walked to the spot where I had seen it, searching for the obvious clues, but the dusty ground gave nothing away. Yet I had witnessed it. I had seen it with my own eyes.

I could tell from the light and where the sun was that someone would be getting up soon to make breakfast.

I stood looking around, and images of what I remembered from last night replayed in front of me. I heard a creak and turned to see Avril's cabin door had opened. No. My mind was screaming run, but my body wouldn't move.

Avril hovered in the doorway. She was smiling warmly. As though nothing had happened. Her eyes were inviting me towards her. She began walking over to me and I felt my body recoil, like a child I closed my eyes as though doing so would make me invisible.

I heard her footsteps, then I could smell her and when she spoke I could feel her breath on my skin.

'Sadie.'

I opened my eyes. She was inches from my face but she stepped back.

'You look tired. Let me make you some tea.'

She walked over to the fire and began to stoke it, then took the kettle and hung it over the fire.

'Please come, sit.'

I was in a dream; I had to be. I could hear Avril speaking but this wasn't real. This wasn't happening.

'Come sit.' She spoke louder this time and I jumped at the sudden change in volume.

I shuffled near to the fire but set myself down on a trunk of wood.

Avril crushed dried nettles as we sat in silence. She put a small strainer over a coconut cup and when the water was boiling she emptied it over the strainer, swiftly removed it and handed me the tea. I took the cup and held it in both hands, staring away past her.

'You have come a long way. Camp life suits you.'

I barely moved. This was not what she had said last night in Adi's cave. She had said she had seen someone who was terrified. She had already seen through me. She was playing games with me. My throat was dry and I needed a drink but what if she had poisoned it?

'You're one of us now, Sadie,' she said quietly.

I could have laughed but I was rigid.

She spoke again louder this time. 'You're one of us now, Sadie. Okay?'

I forced myself to nod. This was what I had wanted, to be accepted, to feel part of something. But I could not accept Avril's words. This was not how it was supposed to be. I moved my face an inch to look at her. My teeth chattered even though the temperature was rising again.

'You are one of us,' she said, laughing whilst she stoked the fire.

My tired eyes were watering from the smoke that had accumulated around us as Avril brought the fire back to life.

She looked at me. Her eyes were dark like deep pools of water. An expression of satisfaction spread over her face.

'You do understand, you must help me now.'

# 53
## THEN

Later that morning, I went to Camp Z. I brought a packet of cigarettes I had found in the pantry. They must have belonged to James and his friend, and I felt sick passing them around the other men, but they were thankful. I tried not to look too hard at their frail bodies or the way their ribs protruded through their skin, as though I could grab a bone at any moment.

'That was very nice of you. Men feel like men when they have a cigarette,' Kai said and lay down on the ground. He patted the ground, an invitation, so I took it and sat down close to the cage.

'She hasn't trained you with a gun then yet?'

I looked away. Guns. Surely that was the quickest way to eradicate all the men at once.

'Just basic point and shoot.' Kai sucked on his cigarette. 'You'd pick it up quickly.'

I didn't reply. He sucked in again, and fell to his side with his hand under his head.

'She came here a few weeks ago. She looked stressed. She didn't speak as such or say anything, but I rarely see her these days. The food rations have halved. No new men are arriving and disappearing. I have very little to focus my senses on here, Sadie, so I am highly and finely tuned to every little thing that is within my reach. I can sense something is happening.' He sucked hard on his cigarette. 'Do you know what is happening?' he asked calmly but I could sense the fear.

'I . . .' I began.

'And don't sugar-coat it, Sadie. Look at me. I have nothing. Just tell me the truth.'

'The deal she had with the island is coming to an end. She has said she wants you all gone.'

Kai nodded. 'Poor little rich girl.' I wondered if he had understood what I had told him.

'You know what I mean when I say gone?' I asked Kai.

He looked at me, took a last long drag of his cigarette, and dropped it on the floor. 'Of course I know what you mean,' he said. 'Which is exactly why you and I need to work together from here on in.'

I felt my stomach lurch. The words that Avril had been saying to me recently were now being echoed by Kai. But I knew in my heart which one I needed to help. It just meant how much was I willing to risk my own life.

'You know you have all the power,' Kai continued. 'She probably likes you a lot, right? You know where the keys are.'

'I don't know that.'

'But you could find out?'

I thought of all the places where Avril could keep the keys.

'Let me go, Sadie. I'll go back to the mainland and find my way home to South Africa. Start that boat business I always dreamed of.'

'Boat business?'

'My papa had a dream to make boats; he died when I was fifteen. I vowed I would start the business. But I never got around to it. Yet.'

He walked to the other side of the cage and stared across at all the other prisons, as though he was seeing beyond them all and watching his dream come to life.

'Find the keys, Sadie; set me free. Do the right thing.'

## 54

### THEN

I was a shell of my former self. I didn't know who I was anymore. I went through each day as if I were sleepwalking. I spoke only when I had to. I ate only fruit, rice and vegetables.

I had nothing to do with anyone. I had become a version of Ula.

But a part of my brain was still functioning just about enough that I had begun hatching a plan.

Ula and I had been spending most days together now; I was as much an outsider as she was.

Avril emerged into camp later and later each morning. She had begun to relieve herself of some of her duties and spent most days down at the shore sorting through the stores, tinkering with the boats with Kali, Mary and a burly woman who was sometimes here, other times not. There were more of them now, the boats, I noted, which stayed here. Usually only two

283

were moored. Now there are five, sometimes six boats. The sight of them made me uneasy. Did Avril have a plan, I wondered? She seemed edgy as though she were making things up as she went along. So far away from what her life had been for the last few years, where she had been able to live carefree and day to day. I wondered about all the other women – Mary, Kali, Precious, the mothers – where would all these women go? How could you leave somewhere like here and then carry on with normal life afterwards?

That night, I immersed myself in camp life by cooking. But even now, I could feel the change of atmosphere. Where before there was any reason to celebrate, now meals were taken without much conversation. The kava was rarely sent around, and most retired to their cabins by eight.

I then had to take the leftovers to Camp Z the next morning. No more fruit and bread. Avril commented that she didn't know why she was even bothering anymore and I felt a weight in my stomach that hadn't been there before. But what I now knew was that I had blood on my hands; I could have saved James and his friend's lives.

I was dealing with a cold-hearted killer, and I had to watch and plan my every move around her from now on.


'Tomorrow Hester, Star and the children will leave the island,' Avril said with a tone of despondency.

'Okay,' I said. 'Will we talk about protocol? About Camp Z?'

She looked at me nonchalantly. 'What about Camp Z?'

'Well, what we are going to do? I mean the women are beginning to be shipped out, what will happen to the men?'

'They will end their days on Totini Island as per the agreement.'

Panic rose in my throat. I had initially thought she was going to abandon them. But now I realised she was going to kill them all.

# 55
## THEN

I knew I needed to find that key and I had very little time to do so. Avril had not left it anywhere where I could find it, and she had not given me any idea where it might be. It was hidden. She was the only one who had it.

The only way I could think to get Avril to tell me where the key was, was to get her drunk.

'I'm cooking a stew tonight?' I said. 'I think we should drink kava and not worry about the future. This has been a beautiful experience; we need to be thankful. Some of the women go tomorrow, so let's drink?'

Avril smiled, and part of me felt like it was the old Avril I knew, when things were sweet and perfect and no one had been murdered.

I handed her a cup of kava. 'A pre-dinner drink.' I laughed and she laughed with me, which was a relief.

'Thank you.' She took the cup. 'I've been distracted recently. There is a lot of stress here. I need to make sure all these women leave and then, after that you know, we must go too. It's time to say goodbye. It's been a long period of my life.'

'Any idea what you'll do?' I asked, topping up her kava without her noticing or paying much attention.

'I have no idea. I have some friends in New Zealand,' she said vaguely.

'Sounds like a good plan.'

'You?'

'I'll go home to England.'

'And never speak of your time here,' she said with a stony expression. I went to laugh then I realised she was of course deadly serious.

'There's nothing to tell. I was on the mainland selling chocolate. That's all anyone needs to know.'

'You're a good woman, Sadie.' But there was something in the way she spoke, in the way she said my name. Nothing felt sincere. Nothing felt right. She did not hold my gaze. She could not look me in the eye. I could feel the building of something. I had been here such a short amount of time, but it felt like years. Avril had seen my concern for Ula, then Clara, then Camp Z. She knew I was the weak link.

For the first time in weeks I now knew that my own life was in danger. I was never going to leave this island alive, not if Avril had her way.

# 56

## THEN

'Tonight's the night, Ula,' I said as I made tea with her. 'You remember the plan?'

Ula nodded. We had been discussing it for some time, but I wasn't sure if Ula fully understood that we needed to implement it tonight. It had come quickly, and with more of the women being shipped off the island, we needed to act – and fast. But Ula had been showing signs of slowing down recently, as though she were ill or maybe giving up herself. I needed her to be strong and stick to the plan.

'I need everyone to stay at the camp. No one is to leave. If you see anyone try, you stop them in any way you can. I will be down there on the beach. You must come when you are done. We will leave together, you understand?'

Ula nodded again. There were days when she was more vocal than others, and today was not one of them, but I knew we had an understanding now, and I knew I wanted to help her as much as I wanted to help myself.

I had been taking a tiny amount of petrol each morning before anyone woke and storing it in a container I'd buried in the woods in a spot no one had ever set foot in before, except maybe Adi.

I had set up bunches of dried grass all around the perimeter of the camp, which I would douse with petrol before anyone arrived. Ula's instructions were to come down to the camp after we had eaten and set the grasses alight. Eventually, the whole of the outside of the camp would go up in flames whilst I made a run for it to the boat, which Ula would have dragged along from the other side by hand during dinner. Prior to that, I was to go to Camp Z and free Kai and the other Cupcakes. Before that, I was to find the key. And that I was going to try and do tonight when Avril was drunk and delirious on kava.

The plan was set.

There was a buzz in the air as the camp prepared themselves for the departure of more of the women. It was nothing I could put my finger on, just a feeling, like they were different people to the ones they usually were.

I hadn't brought much with me in my rucksack, but I made sure I had put a couple of bottles of water in there. I knew I would head straight for the next island, but I could only hope that I could manage it. It would be just Ula and I in the dark, and she was in no state of mind to be guiding us through the South Pacific waters. I had stood at the top of Totini so many times these last few weeks, I knew which direction to head in. I could see the neighbouring island from the cliff edge and had performed the manoeuvres hundreds of times in my mind. All I needed was courage and a little bit of luck.

I had to think of myself and no one else. Trying to save anyone else other than me and Ula was not top priority, yet my conscience could not let those men die here.

It was time for dinner, and my stomach was churning. I was running the plan over and over in my head, worrying about everything. What if Ula decided to stay in her hut? What if she came too early? What if the camp were prepared for ambushes and both Ula and I were to end up as prisoners in Camp Z?

All I knew was it was time to get out of here. I didn't want to exist in this prison anymore. I had to leave.

Avril was sitting at the campfire looking drowsy. I felt the dread spill through my body. I could have choked on the anticipation.

The dinner I had cooked was served and when my bowl reached me, I gazed down at the contents. I could feel eyes on me every minute of every day but I wasn't sure if I was just being paranoid now. The kava came out again. I made sure I poured more for Avril and then other women too so it didn't look as though I were only trying to get her drunk. Avril was showing some signs of looking a bit woozy but nowhere near the level of drunk I needed for her to show me where the key was.

I made my way over to her, and slipped down in a seat beside her. I stayed with her, engaging her in conversation from time to time, making sure she was filled with kava. There was a little music. I tried to pull Avril up to dance.

'Noooo,' she groaned. She was too tired apparently.

When it seemed that everyone was also tired and the women began to retreat to their cabins ready for an early start in the morning, I turned to Avril and asked, 'Shall I walk you back to your hut?'

She looked at me, a glint in her eye. And I realised I had asked in a way that had sounded seductive. Had I wanted it to come out that way? Was I playing with her? Would she succumb, as this could be our last night together? Avril had been playing with me for weeks. I was sure if I entirely offered myself to her, she wouldn't decline me.

She held out her hand and I stood to help her. I caught Lola looking at me, a defeated, arrogant look about her.

She scooped her arm through mine and we walked up the steps to her cabin.

'I'm so tired,' she said and sank onto her bed.

I hovered above her, not knowing what to do, waiting for a sign. My eyes were already scouring the room for where Avril might keep a key. It had been a while since I had been inside Avril's cabin and it seemed as though she had begun to pack a few precious items into one crate. She patted the space next to her on the bed, feebly. I knelt down next to her and then lay my body on the mattress. It felt strange but her arm swept across me and pulled me in towards her so our faces were almost touching. Her eyes flickered; she was barely conscious. My heart quickened. This was my opportunity.

'Kiss me, Sadie.' Avril's voice was barely a whisper, but she nudged her way towards me until her lips were touching mine. I accepted her until our mouths were moving in sync. My gut tightened as images floated through my mind: the men in the prison, Clara, James.

I hated her.

She managed to pull her head back enough so that she could see me.

'You're not as into me as I am into you.'

'I . . .' I went to defend myself, to say I was tired.

'It doesn't matter. I'm afraid it's too late.' She turned her whole body to face the wall. 'I cannot give you the key to Camp Z.' She let out a loud yawn. 'There is no longer a key. I threw it in the South Pacific Ocean weeks ago.'

My heart thumped in my chest, and I opened my mouth to suck in air; the room became stifling hot around me. Avril had spoken to me about the cages, the prisons that the men were in right at the beginning when I discovered Camp Z. Huge deep holes and cage frames complete with built-in steel bottoms had been lowered into the hole, meaning there was no way for the prisoners to dig their way out. Now I know they had originally been for the pigs who like to root and dredge up the ground. Those men could dig all they liked, they would only eventually hit a steel flooring. This I had known and yet I could only hope for the key to help me. And all the while, Avril had known my intentions. I felt sick. But right now, I could hear her breath had softened and she was asleep.

I took myself from the room and straight to Camp Z.

# 57

## THEN

Kai was waiting for me. I could see from the way he was leaning into the bars, looking towards the clearing. I was out of breath by the time I arrived, knowing that I didn't have long until Ula would be along to begin executing our plan.

I stopped in front of his cage. I held my hands out in front of him the way a pet owner would show their dog they had no more treats. It was over. I could not help this man or the others.

Kai sucked his breath in defeat. We both knew what this meant. If I tried to escape before him to make it back to the mainland, somehow, having zero knowledge of driving a boat and not knowing what direction I was going in, even if by some miracle that happened and I could alert the authorities to what was happening, Avril would just shoot the men. There would be no chances taken. The only option was the key and now that was gone.

'I'm sorry,' I said. 'I tried. I was going to let you out. I truly was.'

Kai shook his head. 'This is not your problem. You did not invite this problem into your world.'

I sank to my knees and rubbed my head. It hadn't affected me this much before but to know that these men would perish because I hadn't been faster, slicker to get the key. They might have stood a chance. But it was over. I had no choice. I had to walk away and leave them here. I heard the disgruntled groans from the men, which had grown more prominent the last few days with lack of food and the growing sense of unease. They knew what their fate held for them.

One key fit all; I was sure of that and I would have been able to let them all free. I knew now they were all innocent, and not one of them deserved to die this way.

Kai sat for a while, not saying anything. Just breathing in and out.

'Clara wouldn't have let this happen,' he said with some sort of laugh that made me feel uneasy.

I sighed loudly. I thought of Clara, and what she had endured at the hands of Kali. The fate of that poor woman, who I had started to bond with. But I guessed that was why they wanted her gone in the end because she was more like me than them. Then I sat up, dropped my hands from my face and looked up at Kai.

'Clara. She used to come here, to visit you.'

Kai nodded.

'She let herself into your cage?'

Kai shook his head. 'We didn't reach that part. But she was planning to. I don't know what would have happened, whether

I would have tried to bypass her and escape, but we had built up a rapport, a trust.'

I wasn't listening to Kai anymore; I was thinking about the time I walked into my cabin and found Clara trying to conceal something in her bag. I should have looked but I didn't think that was the right thing to do. But her rucksack was still shoved in the corner of our hut; no one had come to claim it and I had sought comfort from it being there. I bet that was what she had been concealing. The key to every cell in Camp Z. She had been struck out for getting too close to Kai, but maybe they didn't know she had a key.

I stood up.

'I need to get back to camp. Quickly. We're running out of time.'

I raced through the woods to the camp, each way was twenty minutes at a fast pace and I was exhausted. I slowed when I reached the cabins. A few women were still milling about, and I didn't want to alert any of them to what I was doing. I smiled and walked slowly to my cabin, almost tripping on the step, but I made it inside without anyone approaching me and questioning where I had been. Everyone was preoccupied with leaving now.

I fell to my knees, conscious of time ticking, not knowing if Ula would show up on time, but knowing that she very well could. That was what I had been hoping for all this time at least. I pushed my hands into the rucksack, and felt around amongst a hoody and a watch, a small notebook that I had seen addresses in, some can headphones and an iPod. So retro, but the only way to listen to music. Next I spilled the contents out to get a better look, and as I did I heard a loud clang on the wooden floorboard. I looked next to my foot, and there was a large, heavy metal key.

As I stepped out of the cabin again, I took a moment to look around the camp one last time. This was the last time I would see everyone, the last time I would see this fireplace, which had burned non-stop since I arrived, apart from the day of the storm. There was no sadness, no remorse, no anger anymore. I was scared.

My rucksack was hidden in a bush that led down to the beach. I had marked the spot with a stick so everything was packed ready to go. All I had to do was head back to Camp Z and release the men.

# 58
## THEN

Kai was looking anxious this time when I returned. I hadn't really explained about the key; I had just run. I held it up to show him and he threw his hands up in the air and then over his head and ran them down his scalp.

'We don't have long.' I pushed the key into the lock. It fit. Kai's eyes were on the lock. I heard the motion of other men, the sounds of them growing louder.

'Shhhh!' I called to them. 'You want to get us all killed? Have patience.'

I held the key in place. Kai looked from my hand to my face.

'Don't fail me now, Sadie.' He looked as though he might shove his hand through and try to grab the key.

I paused for a moment, my mind playing tricks on me. I was doing the right thing, wasn't I? These men, they were all innocent. Weren't they? They were all part of Avril's game, her desire to build paradise, a world without men. And Clara had known the truth too.

The men's protesting voices began to get louder. I tried to block them out. I could hear a countdown beginning. I knew I had very little time left. It was now or never. I stared at Kai, willing him to speak, willing him to let me know that I was making the right decision.

'My name is Kai. Kai Jackson. I was born in Cape Town in 1989. I am from a good family. I had hopes and aspirations. I should never have been here.' He bent down a little so that he was facing me. 'Sadie, please let me out.'

I turned the key, the cage door opened and Kai fell forward. His hands were on the ground, rubbing the soil over his face.

I handed him the key. 'Save your men.'

He was on his feet and opening cage after cage. I began running. I was halfway back when I heard the first screams coming from the main camp.

Ula had arrived.

Ula was in the centre of the camp. Flames licked around the edge in the dry foliage. There was no routine involved, no planned structure, just her presence there was enough to make the campmates uneasy. If I had waited another day or two then the rain would have come and the bushes would have been too wet to light.

I heard the strained voices of the campmates as Ula put herself amongst them. They would all be watching her until they realised the bushes were burning.

I watched as the flames rose higher and began to reach the cabins. But I was headed to the back beach where I had moored a boat earlier.

I took one last look at Ula, then I ran.

# 59
## THEN

I found the boat as I had left it thank God. I needed to wait for Ula. She had promised she would be here.

I waited, pacing the sand for what felt like hours, but it was only a few minutes until finally a figure appeared at the mouth of the forest.

'Ula.' I raced towards her. She was hurt. Blood was dripping, no, gushing from her stomach. She fell to the ground in front of me. I needed to get her to the boat. But she was too tall, too bulky. I couldn't lift her.

What was prevalent was the dark streaks of blood all through the sand, and the smell. The smell of blood. Even in the time it had taken me to run through the woods and retrieve my things from a spot amongst shrubbery, it had not subsided.

Ula looked so serene just lying there and I wondered how it was that I could walk away and just leave her there. What kind of monster was I? I bent down by her side. I observed the blood across her dress, and down her legs. I was responsible for all of this. I sat back on my heels and held my hands in a prayer fashion. Then I looked down at my own hands and saw the blood all over them, I could see it even in the half-light of the moon.

I only had a few more minutes. I needed to get onto the boat, and I needed to get away soon. I looked behind me, the boat was moored already for me as we had arranged. Now all I needed to do was get in it and leave. I looked once more at her lying on the sand, the dark streaks marring her clothes, so I was barely able to see what the pattern once was. I quickly bent down next to her and then I moved towards her forehead. I kissed her gently; I felt her flinch. She wouldn't survive much longer; that I was certain of. How much time she had though, I wasn't sure. But I couldn't think about it anymore.

I had to take myself from the island and forget about her and everything that happened here. What kind of person would that make me? It's too late for me; I had too much blood on my hands. I have done too much. I would never truly be able to escape the horrors of what happened here, what I was responsible for. The terrible things I had done. And this one last act, a kiss as though that may solve everything, make everything I have done better. I knew it wouldn't. I stood and pulled my rucksack onto my back, so I had two free arms for balance to wade out to the boat and get on board. I knew every second counted now; they could be coming for me as I wasted precious time with sentimental moments.

I looked down at her almost lifeless body once more, then I stepped around her. As I did, I heard a rustle in the bushes. I didn't flinch; I simply waited. Then a head appeared, with those glittering eyes. Then the smile, that smile. Adi looked at me with his sparkly eyes and I smiled back. I wondered if he wished he could come too. I guessed I would never know. I turned towards the shore, then I slowly waded out into the shallows until I reached the boat. I threw my rucksack inside and climbed on board. I sat down on the plank of wood nearest the engine and before I started it, I took one last look at the island; this was the last time I would see it close up. Now it was time to go.

I saw the eyes peeking from the bushes and I raised my hand to wave, even though I was sure he would not wave back. I looked at the body on the sand, and as I started the engine and the boat began to chug away, I kept looking at Ula and didn't take my eyes off her until she was just a tiny speck on the small stretch of sand in the faraway distance.

# 60
# NOW

*Seven months later*

A cup of coffee arrives in front of me and I look up and smile at the man who has just put it there.

We've been spending every day together for the last six weeks, and I have learned so much more about him than I could have ever imagined.

We had met in the foodbank where I had been volunteering for the last few months. It shocked me and gave me satisfaction in equal measures to work there. Having come from a place where I knew how easy it was to live simply with just the basics yet there were families unable to provide a meal for their children here in the UK.

I wasn't having the reoccurring flashbacks or terrible nightmares, but I still dreamt of Avril often. A few weeks ago I read online about an uninhabited island in Fiji that had just been reclaimed by the people of the country. There was no mention of cages or men or dead bodies. But I knew it was Totini. Where had everyone gone? I hoped that they had buried Ula before they all left. I hoped that Adi was okay and was safe and happy wherever he was. But as I thought of these people, they quickly began to fade in my mind, as though it was a movie I had watched a long time ago and I could no longer remember much of the storyline.

I had not committed a crime, I had not killed anyone, and I was not the one to blame for what happened to James and Clara or anyone else who died on Totini Island.

This I now knew. The terrible images I had drawn had been the memories of something I couldn't understand, something I had been forced to be a part of. My brain had been trying to make sense of it all and process my time on Totini. The island had held me ransom for a while as I tried to make sense of the horrors I had witnessed so they normalised in my mind. When I fled Totini my mind became a torrent of images and sounds and words that I couldn't put into any order or make sense of.

Until I met Callum. He was everything that Bruno wasn't and more. After I had asked him to leave my parents' house that day I had never heard from him again. Except through a friend who had told me he was engaged. Good luck to whoever he is marrying. I sometimes felt I needed to find her and warn her. I never told my parents about what he had done. The time passed and so did the right moment. I have no need to ever bring him into conversation again.

Callum and I both want to give back for our own reasons. He could understand and nurture my weak spots; he was the real catalyst for my recovery. Once I knew why I had left to go to

Fiji, I was able to fit everything in place. Trauma had held me captive for months, but love had rescued me.

Callum sits opposite me. The sound of the sea is the soundtrack to our morning, something I had to get used to hearing again without making the connection between the ocean and the nightmare I had lived through. There is a chill in the air, the dire effect of living in the south of England, but I relish it by wrapping up in layers so I can be outside, seated at this table outside the café. Callum and I come here every morning. It is part of my therapy he says, but I joke it is now part of his caffeine habit.

I sip my coffee and watch an elderly couple walk past with their Cavalier King Charles, chuckling with one another. I wonder if Callum and I would still be as happy at that age as we are now.

I am thrust out of my thoughts by a loud clatter as a tray falls from a nearby table and cups and saucers smash across the concrete. The family at the table are on their feet immediately and then I hear the soft voice of a man with a South African accent. I freeze, thinking of him and all the men, and I wonder what they are all doing. Did they get to return to their normal lives after spending so many years away from them?

'I am so sorry,' the man mutters, and I strain to see his face past the small crowd that has suddenly appeared around the table as waiters and customers pick up broken pieces of crockery and try to wipe up the mess of several cups of spilt teas and coffees.

'I'm sorry again,' the voice says, and this time, it sounds more familiar. Then, amongst the crowd, I momentarily see the flash of faded and worn tattoos. But as soon as I see it, it's gone. Was it really there at all?

I stand and try to look past the table busy with staff and customers trying to manage the mess. I catch sight of a tall but slim-built man walking away, his shirt sleeves rolled up, a strong tan on his arms and neck from working outdoors. He walks slightly bow-legged as though he is used to crouching a lot. His frame seems familiar, almost as if I had seen it only yesterday.

He reaches the corner of the road where the path turns to meet the sea and there he is joined by a woman, a flash of red hair escaping from a thick woollen hat. She holds the hand of a small child. Someone shouts and they all turn and they are facing me. Of course, they are just a normal family and no one I know.

Callum taps his coffee cup the way he does when he has just finished stirring in his sugar.

I swing my head back at the sound then immediately turn my head back to the end of the road where I had just been watching what seemed to be a very normal little family going for a walk.

'What's got your attention?' Callum says half looking at me, half concentrating on his morning coffee.

I shake my head. 'Nothing,' I say and I watch the gulls swooping and landing on the sand and being chased away again by dogs.

Callum finishes his coffee and stands up. 'Ready to walk?' he says.

He leaves cash on the table and holds his arm out for me to link mine in with his.

Then we walk in the direction I had held my gaze for the last minute, the wind blowing a gentle breeze behind us, trying to help me clear away those memories but somehow still pushing me towards them.

# ACKNOWLEDGEMENTS

I visited Fiji twenty or so years ago, and it was one of the most beautiful and serene experiences of my life, not anything like Sadie's experience on Totini Island.

Totini Island does not exist, but small remote islands like it do, and I gained my inspiration after spending some time on a round-the-world trip.

When I woke at dawn to the sound of falling coconuts and roosters crowing, I would never have thought I would write a novel set on an island in Fiji and then have it published.

I must thank Audrey Linton for her unwavering faith, belief, and passion. She championed the book from the beginning, and I am forever grateful for that.

Thanks again, Mum, for always taking me to the library, where my love of reading began. This has shaped me and given me the tools to do something as extraordinary as writing stories.

Thank you to my lovely family for sharing my joy and being there for this experience. I love you all, and I promise I will try to get us back to Fiji one day.